THE LIAHONA LEGACIES

A Traitor In Our Midst

VOLUME II

A Novel by TINA MONSON

Acknowledgements

I owe a special debt of gratitude to Paula Mitchell and Lisa Peck whose true friendship, support and encouragement gave me the ability to complete this volume quickly. Thank you.

In addition, I need to sincerely thank Suzette Jensen, my sister and editor who once again offered her invaluable support, long hours and effort in helping me to meet my deadlines.

I wish to extend a deep heartfelt thanks to Doyl Peck who has spent countless hours reading the manuscript, offering suggestions and providing optimistic encouragement. I couldn't have done this without your help.

Last, and most importantly, I wish to thank my husband, Kreg, and my children Carson, Carter, Sierra and Bristol. I sincerely appreciate their help, love, and patience. They have truly allowed me the opportunity to write this story.

Chapter One

The glimmering of pale lights from the stars in the sky was not enough to stop the uneasy feelings Hero, Bubba, KP and Bean shared as they ran further into the darkness ahead. The moon cast no apparent light tonight as it hid restlessly behind the eastern mountains, as though waiting for its moment to climb high into the sky above the mysterious clouds. Bean watched the landscape around her continue to change, as the four teammates ran for their lives. The only scene that remained constant was the glow of faint lights in the sky.

❋

The Timber Creek Titan's Baseball Team began the day with grand expectations. After all, they had overcome perilous obstacles, defeated escaped prisoners, and even bridged ancient language barriers. Nothing had stopped them from finding Moroni's Treasure.

The Team's adventure began as the long awaited championship baseball game was canceled, and the Team was called on to repay a debt. While cleaning the attic of their old friend, Mr. Jensen, the Team stumbled upon an ancient map. Moroni's Treasure map promised excitement, riches and danger, and had delivered on all three expectations.

Having located several clues on the map, the Team could see a treasure was within their grasp. Suspense mounted as they recovered a small box, surely full of riches. Carefully, they opened the lid to reveal its contents. But to their dismay, the box contained no jewels, no gold coins — only a curious round ball. Hesitantly, Hero reached into the box to retrieve the object. Suddenly, a flash of light filled the Treehouse, leaving Tater, Red, Runt, Butch, Stick and Squeaks wondering where the other four members of their Team had gone.

❋

The dark, ominous shadow of a powerful soldier was suddenly over them. One hand pointed eastward, and the other firmly grasped his spear. In a deep booming voice, he ordered Hero, Bubba, KP and Bean off the king's land immediately. The intense fear of this horrifying moment burned a picture in Bean's memory that she would never forget.

"Where in the world could we be?" she questioned, afraid to stop running. Her aching feet continued to carry her further into the empty darkness that loomed ahead. Thorns from bushes and vines tore at her skin as she ran, leaving burning scrapes and painful cuts all over her body. The unfamiliar surroundings frightened her and kept her imagination filled with spine-chilling images. Tears streamed down her face as the memory of the soldier's booming voice continued to push her forward.

"How did this happen?" Bean wondered, her ponytail snagging several branches and vines as she ran past them. "Moroni's Treasure did this to me," she thought angrily as she ran.

She shivered from the chill in the air. Feeling the burn in her legs from running, she knew they must have run at least three miles by now. As long as the terrain did not get much worse, she could continue at least another three miles without any problem. "The boys will be another story," she thought.

Just then, KP stumbled over the uneven landscape. He fell to the ground exhausted, crying, "Stop! Please, stop. I can't take one more step."

Hero, following immediately behind KP, slipped on the wet moss that covered the ground. Too exhausted to stand up, and struggling for breath, he said, "Yes, please. Let's stop for a minute."

Pausing a moment to look at her weary teammates,

Bean insistently yelled, "NO! Get up. I don't want to die here tonight. We've got to keep moving. You heard the soldier."

"Moving to where, Bean?" asked KP, shrugging his shoulders. "We have no idea where we're going."

The terrain had changed slightly, and running had become more difficult. Mounds of dirt were hidden underneath the grasses. Trees were everywhere, and the vines that hung from them were dangerous. The shadows from the sparse light between the trees played tricks on the kids' minds. At every turn, they were sure the warrior was still following.

"Whether the warrior is behind us or not, I have to stop. I can hardly lift my feet, Bean. We've got to stop and catch our breath for a minute," said Hero.

"NO! We can't stop," said Bean insistently. "What if the soldier is close?"

"I've looked, but I can't see him anymore," said KP. "I'm sure he didn't follow us."

"I think you're right, KP. We've run into what looks like a jungle," replied Bubba. "The soldier probably guards the meadows where the king's crops grow and livestock graze. I don't think he's following us anymore."

"If we don't slow down, one of us is going to get hurt," replied Hero as he examined the scrapes on his hands from falling.

"So what! The king could own the jungle land, too," Bean persisted.

"We have been running non-stop for an hour, Bean. We've got to be off the king's land by now," reasoned

Bubba, holding his chest as his heart pounded rapidly.

"But what if we're not off his land, Bubba?" Bean asked, looking over her shoulder. She was absolutely positive she could see the shadow of the mighty soldier still behind them.

"Bean, whether we are off or not, we've got to stop," Hero stated firmly. He pulled off his backpack and retrieved his water bottle.

"Can you see the warrior behind us anywhere?" asked Bubba, nervously looking back at the darkness. He was suddenly fearful that Bean might truly see something.

"No, I can't see anything except trees and hanging vines everywhere. I think we're safe," replied KP.

"Safe? What is the matter with you guys? We're not safe. Some huge man with leather bands on his arms shot an arrow at us. Then he threatened to kill us if we didn't leave the king's land," Bean said heatedly.

"Sorry, Bean. You're right," KP replied. "I'm scared, too. But I'm looking, and I don't see anyone behind us. I think we will be safe to stop for a minute."

"Only if someone stands guard will I agree to stop," replied Bean firmly, placing her hands on her hips.

"Okay, Bean. I'll do it," announced Hero. "I'll stand guard."

Bean looked at Hero and tentatively agreed. "All right, let's stop and rest — but only for a minute. If the soldier is behind us, I don't want him to have time to catch up."

"Okay, only for a few minutes," agreed Hero.

Bubba and Bean collapsed into the moist grass next to KP, trying to catch their breath. The sky was dark and filled with small speckles, which resembled stars. The clouds stirred swiftly through the sky tonight and formed beautiful designs below the faint light of the stars. A stiff wind came from the north, swirling about their bodies and providing much needed relief from the heat and humidity.

As Hero stood watch, he noticed the clouds building in the sky. "At least it's not raining here like it was back home."

"I wish I was back home where it was raining," Bean said solemnly.

"Hero, what was that soldier talking about anyway?" asked Bubba, still breathing hard.

"I don't know for sure," Hero replied, passing his water bottle to Bubba.

"Why do you think he thought we were Nephites?" asked KP, listening to every terrifying sounds made in the wilderness.

"I don't know if he thought we were Nephites. He thought that we had come from the North," Hero answered. "I guess that must be Nephite territory."

"Or maybe an unknown territory?" asked Bubba.

"Nephites? What do you think he meant? Where are we exactly?" interrupted Bean, still gasping for air as the tears started to stream down her face. "Why would he think we are Nephites? Don't we live in the twenty-first century?"

"We're no longer in the small town of Timber Creek," said KP, trying to lighten the mood.

"No kidding," responded Bean angrily. "Where are we, guys? I'm scared. Being lost is not a joking matter."

"We've traveled to the past and landed in Book of

Mormon times; I'm sure of it," replied Bubba casually, as he placed his hand on Bean's shoulder and attempted to comfort her.

"But how could we realistically be in Book of Mormon time?" she asked, pushing Bubba's arm away.

"Time travel, I guess," he replied coolly.

"Funny, Bubba. Tell me, how did we travel back in time?" she asked, obviously bewildered.

Bubba shook his head back, shrugged his shoulders and said, "I'm not sure how, but I'm sure we have."

"How are you sure?" she whimpered, as tears started to well up in her eyes again.

"I've been thinking about what happened since we started running, Bean. I think traveling in time has got to have something to do with the treasure we found back at the Treehouse," said Hero. "The treasure is the only thing I can think of that would have the power to bring us here."

"Well, how do we use it to get home?" she asked between sobs. "I want to go home. Can you hear the scary noises out here? I hate to think what they're coming from."

"Don't worry, Bean. We'll figure out how to get home," replied Hero reassuringly. "If the treasure brought us here, it has to be able to take us back."

"Where is the treasure?" KP nervously asked.

"Safe and sound in Bean's backpack," declared Hero.

"If we're going to need it to get home, we better take good care of it," stated KP.

"Don't worry, KP. I will — especially if the treasure is our only way home," said Bean, as she patted the side of her backpack.

"Are you sure you don't want me to carry your pack for you? You're only a girl, and I would hate for you to be responsible for losing the treasure," KP teased.

"I won't lose it, and if you guys aren't nice to me, maybe I will leave you here and go home as soon as I can figure out how to use it," she responded, as a big smile crossed her swollen, wet face. "So, tell me smart guys, if we are in Book of Mormon time, how did the soldier understand anything we said?"

"Hey, good question — I hadn't thought about that. How did he understand us?" questioned Bubba. "I'm sure he doesn't know English."

"I'm not sure you understand English very well, Bubba," said KP jokingly.

"Cute, KP," answered Bubba. "Are you sure you're not talking about yourself?"

"Come on, you two," said Hero. "I'm sure the Lord helped us to understand his language and helped him to understand us," suggested Hero.

"You mean we're speaking Hebrew or something like that?" asked Bubba, a little confused.

"No, Bubba. The soldier heard Hebrew."

"I thought the hieroglyphics we translated back at the Treehouse were Reformed Egyptian," said KP.

"They were, KP, but Lehi's descendants spoke Hebrew or some form of Hebrew," he answered.

"So, we spoke English, but he heard Hebrew, and he spoke Hebrew, but we heard English?" asked KP.

"Yeah, I think so. How else could that soldier have known what we were saying?" answered Hero.

"Maybe because he understood us, he didn't kill us," suggested Bean. "I bet when we spoke, the soldier heard the language he speaks."

"Maybe," said Hero, hoping she had guessed right.

"See, the Lord is already helping us on our journey," KP added, trying to be positive.

"How about He helps us go home!" said Bean.

"I'm sure He will, as soon as we figure out why He needs us here," replied Hero.

"How are we supposed to figure what we need to do here, anyway?" asked Bubba.

"I'm not sure, Bub," replied Hero. "But, I am sure the Lord will provide a way for us to make that happen."

"Do you think the treasure has the answers we need?" asked Bean.

"Well, from what I know of the Liahona — which is what I believe the treasure is — the Lord used it to show Lehi and his family the direction He wanted them to travel. Maybe it will show us the way, too," Hero suggested.

"Do you think the treasure is why Mr. Jensen's great-grandfather, Ole, was always on an adventure?" asked Bean.

"That would make sense," Hero responded. "I kinda wish I had paid closer attention to Mr. Jensen's photo albums. I'm sure the answers to some of our questions were in them."

"The pictures make more sense now than they did when we were looking at them," said KP.

"I wish I knew more about what the treasure is and how it works," said Bubba.

"I'm sure we'll figure it out," replied Hero, trying to reassure everyone.

"I think if we knew more about it, that would help us get home faster," said Bubba.

"Hey, we might have a lot of fun on this adventure. I don't think Ole would have gone on adventure after adventure if he had really bad experiences every time," reasoned Hero.

"I'm sure you're right. I guess time travel is a little intimidating because we don't know exactly what to do," said Bean.

"Wait, I just had a thought," said KP excitedly.

"Wow, that's new for you, KP," said Bubba. "Maybe this clean air is helping your brain to finally work."

"Ha, ha. Very funny, Bubba," said KP.

"Come on, guys," said Hero. "Tell us, KP — what was your thought?"

"Okay, if Ole used the treasure to go on these adventures, he evidently knew how to come back after each one, right?" KP asked.

"You're right, KP," said Hero. "I guess we've got to figure out how to use the treasure. Bean, maybe you can be in charge of doing that?"

"Quiet, everyone," said Bean, as her eyes grew bigger and bigger.

"What? Do you hear something?" asked KP.

"Listen!" she snapped. "Be quiet and listen."

"What are we listening for, Bean?" asked Hero.

"The noises of the jungle are getting louder. They're almost frightening, and they don't stop. Do you think the animals out here could hurt us?" she asked, nervously looking around.

"I'm sure tons of animals are out here," said Bubba. "But I'm not sure any would hurt us."

"Hurt us? Some animals in the jungle might want to eat us," said KP grinning, trying to frighten Bean.

"No animals out here are going to eat us. We'll be all right, as long as we stay together," Hero replied, trying to comfort Bean.

Bubba sensed Bean's fears and said, "Don't worry, Bean. I know Tater's not here, but I will protect you," he said, as he held up his arms and flexed his muscles.

"Those muscles aren't quite as big as Tater's are, Bubba," she replied, showing a small smile.

"Not quite," Bubba replied. "But, I'm twice as fast as he is."

"You're right. Thanks, Bubba," she softly whispered.

The teammates' nerves seemed to settle slightly as they sat and relaxed for a few minutes. Unable to focus on anything in the overwhelming darkness, they speculated on what might have happened, why they were here and how they were going to get home. The conversation dwindled as they pondered what they should do next.

Hero, still standing guard, looked cautiously around his surroundings and concentrated on the sounds of the jungle. Concerned the noises were getting softer, he whispered, "Everybody, listen a minute. The animal noises seem to be quieting."

As Bubba, Bean and KP watched, Hero quickly moved behind a tree. He took a deep breath, pulling in his non-existent stomach, and tried to hide behind the tree. He squinted his eyes and attempted to focus on the darkness ahead.

"What in the world are you doing, Hero?" asked Bubba.

"When the noises in the jungle get quiet," he responded, as he jumped like a cat behind a bush, "that typically means someone or something has scared off whatever was making the noise."

"Maybe the noises have stopped because we're here," reasoned KP, as he stood up and surveyed the area.

"Possibly," replied Hero, still moving covertly around the area. "But then, why weren't the sounds quiet earlier?"

"Oh, good question. Maybe someone is watching us," replied Bubba looking around the darkness.

"The trees are so big around here. I can't tell for sure, but I think I can see lights not too far in the distance," KP quietly whispered.

"They could be lights from the city that the warrior talked about," Bean added.

"I'm sure it's a city, but what city?" replied Bubba. "I don't want to end up in the hands of the Lamanites."

"Lamanites?" asked Bean worriedly.

"Yes, Lamanites. We've got to be careful out here. Scary stories about the Lamanites are written throughout the Book of Mormon. I don't know for sure what's happening during this time in the Book of Mormon. But, if we're in the war times, we could be mistaken for Lamanites, Amalekites or Zoramites," said Bubba.

"Dressed like this?" asked Bean, pointing to her jean shorts and bright red shirt.

"Good point. We're really going to stand out to the people around here if we don't find some different clothes to wear," said Hero.

"We're going to have to find some modern clothes," said Bubba.

"Modern clothes. Didn't the people in the Book of Mormon wear loincloths?" asked KP.

"Not all of them," said Bubba. "We'll have to find something that blends in with what the people in the city are wearing."

"How do we do that?" Bean demanded. "We have no money — at least no money they would recognize. We have nothing of any value. We don't know anyone here that can help us, and we don't even know what we're doing here!"

"We'll figure out why we're here. Maybe we'll even get lucky and spot some people from the city so we can see how they dress," suggested Hero. "Then we can borrow some clothes or something."

"I'm not wearing a loincloth! I don't care if I stand out and get captured," replied KP.

"Don't worry, KP," said Bubba smiling. "I think that only the Lamanites wore loincloths."

"Why are we talking about clothes? What about dark hair? We all have light skin and light hair. Lamanites had dark skin and hair, didn't they? I'm not sure about the character traits of the Nephites," said Bean, "but I doubt fair skin and blonde hair were common."

"Hopefully they look a little like us," answered Hero. "Be positive for a minute."

"Hey, I just had a thought," interrupted Bubba.

"Good, Bubba. Is the clean air helping you to use your brain?" asked KP jokingly.

"Funny, guys. Tell us your thoughts," demanded Bean.

"Now I know why Mr. Jensen had all of those cool clothes in his attic," he replied.

"Why?" she questioned gruffly.

"I bet his great-grandfather, Ole, would dress up in character before he would use the treasure to travel back in time," he answered.

"I bet you're right," replied Hero, nodding his head in agreement.

"Yeah, me, too. I bet he knew exactly how this thing worked and what to do with it," said KP, holding up Bean's backpack for everyone to see.

"How do you think he knew what to wear?" asked Bean, a little puzzled.

"Maybe he would bring more than one outfit with him to wear," answered Hero. "He probably carried a pack or something with all sorts of stuff in it for these adventures."

"Well, we don't have clothes with us, so we are going to have to find something here to wear," replied Bean.

"Let's figure out where we are," said Hero. "Then we will know what to do and how to dress."

"We've got to figure something out before the sun comes up. I don't want to be mistaken for a Lamanite," said Bubba, looking over his shoulder. "And Bean's right — we don't look like we belong here."

"We better keep moving," said KP nervously. He

picked up his backpack, threw it over his shoulder and started walking toward the lights. "We have been here too long, and I don't want any other soldiers to find us."

"Wait a minute. What's our plan? Shouldn't we at least make a plan?" asked Bean, standing up quickly and cautiously looking around, worried about continuing on into the darkness.

"Bean's got a point. Hold on a minute, KP. Let's make a plan," said Hero. "It doesn't need to be elaborate, but I do think we should have some sort of direction."

"Hero!" shrieked Bean.

Hero spun around quickly, petrified of what might be behind him. His heart raced wildly. "What is it, Bean?" he asked, shaking from the adrenalin rush her scream had caused.

"What is it? What is it?" she screamed, pointing to the broken tree lying on the ground.

Squinting to see what she was pointing at, Hero walked toward the tree stump. Searching intently, Bean caught Hero off guard when she screamed again.

"Hero! Stop!" she yelled, pointing to the log.

"What is it? I can't see the anyone," he complained, holding his chest from the shock of her piercing screams.

Bubba smiled and yelled, "It's on the log, Hero."

Hero, not looking for a soldier anymore, glanced down at the log. Sprawled out across the length of the log was the biggest iguana he had ever seen.

"Wow, it must be at least four feet long," Hero said, moving closer to see the vibrant green, brown and yellow colors.

"Don't get too close, Hero," warned Bean. "I'm sure it could bite your hand completely off."

Hero smiled and said, "Don't worry about me. KP, Bubba, can you see this thing?"

"Yep, and I can see another one over on that rock," Bubba replied, as he pointed further to the north.

"This is so cool. When we go home, I want to take one with me," Hero said, grinning.

"No way!" shouted Bean. "That thing is too big."

KP, ready to get moving, said, "Come on guys, please. What's the plan? I'm ready to go."

Hero walked back over to his teammates, smiling. "KP's right. What's the plan?"

"I think our first plan of action should be to build some shelter," suggested Bubba. "That way, we will at least have a place to sleep."

"And a place to hide," added KP.

"Yes, we do need to do that," agreed Bean, still staring at the huge reptile.

"Okay, I think we need to move closer toward the city. Then we can see what the people are wearing and determine if they are friendly or not," replied Hero.

"As we move closer to the city, we can watch for a secluded area that we could use as a shelter," suggested KP.

"And we can also try to figure out where we are and why we're here, right?" asked Bean.

"Yes, Bean," answered Hero. "Everybody all right with that?"

"Yep," said Bubba.

"That works for me," replied KP.

"Maybe we'll be able to figure out how to get home, too," said Bean, shrugging her shoulders.

"Hopefully," answered Hero. "You're in charge of figuring out how the treasure works."

"Okay, you can count on me. I'll figure it out," Bean replied.

"Come on, guys. I'm getting nervous, so let's move," suggested KP, uncomfortable with the surroundings. "Follow me to the city," he said. He tried to relieve the tension by swinging his arms, stomping his feet, lifting his knees high and marching like a soldier toward the lights.

"Quiet, KP. Quit messing around. We could still be in dangerous territory, and I don't want anyone to get hurt," said Hero.

"There could be animal traps out here," said Bubba. "You don't want to be careless and get caught in one."

"Animal traps? I bet there are people traps," said Bean, cautiously looking around.

"Bean's right. I bet we will see traps and guards everywhere. We need to move slowly and cautiously through the jungle," said Bubba. "We don't want to make a dumb mistake and get hurt."

"Or die," added Bean.

"Yeah, KP. Wait a minute, and we'll all go together," said Hero. He put his water bottle back into his backpack and zipped it closed.

As they stood and gathered their belongings, the clouds burst and the rain poured down. The noise from the drops made a song that, when added with the animals, was truly musical. With no shelter from the downpour,

Bean searched her backpack for a rain jacket. Struggling with the zipper for a moment, she knelt down, dropped the bag and tried again. Finally getting the backpack open, she fumbled through the contents in the pack.

"I've got two jackets. Who wants one?" she asked.

Before anyone could respond, a loud scream pierced the silence. "Ooooouuuch! Ouch! Ouch!" yelled Bubba, jumping to his feet and shaking his arms and legs wildly.

"What's the matter?" asked Hero, quickly standing up and moving toward Bubba.

"There are bugs all over me," he replied, still shaking his arms wilding. "Help me! Help me! Get them off!"

Bean rifled through her already-opened backpack. She pulled out her small flashlight and shined it on Bubba. Hero grabbed Bubba's arm and started brushing off the bugs.

"Oh, they're just ants, Bubba," said KP. "You'll be all right. Quit jumping around, you wimp."

"They're Red Ants, KP," said Bean, as she inspected them with her flashlight. "BIG, Red Ants."

"Yeah?" he answered. "So what? They're still ants."

"Red Ant's bite, and their bites sting," answered Bean, as she glared at KP.

"In the jungle, I think they are called Fire Ants," added Hero, as he continued brushing them off of Bubba's pants.

"Fire Ants? What does that mean?" asked KP.

"They sting when they bite, KP!" yelled Bubba. "I feel like I am on fire everywhere."

"Pull off your clothes, Bub, quick!" Hero screamed. "We'll never get them all off this way."

Bubba stopped jumping, looked over at Hero and

said, "Are you crazy? Bean's here, and I'm not taking off my clothes — even if the ants are biting."

"Bubba, you are getting bitten all over your body. You could have a severe reaction to all the poison. Take you clothes off, now!" Hero yelled. "I don't care if Bean is here. Just leave your boxers on."

Bean quickly grabbed her backpack, smiled at Hero and said, "Bubba, Hero is right. You need to get your clothes off. I'll move over and stand behind that big tree," she said as she pointed. "Shake out your clothes, and get those ants off you." She smiled and quickly turned toward the tree.

Bubba, on the verge of tears from the pain caused by the ant bites, managed a small grin. "Thanks Bean," he whimpered.

"Yeah, thanks, Bean," said Hero. "I'll call you as soon as we have him taken care of."

Bean turned and quickly ran behind a huge tree yelling, "Hurry, I don't want to be alone for very long."

As soon as she was out of sight, Bubba frantically peeled off his shoes and socks, then his shirt and pants. Standing in the rain in his boxer shorts, still brushing off the ants, he looked at Hero and said, "Do we have a first aid kit with us?"

"I'm not sure. Why?" he asked.

"I think I'm gonna need some anti-histamine, or some anti-itch ointment or something," Bubba answered through a crackling voice. "I hurt everywhere. I've never felt pain from bug bites like this before! I wish Mom were here to take care of me."

"Hang in there, Bubba. I'll check my backpack," Hero replied. "KP, check your backpack too, please," he called.

KP pulled off his backpack and checked the contents. "Nothing here. I don't have one," he said.

"Me neither, Bubba. I'm sorry," said Hero.

"Maybe Bean has one in her pack," suggested KP. "I'll go ask her as soon as we're sure all of the ants are off you, okay?" said Hero.

Bubba nodded his head as tears streamed down his face. "My body is on fire, guys," he said. "We've got to be more careful out here."

KP and Hero helped check Bubba's hair for any remaining ants. Then they took Bubba's clothes and started shaking them. The half-inch-long Fire Ants remained stuck to the clothes. When violently shaking the clothes did not work, the boys beat the clothes against a nearby tree. Then they turned out the pockets and checked the waistband for any stragglers.

Finally, Hero handed Bubba his pants and said, "I think your pants are okay now."

"Your t-shirt's okay, too," said KP, holding it out for Bubba to take. As Bubba took the shirt, an ant crawled up KP's arm. He screamed as the ant bit him. "Ooouch!" he yelled, smashing the ant. "These ant bites do hurt."

"Thanks, guys," replied Bubba trying to smile. He carefully pulled his shirt over his head, and cringed from the pain as it rubbed against his burning shoulders. He slowly worked up the courage to pull his pants over the hundreds of bites covering his legs.

A startling scream brought the boys' attention back to their surroundings. It shattered the quiet sounds of the animals, bringing the jungle life to a standstill.

"What is it, Bean?" shouted Hero. "Everything okay?" he called, looking toward the tree where she was waiting.

"Her-..." Bean yelled, not quite finishing his entire name.

"Are you okay?" Hero called.

"Probably a snake or another iguana," replied KP, slowly walking toward the tree.

"Her..." Bean shrieked again.

"Bean, are you okay?" asked Hero again. "What's wrong?"

Hearing no response, KP, Hero and Bubba, who was now dressed, started running toward the tree where Bean had been waiting for them.

"Bean, where are you?" Hero called, as they reached the tree.

They could see no sign of her anywhere. Turning in circles, Hero checked the entire area. No sounds, no movement, nothing. Even the animal noises had stopped. The silence in the jungle was more frightening than any of the noises that had previously filled the air.

"Bean!" shouted Bubba frantically. "Where are you?"

"She's not here," said KP. "She'd better not be playing a trick on us."

"No way. She's too scared to do that," replied Hero.

"Where could she be then?" asked Bubba searching the area. "She has to be here."

"Bean," Hero shrieked. "Where are you?" he hollered. "She can't be too far; she just called my name."

"Oh man, you've got to be kidding," said Bubba, frantically searching the area. "She's a girl, Hero. She could really get hurt out here. We should've kept a closer eye on her and protected her better."

"It's not my fault you sat on an ant hill, Bubba," Hero responded angrily.

"Hero, what do we do?" asked KP, running through the surrounding trees and bushes searching for her.

"How am I suppose to know? I thought she was close enough that she would be okay for a minute or two," he replied, feeling responsible for her disappearance.

"Bean! Bean! Where are you?" Bubba continued screaming. "Answer me!"

Faintly in the distance, the boys heard a muffled cry. The muted sound was hard to locate. Fighting the urge to start running, they listened and hoped they could hear her cry again.

"Wait! Don't move. What was that noise — Bean or an animal?" asked Hero, holding out his arms and signaling KP and Bubba to remain still.

"Probably the animals in the jungle," said KP. "They're starting to get noisy again."

"Be quiet and listen!" demanded Hero. "The sound might be Bean."

As they stood completely still, almost holding their breath, they waited patiently for another sound.

"There it is again. The noise kinda sounds like a scream," said KP.

"Could it be Bean?" asked Bubba.

"It has to be her. Let's go check it out," said Hero.

"Which way?" asked KP.

"This way," hollered Hero, as he headed east, deeper into the jungle. "Follow me, and stay close."

Chapter Two

Cautiously following the occasional muffled noises in the distance, Hero, KP and Bubba maneuvered deeper and deeper into the dense growth of underbrush, grasses and vines. Though they were nervous, they pressed forward into the darkness, desperately searching for Bean.

"The noises in the jungle are kinda frightening at night, don't you think?" KP asked, fearfully looking over his shoulder.

"A little, I guess," replied Hero, as he stumbled over the roots of a tree and fell to his knees. "I haven't paid much attention. I'm worried about Bean."

"Are you all right, Hero?" asked Bubba, as he helped him up from the ground.

"Yep, I'm fine. We need to be really careful out here," he said. "It's getting harder and harder to see."

As they traveled further into the jungle, Bubba noticed a footpath worn in the grass. Sure he was on to something, he started looking for broken branches or any sign of a struggle.

"Look!" shouted Bubba, startling Hero and KP.

"What? Look at what?" asked Hero eagerly. "Do you see her?"

"Isn't this a clip from Bean's hair?" he asked excitedly, as he pulled it off the tree branch.

"It has to be," answered KP.

"I can't imagine people from the Book of Mormon know how to mold plastic," added Hero. "Nice work, Bubba."

Realizing they were on the right track, the boys continued forward, carefully working their way through the maze of trees. The rain began again, but the canopy of trees acted as an umbrella and shielded the boys from most of the water. The rain collected on the leaves, forming little pools of water, which cascaded down like a waterfall to the leaves below. In a short time, despite the cover, the boys' clothes were soaked again. But, in spite of the undesirable conditions, they pushed forward and followed the path. They knew they had to locate Bean quickly and bring her to safety.

"Holy cow, I walked through a spider web," said Bubba, flailing his arms in the air. "What kind of spiders do you think are in this jungle?" he nervously asked.

"Probably spiders that can kill you," answered KP.

"You're probably right, KP. Get the flashlight out, and let's check to make sure Bubba doesn't have a poisonous spider on him," said Hero.

KP unzipped his backpack and retrieved the flashlight. Bubba pulled off his backpack and continued to wipe away the icky feeling of the spider web on his arms. Shining the light directly on Bubba's head, Hero quickly checked for any poisonous spiders on Bubba's body.

"Hurry, Hero. The web is making me nervous," said Bubba.

"Well, watch where you're walking then," Hero replied, smirking.

"I can hardly see my feet, let alone where I'm going, Hero," retorted Bubba.

Hero grinned and said, "I know — just teasing. Wow! Here it is, Bubba," he said, knocking it quickly from his back.

"Why don't I believe you, Hero?" Bubba asked, looking at him skeptically.

"'Cause there are no spiders anywhere on you. Now, check your pack, and let's keep moving," replied Hero.

"I don't like the unknown, Hero. I wish I had a clue where we are," said Bubba.

"We know where we are," answered KP.

"We do?" questioned Bubba.

"Yep, we are in a jungle," he replied.

"Man, KP. You are on one today," said Hero.

KP's smile turned to concern as he said, "Guys, I

thought the noises here in the jungle were just animals. But listen to that sound. I've heard it before," KP stated.

"Hey, you're right. The noise does sound familiar," replied Bubba. "What is it?"

"Are we in danger?" KP asked anxiously.

"Danger? Yep, I think so. We're in the middle of a strange jungle with no light to follow, and we can't find Bean anywhere," Bubba answered, taking a deep breath. Then he continued, "We don't have a clue where we are or why we're here, I'm starving, and we haven't had time to figure out how we will get home. Yep, I'd say that's a little bit of trouble."

"Whose fault is all of this anyway, Bubba?" snapped KP. "If you hadn't stepped on the wire back at Mr. Jensen's house, we'd probably be playing ball right now."

"Well, soooorrry, KP," responded Bubba. "You could've stayed home. You didn't have to search for Moroni's treasure."

"Come on, you two. We've got to work together," declared Hero. "Be quiet, and try to get along."

"Hey, now you're kinda sounding like Mom, Hero," said Bubba, as he threw on his backpack and continued to follow the footpath. "That makes me homesick. I wonder if she even knows we're gone."

"If she does know, the world is coming to an end in Timber Creek. I'll bet she has the Police, National Guard, FBI and CIA looking for us," Hero chuckled.

"Not to mention the Relief Society and the Elder's Quorum," said Bubba smiling.

"And anybody else she can think of," added KP.

"And I bet your mom is right there with ours, KP," said Hero.

"I can imagine how crazy it is at the Treehouse. I hope our parents haven't destroyed our clubhouse and everything in it," said KP.

"That would be a crazy scene, with everyone looking for us, huh?" Bubba replied, as he tripped over a maze of vines on the ground.

"Yeah, that would," whispered Hero, fearful he might never see his mom again. "I hope Tater has things under control."

"Me, too," said KP.

"Wait guys — help me. My foot is caught. Someone, get the flashlight out," said Bubba, sitting on the ground. He pulled on his leg, trying to free it from the vines.

"You need the flashlight again?" asked Hero.

"Sorry, guys. Walking through a dark jungle is hard," said Bubba.

"Well, you better be careful," suggested KP. "You don't want to sit in a pile of Fire Ants or walk through a spider web again," he said, as he handed Bubba the flashlight.

Bubba grabbed the light and swiftly switched it on, scanning the area for insects. With none in sight, he held the flashlight in his teeth and tried to untangle the maze of vines around his foot. As he pulled at them, they moved only slightly. They acted as though he was their prisoner, and freedom came only to those who fought for it.

"Hurry, Bubba. We need to leave the light off as much as possible. Someone might see it and come to find out what it is," explained Hero.

"Just a minute — my foot is almost untangled," replied Bubba, still pulling at the vines wrapped around his feet. As the last vine finally gave way, Bubba's hand flew back and hit KP squarely in the stomach.

"Sorry, KP," Bubba whispered, as he watched him hunch over, moaning from the pain of the unexpected blow.

"You did that on purpose, Bubba," KP whined, trying to catch his breath.

"No, I didn't. I promise," he replied. "It was an accident."

"What is the matter with you two?" Hero asked. "I've never seen you act this way."

"I guess I was unprepared for this adventure," squeaked KP, still holding his stomach. He longed to see something that reminded him of home.

"I'm a little on edge, too, Hero," said Bubba. "Sorry, KP. I really didn't mean to hit you."

"That's okay, Bubba," replied KP. "I'm sorry, too."

The boys wandered on through the jungle, listening for any sounds that could lead the way to Bean. Hero figured they had walked nearly two miles. Forging through the dense jungle was more difficult than they had expected.

Still uneasy, the boys maneuvered down the side of a hill, holding onto the vines as they repelled down. Then something in the jungle caught their eyes.

"Hey, did you see that?" asked Hero.

"Or hear that?" asked KP.

"See and hear what?" whispered Bubba, as he tugged at the sticker weeds stuck to his pant legs.

"It's getting louder. It sounds like a crackling noise," Hero responded. "Turn off the flashlight before we're spotted," he ordered, nervous someone might be very close.

"And look — I think that's smoke," said KP, pointing to an area approximately two hundred yards in the distance.

Bubba quickly switched off the flashlight and squatted down next to a bush. He looked for the smoke and listened intently for the sounds Hero heard.

"Those could be clouds," said Bubba, pointing to a smoke cloud.

"I hear something," replied KP. "What is it?"

"I hear it, too. I know that sound," replied Bubba. "That's the sound of a crackling campfire."

"It does sound like a campfire," said KP. "Where is it? The smoke is wandering, and I can't see any fire."

Hero carefully searched through the almost impenetrable thicket of trees, canes and reedy vegetation. He spotted the fire fifty yards further east into the jungle. The light from the fire offered the boys' first look at their jungle surroundings.

"I see animals everywhere," said Bubba. "We could have been hearing noise from them this entire time."

"Guys, come here and look," whispered Hero, as he moved some branches of the tree for them to see.

Laying flat on their stomachs, KP and Bubba squeezed under the bush with Hero. For the first time, they felt completely hidden and safe.

"What is it?" whispered Bubba.

"It looks like a small camp or..." replied KP.

"Or what?" asked Bubba.

"Or an army camp," finished KP.

"There is the crackling we kept hearing," said Hero,

pointing to the fire in the center of the camp.

"Look at all the tents," said Bubba. "They're like the tee-pee tents at scout camp."

The boys gazed at the camp in awe. They would have never found this camp in the daylight. The entire camp was made out of foliage from the jungle. Nothing but trees and vines were used in the construction. Most of the tents were small in size. They saw a few large tents that were probably used for the army's leaders. The fire provided the only non-green color in the area. No spears, machetes, pottery or animal skins were anywhere to be found.

"These tee-pees are made with bamboo sticks and palm fronds," said KP.

"And they're pretty small," said Hero. "I bet you could only get two or three warriors inside each one."

"That's good for us, right?" asked Bubba.

"Why?" KP asked.

"Not as many warriors," answered Bubba.

"That's good, but I'm not sure that fewer warriors will make freeing Bean any easier," said Hero.

"Do you think they have Bean in one of the tee-pees?" asked Bubba.

"It's possible," replied Hero. "We didn't see who took her, so it's hard to know for sure. But we did find her hair clip, so I'm hopeful."

"How many tee-pees do you see?" Bubba asked.

Hero surveyed the entire area, which was nearly half the size of a football field. He counted the tents in his head, trying to determine how many warriors were in the camp.

"The tents circle the small meadow area. I think I can see about fifteen or sixteen," Hero answered, still searching the area intently.

"So, there might be forty to fifty warriors?" asked KP. "That's a pretty small army."

"Probably," Hero replied. "I'm wondering if they're a spy group or something like that?"

"What would a spy group do?" asked Bubba.

"Find the enemy spies, and take them back to the leader of the camp," he replied.

"Do you think Bean is considered a spy?" asked Bubba.

"Probably not," answered Hero. "She's a girl, so I'm not sure what they would think."

"How are we going to check all the tents without getting caught?" asked KP.

"Very carefully," joked Bubba.

"Everybody's a comedian tonight," laughed Hero.

"I can't see any soldiers anywhere," said Bubba.

"Well, searching the tents should be easy then," replied KP. "Let's go check."

"Hold it — not so fast," said Hero. "Something doesn't seem right here."

"Why?" Bubba asked. "It's late at night. They could all be asleep in the tee-pees."

"I'm sure they would have guards on patrol. And with the capture of Bean, I'm sure the warriors would be celebrating in the camp. But I can't see anyone — not even a guard," replied Hero. "That doesn't seem right."

"This could be a trap to catch us unprepared," said

Bubba. "The warriors must have been watching us before they took her. They would have to know that we'd come to get her."

"The warriors probably had an easy time kidnapping her. I bet we looked hilarious out there, with you jumping up and down, and KP and I shaking out your clothes. Maybe they figured they had nothing to worry about," said Hero.

"That's true," admitted Bubba. "I'm glad they don't have cameras here. That would be a picture I'd never want anyone to see."

As the fire burned in the camp, it cast a soft, spooky glow in the jungle, causing daunting shadows to dance on the ground. The boys watched the camp silently for thirty minutes, but they saw no movement. Bubba was so tired and bored, he laid his head on his arm in the grass and almost fell asleep.

"Maybe Bean's not here," said KP. "This could be a deserted camp."

"That's true — she may not be here," answered Hero. "Maybe whoever captured her kept moving past this camp. But, there's no way it's deserted. Remember — a fire is burning."

"Yep, that makes sense," agreed KP. "I forgot about the fire."

Bewildered, the boys huddled together for warmth. Their clothes were still damp from the earlier rain, and the chill in the air caused every breath to form a puff of white mist. The boys hid safely in the dense foliage of the trees and bushes, concealing their breath the best they could, while they considered what to do. They could risk searching each tee-pee under the cover of darkness, or they could wait to see what the morning would bring.

"If Bean isn't here, we run the risk of falling further behind her kidnappers if we wait," said Bubba, nervous because they had not seen her in the area.

"But if she is being held captive in one of those tents and we leave, we could lose her forever," said KP.

Hero sat quietly for several minutes, pondering their next move. Suddenly, the silence was broken with the loud sound of beating drums.

"What's that?" whispered Bubba, his heart racing. "Where's it coming from?"

"SHHH! Be quiet," ordered Hero. "Let's watch."

"Aye, yi, yi, yi. Aye, yi, yi, yi," called several warriors, as they jumped out of the tee-pees and moved toward the fire. The beating of the drums stopped momentarily as the warriors circled the fire pit. Several anxious seconds passed before the drums began again. Then the warriors began to dance.

The boys sat motionless, afraid that the warriors might spot them at any moment. They were shocked at the appearance of the warriors, who wore only loincloths and tie-on sandals — nothing else. Their faces were painted with several colors, like bright yellow, orange and red. Some of the men had even painted blue and black stripes around their arms and legs. Their hair was partially shaved on top, with the remainder pulled back into a ponytail. Only one or two had a full head of hair.

"Can they see us, Hero?" whispered Bubba, covering

his mouth with his hand to hide his breathing.

"I don't think so," he replied. "We're hidden pretty well in these trees and vines."

"What are they doing?" asked KP. "I've never seen anything like this before."

"They look like they're dancing around the fire. Maybe they're doing a ritual dance," answered Hero.

"A what?" KP asked, staring at the crazed warriors.

"A ritual dance is a dance Native Americans used to do. Some of the dances were done to bring rain, good crops, or other things like that," answered Hero.

"Why?" he questioned, making a funny face. "It's the middle of the night."

"I don't know," said Hero. "Maybe they're doing a dance of celebration because they just captured Bean."

"We don't know that for sure," said Bubba.

"We haven't seen anything else in the jungle besides this camp," said Hero. "She has to be here; I'm sure of it."

"I hope so," replied Bubba.

"Do you think these warriors are Nephites?" asked KP.

Hero looked over to KP and asked, "Are you kidding, KP?"

KP shrugged his shoulders and said, "We don't know anything about this specific time in the Book of Mormon. I was just asking."

"I don't think so. I never remember reading anywhere in the Book of Mormon about righteous people painting their faces and doing ritual dances," said Bubba.

"Have you read the whole book?" asked KP, smiling.

"Oh, you are really funny tonight," responded Bubba.

"So, you don't think that these warriors would help us, then?" asked KP, somewhat serious.

"No, they don't look like they would help us," Bubba replied. "They're probably warriors that would kill us, though."

The three boys sat and watched the warriors. They danced, screamed, and shook their fists and spears in the air for almost twenty minutes. As the boys watched, they could see no sign of Bean anywhere. A dark feeling covered the area and made Hero very uneasy.

"What should we do?" asked Bubba. "Do we wait longer?" he asked, afraid to stay in the area. "It's creepy here, guys. If I didn't know better, I would say that Satan is influencing this camp."

"We better get out of here before one of them spots us," suggested KP, confused by the evil feeling in the air. He started crawling recklessly on his hands and knees out of the bushes and away from the commotion.

"Wait, KP. We need to make sure Bean is not here before we move on," said Hero. "If these warriors have her, we have to save her!"

"Maybe if we make it back to the city we saw before, we could find someone who would help us," KP replied.

"We don't even know where the city is for sure, anymore," said Bubba. "I don't want to leave if Bean might be here."

"Slow down, KP. Let's watch a few more minutes, and maybe we will catch a glimpse of Bean."

"Or the warriors could get a glimpse of us," he replied, crawling uneasily back under the bush.

As they waited impatiently and watched for another five minutes, they heard a blood-curdling scream. Then a frantic beating of the drums roared for at least a full minute, which was followed by dead silence. The huge palm frond that covered the opening of the largest tent was thrown open.

Two mighty warriors in loincloths emerged. They had leather bands around their arms and war paint all over their bodies. They wore beautiful headdresses with hundreds of feathers that ran the entire length of their backs. They were followed by two small women. The first woman had thick, beautiful, long black hair, which she pulled into a ponytail. She was older like the boys mom's and looked to be the servant of the leader. The second woman had shoulder-length, sandy-blonde hair, with two bright yellow feathers sticking straight up from the back of her head.

"Hey, that looks like Bean," said Bubba.

"Yeah, but she's wearing a long dress and moccasins," said KP. "Bean would never do that."

"That's right," agreed Bubba. "The only time I've ever seen Bean in a dress is on Sunday at church."

"I've never seen Bean without her hair tied up in a ponytail," added Hero.

"What if she didn't have a choice?" asked KP, watching every move the girl made as he tried desperately to get a good look at her face.

"It doesn't look like she did," reasoned Hero. "Her hands are tied behind her back."

"That is Bean!" declared KP.

"Looks like her to me," said Hero. "I haven't seen her face yet, but she is the same size, she has the same hair color, and she is tied up. That has to be her."

"What are they doing?" asked Bubba. "Why are they dragging her around the fire?"

"Looks like they're celebrating her capture," replied Hero. "They're showing her to all the warriors."

"Why do you think they made her change her clothes?" asked Bubba.

"I don't know," Hero replied. "Could be that her shorts and shirt are not appropriate clothing for a girl in their tribe."

"Where is her backpack?" asked KP frantically, realizing she did not have it with her. "She's got the treasure inside it. We can't get home without that treasure. What do we do now?"

"I'm not worried about the treasure right now," answered Bubba. "How are we going to rescue her?"

"We're gonna have to wait until the warriors fall asleep," said Hero. "Then we'll have to try to sneak in and save her."

"I wish I could think of a good western movie with cowboys and Indians, where the cowboys rode in and saved the girl," said KP. "That might give us some good ideas on how to save Bean."

Bubba looked at KP and smiled. Then he asked, "Hero, how are we going to save her if they have guards on duty all the time?"

"I'm not sure yet," he replied. "Let's watch and see what they do first."

Hero, KP and Bubba watched in horror as the warriors danced around Bean. They pulled at her hair and moved her around the fire for all the warriors to see. The tears on her face glistened in the firelight, infuriating the boys. The dance continued for at least an hour as they picked and pulled at Bean. The boys could do absolutely nothing but wait.

"What are they doing?" asked Bubba. "Can't they see she's upset?"

"I don't think they really care," said KP. "I don't know what I'm gonna do if they hurt her."

"Maybe they're trying to show her their strength so that she doesn't try to escape," Hero replied.

"They don't know Bean very well, then. She doesn't get intimidated easy," Bubba said.

"What do you think they are going to do to her?" asked KP. "They're not going to kill her, are they?"

"No, I don't think so," Hero replied slowly. "I hope not."

"Hero, what aren't you telling me?" Bubba asked. "I know that face, and you know something."

Hero paused only a moment before he answered. "I've studied the Book of Mormon, and the Lamanites weren't always nice to their prisoners. I'm just afraid for her. I'm really not sure why they are pushing her around."

"If I stood up and screamed, would they follow me?" asked Bubba. Tears welled up in his eyes as he watched. "Then maybe Bean could escape," he finished.

"All that would do is give them another prisoner to torture," Hero replied. "Stay down, and be quiet — both of you."

"I hate this, Hero," said Bubba. "And it's all my fault."

"This is not your fault, Bubba," said KP. "Any of us could have sat in that ant hill."

The drums and dancing stopped when the leader held up his hands and yelled, "SILENCE!"

The warriors quickly moved to the opening of their tee-pees and sat down.

"Men, as you can see, we have stolen this Nephite daughter from our enemies tonight," the leader said.

A roar of excitement followed from the warriors. Again the leader held up his hand for silence.

"We have also penetrated the city and stolen our enemies' sacred records," he said, holding up something the boys did not recognize. "This Nephite daughter wore special clothes and carried a bag full of treasures from our enemies, the Nephites," he said, pausing at the yells of the men. "Their prophet Alma sent for captains from other cities to help the great Captain Moroni, and we have stolen one of their daughters. As she traveled, she was guarded by three of their best warriors."

"Is he talking about us, Hero?" Bubba asked.

"Shhhh. Be quiet and listen," Hero responded, afraid he might miss something.

"When our mighty warriors, Matoki and Coninihah, were returning from stealing Alma's sacred records, they found her and captured her for us!" their leader exclaimed, patting the warriors on the back. "Now, with the great price she will bring in the war with Captain Moroni, and the records his men will do anything to save, three moons from tonight we will be victorious."

Once more the warriors screamed in delight.

"In three days, we will join our brothers on the battlefield against the Nephites. We could have struggled and lost many men, but I now believe we will be victorious, for we have a strong weapon against them. They will not want their daughter to die, nor to have their records destroyed."

The leader turned to Bean and grabbed her arms, which were tightly tied together. He pulled her to the front for everyone to see. "This girl, the treasured daughter of a Nephite Captain, is more valuable than gold to them. Not only will she bring us good luck. But we will be able to trade her and the records for this land. Then we will require the Nephites to depart into the wilderness," he explained.

Again, the warriors cheered in delight. They jumped up, waved their spears above their heads, and chanted in unison, "We will conquer! We will conquer!"

"What do we do?" asked KP. "This is terrible."

"They are using her as a hostage," replied Bubba. "And what records are they talking about?"

"This is not how the war was fought against Captain Moroni. If he doesn't win the war against Zerahemnah, the outcome of this war and the Book of Mormon will be changed," said KP.

"We've got to figure out a plan for her rescue, and quick!" said Hero.

"I guess we know for sure where we are now," added Bubba.

"I was really hoping we were in a more peaceful time," said Hero.

"What should we do?" asked KP. "We've got to save her," he said, watching the warriors dance around her and the fire.

"Wait, just a minute," responded Hero, again trying to hear what the Lamanite leader was saying.

"Men," he started, holding up his hand to get their attention. "I know the three warriors who were guarding the girl have announced her capture to the captain. And they most certainly have discovered their records missing. The Nephites are surely planning her rescue at this very moment. We must keep this girl and the records protected from the certain rescue attempt Captain Moroni's army will make to get her back. For that reason, both will be guarded in this camp at all times until the third moon rises. Then we will take them before Captain Moroni, and we will demand this land."

"We'll never be able to rescue her if she is under constant guard," said KP.

"Well, we will have to find a way," replied Bubba. "History in the Book of Mormon will be altered if we don't."

"What should we do?" asked KP. "We really need a plan."

"Okay, let's make one," said Bubba, extremely nervous about Bean's safety. "We know they will not kill her, and that is good."

"But they could hurt her," said KP.

"I don't think they will. They believe she is too valuable," said Hero. "We still need shelter, and we cannot stay here tonight — guards will be posted everywhere."

"You're right. We might get caught," said KP.

"Where should we go?" asked Bubba. "I don't want to get too far away from Bean."

"I think we need to be far enough away to not get caught, but close enough to keep an eye on Bean. We need to figure out what the Lord wants us to do," said Hero.

"I agree. Why don't we move further south and look for a place to hide," suggested Bubba.

"That's not a bad idea," said Hero. "Then we can be out of sight, but still close to Bean."

As the Lamanites continued to dance around the fire, the leader untied Bean's hands and pushed her into one of the tee-pees. He posted a guard at the door. Hero knew it was time to find shelter before the leader sent warriors back to look for them. The boys crawled out of the bushes and moved southward. As the light from the fire started to dim, and the sounds of screams and drums faded, the boys looked for a temporary shelter.

The moist, humid air in the jungle still made breathing difficult for the boys. Every breath was labored, as they struggled to move through the thick trees and vines. Each step the boys took was more difficult than the last. Ready to pass out from lack of sleep and food, they continued looking for the city. Hero knew they could be caught and killed at any moment. They had to get a shelter built fast — Bean's life depended on it.

Chapter Three

Tater crawled nervously back through the hidden opening of the Team's tree to the outside. Surprised to see the midday sun, he paused and turned his face toward the warmth. He closed his eyes for a moment and contemplated the turmoil Moroni's Treasure Map had already caused. "We are in so much trouble. Where could they be?" he thought anxiously.

Tater, the Titan's catcher and the Team's mighty protector, had valiantly kept everyone safe during their search for treasure. He had protected them from treacherous obstacles and escaped prisoners. But suddenly, a little brass ball had mysteriously taken Tater's friends and teammates. Where were Hero, Bubba, Bean and KP?

"What could that little brass ball have been? What was that blinking number and that blinding flash of light? Was it an explosion?" Tater wondered, as he walked thoughtfully back to the Treehouse ladder. Grabbing hold of the ladder, he quickly motioned for Runt, Stick, Red, Butch and Squeaks to climb up to the Treehouse. Somberly watching them climb, Tater knew the remaining teammates would look to him for answers. He had to figure out what had happened — quickly.

Questions rolled endlessly through his mind. "How could I have let this happen. I should've watched closer. Where in the world could they be? What am I going to do? How am I going to tell Hero and Bubba's Mom that something happened and they've mysteriously disappeared?" he wondered, desperately trying to make sense of the events that had just transpired.

As they reached the top of the ladder and climbed into the Treehouse, the Team waited anxiously for Tater's recommendation of what they should do next. After all, he was the next oldest player on their baseball team.

The Treehouse felt empty and lost without the entire Team. The search for Moroni's Treasure was supposed to end with excitement, new adventures and the possible discovery of an unbelievable ancient treasure — one the Team would use to do service for the Lord. But instead, they were left with fear, anxiety and unanswered questions.

"Tater," whispered Squeaks, breaking his intense trance. "Would food help you to think better? I could go to the house and get us some," she offered.

Tater looked up and smiled, hoping to put his friends at ease. "I'm okay, guys. Don't worry about me," he replied. "I'm just trying to figure out what our first move should be."

"Do you think they're okay?" Squeaks timidly asked. "I'm really scared for them."

"I'm sure they're fine, Squeaks," reassured Tater, although not totally convinced himself.

"Where do you think they could be?" she asked, obviously frightened.

"I honestly don't have any ideas yet," he replied. "I've been tryin' to figure it out, but I'm just not sure."

"Maybe we should put our heads together and see what we can come up with," suggested Runt.

"First things first. What are we going to tell Mom?" Squeaks asked. "You know she's gonna want to talk to Hero soon."

"I know she will, but I don't think we should say anything yet," replied Runt.

"We can't tell anyone anything," interjected Red. "They'll think we're crazy."

"Yeah, I can just see it now," said Runt. "Hello, 911… Our friends just magically disappeared in a burst of bright light from inside the trunk of our Treehouse. We were following an ancient map that led us to a treasure that nobody believed existed. Could you come save them, please?"

Everyone chuckled, grateful for the break in tension.

"I know for sure the police would believe that 911 call," giggled Stick sarcastically.

"Do you really think so?" asked Squeaks excitedly. "I

know the number to call 911. I could call them for us."

"No, Squeaks. Thanks anyway. Guys, nobody says anything until we have some sort of game plan," demanded Tater. "I don't want all of the adults searching around here until we know for sure what happened to Hero, Bubba, Bean and KP. Agreed?"

"Besides, do we really want adults to see the inside of our tree?" asked Red. "Or any of the other cool stuff we found?"

"That's true. The hieroglyphs, warm springs, Lehonti's cave and the tree wouldn't be secrets anymore," admitted Stick.

Squeaks, confused by the conversation, asked, "So, I should just tell Mom? I won't call 911 until you tell me to, right?"

"No, Squeaks," replied Tater nervously. "You can't tell anyone — not even your mom — until I tell you to, okay?"

"Really? Not even Mom?" she questioned.

"No, not even Mom," replied Stick, as he put his arm around her trying to comfort her. "We need to figure out what happened first, okay?"

"Okay, I won't say anything until you want me to, Tater, if that is what you think is best," she agreed, starting to cry. "Do you think Hero, Bubba, KP and Bean will come back soon? Do you think they are going to come back?"

"They will, Squeaks. I know it," Stick replied. "Don't worry. I'm sure this is the Lord's plan."

"I hope so, Stick. I miss Hero and Bubba already," Squeaks sniffed.

Tater turned and looked sternly at the Team. "I'm the oldest, and I'm fixin' to take charge until Hero gets back. Okay?"

"I think that's a good idea, Tater. I want you to be in charge," said Stick.

"Hero would want that too," said Butch.

"Yeah, he would," agreed Runt, with a nod of his head.

"I want you to be in charge. I don't have a clue what to do," joked Red.

"So, what is our next move? How do we find them?" whimpered Squeaks, as a tear rolled down her face.

Tater recognized her nervousness. He walked over to Squeaks and gently wiped the tear from her face. He picked up her tiny body from the chair and gave her a big, teddy-bear hug. Then he whispered, "They're gonna be all right. I'll make sure of it. In fact, I'll bet they're on a grand adventure," he said, setting Squeaks back down. "I know they're doing something the Lord wants them to do. They are probably on a noble mission of service right now."

"That's an interesting idea. Let's assume they're on a mission. What kind of mission do you think they could be on?" asked Butch inquisitively.

"And how do they get home from the mission?" asked Red.

"There has to be a way for us to figure out what that ball did with them," said Runt.

"Yeah, I wish I had gotten a better look at it," said Stick. "There could've been a clue to help us figure out what happened."

"Could we have found the wrong treasure? Maybe the flash of light that took them away was our punishment for doing it all wrong," said Squeaks, with a petrified expression on her face.

"I don't think so. I think we found the right treasure; we just need to figure out what its purpose is," replied Runt.

"Do you think it has a purpose?" asked Stick.

"I think it does. I think it has something to do with service for the Lord," replied Tater. "In fact, I think that ball might have been the Liahona."

"If it is the Liahona, what does that mean?" Red asked. "The Liahona was used for direction, not disappearing."

"Well, grab your scriptures. Let's look up Liahona in the index and see what it says," suggested Tater. "All of the other clues required the Book of Mormon. Maybe the clue to solving where they went requires the scriptures also."

"Great idea, Tater," said Stick. "The scriptures always have the answers."

Red opened his backpack and rifled around for his scriptures. He found them and quickly turned to the index. "All right, it reads, 'Liahona — compass given to Lehi', and then it quotes several scripture references."

"Read a few of them," Tater suggested.

Red looked up at the Team and said, "Oh, okay. The first reference reads, '1 Nephi 16:10, Lehi finds brass ball of curious workmanship, with two spindles.'"

"Well, the ball we found was brass, wasn't it?" asked Butch.

"Yep, and it had curious workmanship. According to Hero, the ball had ornate engravings and two spindles," declared Squeaks, excited to help find her brothers.

"Hey, that's right," exclaimed Red. "Hero did say that."

"That description seems to match. Maybe you're right, Tater. Maybe the treasure is the Liahona," said Stick.

"What is the next reference in the index? Does it give us any more clues?" asked Tater excitedly.

Red looked up from his scriptures and said, "The next references read, '1 Nephi 16:10, points the way Lehites should go into wilderness; 1 Nephi 16:28-29, writing on the Liahona gives understanding of the Lord's ways;' and 'works according to faith and diligence.'"

"Red, read 1 Nephi 16: 28-29 so we can hear exactly what it says, please," suggested Runt. "Good idea, Runt," said Stick. "I bet we'll find more information in the scriptures."

Red flipped the pages of his scriptures to 1 Nephi 16: 28-29 and hurriedly started reading. "Verse twenty-eight 'And it came to pass that I, Nephi, beheld the pointers which were in the ball, that they did work according to the faith and diligence and heed which we did give unto them.'

"Verse twenty-nine, 'And there was also written upon them a new writing, which was plain to be read, which did give us understanding concerning the ways of the Lord; and it was written and changed from time to time, according to the faith and diligence which we gave unto it. And thus we see that by small means the Lord can bring about great things.'"

"Hey, I think that's it," interrupted Butch. "I bet the writing inside of the Liahona gave instructions from the Lord on what the treasure is and how to use it."

"Team, is it possible that the hieroglyphs inside of the tree could be instructions on how to use the Liahona as well?" asked Stick.

"What a good idea! Could the writing down there really help us, Tater?" asked Squeaks excitedly.

"I'm not sure, but I bet it's possible," he answered. "Should we go look at them?" asked Butch.

"That couldn't hurt, right?" asked Squeaks.

"You're right, Squeaks. Let's go check it out," Tater said, excited for a possible clue to finding their teammates.

The remaining Team eagerly scurried down the ladder and rushed back toward the secret passage into the tree. One by one, Tater, Butch, Runt, Stick, Red and Squeaks crawled in through the narrow gap.

"I can't believe how cool it is inside here," said Butch, as he climbed up the contorted interior of the tree. "I didn't get to see all of these hieroglyphs earlier. They are remarkable."

"I wonder what they mean," said Runt, running his hands across the carvings.

"I bet Stick's right. They must have something to do with the Liahona," said Squeaks, trying to be positive.

"I'm sure they do," said Tater. "I bet they tell all about it and what it does."

"I wonder if the hieroglyphs tell what our teammates have to do to get home," said Squeaks.

"It's possible, Squeaks," said Red. "Hang in there, and we'll figure this out."

"But how do we find out?" she asked. "We can't read Egyptian!"

"No, we can't, but Cheri can," suggested Red.

"That's a great idea. We'll get Cheri, the librarian, in here to translate the hieroglyphs for us," said Runt.

"Are you crazy? She's like, *old*," joked Red. "And an adult."

"Do you think she would try for us?" asked Squeaks hopefully.

"She's like seventy years old, Squeaks. Don't get your hopes up. Besides, she would have to crawl in here and then climb up these ledges to read them all," said Red. "I'm not sure she could, or would."

"It wouldn't hurt to ask, right?" she questioned excitedly.

"We could ask her," said Tater. "But then we would for sure have to tell her what is going on. That could be a big problem. I'm not sure she would believe everything. This is kind of an unbelievable story — even if it's the truth."

"Do you think she would tell anyone?" asked Runt. "She kept our secret when we were searching for Moroni's Treasure."

"Yeah, but kids weren't missing then. This is a little more serious than just searching for a mysterious treasure," snapped Butch. "We've got big issues now."

"I think she would help us and keep our secret," said Red. "Besides, I like her. She's old, but she's cool!"

"I guess we have nothing to lose. The worst she could do is say 'no'," admitted Tater.

"Saying 'no' isn't the worst thing she could do. If she went to the authorities or our moms about our missing teammates, the consequences could be really bad," said Red.

"Life will be bad if she tells Mom," Squeaks agreed.

"So, do we want to ask for her help and take the risk?" asked Tater. "Or do we want to try and do this on our own?"

"We could try it on our own. But I'm afraid if we try to translate the drawings ourselves, we'd only be wasting valuable time. We can't translate all of this without her help," said Runt.

"Let's vote," suggested Squeaks.

"Okay. All in favor of asking Cheri — raise your hand," said Tater. "All right, then. The vote's unanimous. Let's go see if Cheri will help us again."

"What should we tell her?" asked Butch.

"Let's tell her that we need more help translating. After she agrees to help, we can tell her more," suggested Stick.

"Good idea," said Runt.

"Let's go see if she's at the library," said Stick.

"Remember, guys. No one says anything about our missing teammates to her until she agrees to help us," said Tater.

Everyone hastily climbed out of the tree, grabbed their bikes and started the two-mile ride north through town toward the old Timber Creek library. Passing the retirement home, the Team waved at their friends as they always did. When they reached the library, they quickly jumped off their bikes and locked them up to the bike rack outside, as they had done so many times in the last several days.

They entered the library, and Tater quickly spotted Cheri on the floor reading to several young children. He frantically motioned for her to follow them to the back room. But to the Team's surprise, she kept reading the book *Hungry Little Caterpillar,* and simply motioned for everyone to sit and listen to the story.

Cheri slowly read each word in the book, carefully enunciating each syllable. After several minutes, she finished the story and set the book down. Then she invited the children to look for a book that they wanted to check out and take home. She climbed off the floor and pointed to the Children's Section. "Parents, all of the easy readers are over there. If you have any questions, please don't hesitate to ask." Then she turned to the Team and said, "May I help you now?"

"Cheri, we need your help — we have an emergency! Can you come to the Treehouse with us?" asked Tater.

"What is it? Is everything okay?" Cheri questioned nervously.

"Everything is fine," replied Tater. "But, we have a problem, and we're in dire need of your expertise," he said with a grin.

Cheri looked down at her watch and smiled. "You're in luck," she said. "Wait by the front door, and I will be able to go with you in five minutes."

The Team swiftly moved to the front door and waited for her to join them. Several slow minutes passed with no sign of her.

"I thought only my mom meant an hour when she said five minutes," said Stick.

"Nope, my mom does the same thing," said Red. "When she says five minutes, we still have a good thirty before she's ready."

"Hang in there, Team," said Tater. "We need her help, so we've got to wait for her."

With their patience running thin and worry building about the rest of the Team, she finally arrived out front.

"I'm ready," she announced. "Now, what is so important that you need me right now?"

"We found the treasure!" announced Runt.

"And lost it, too," added Red.

"What?" Cheri asked, confused by their comments.

"We found and misplaced the treasure, all in about five minutes, Cheri. Would you follow us to the Treehouse? There are some hieroglyphs we need you to translate for us," said Tater. "We will explain everything when we get there. This is a matter of life and death."

"Life and death? Are you sure?" she asked smiling.

"Positive," replied Red. "We really need your help."

"All right, then let's get moving to the Treehouse," she said, a little puzzled at the Team's urgency. "I'll follow you there, so don't lose me."

Chapter Four

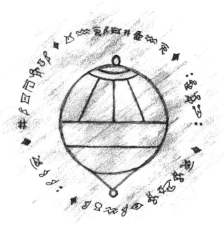

The Team waited patiently for Cheri to walk to her car. She climbed in, turned on the motor, put on her seatbelt, adjusted the mirrors, looked both ways twice, and then finally backed out of her parking space.

"This is going to be a long ride home," said Red, as he tapped his foot on his pedal.

Tater smirked at Red and said, "The ride home would be funny if she got on the main road and drove so fast that we couldn't keep up with her."

"No, that would be great!" replied Red.

The Team waited as she pulled onto Fort Street. They hoped she would at least go the speed limit.

"No such luck, Tater," said Red. "I guess we're goin' home slow."

"I was hoping," hollered Tater.

The ride home took twenty minutes. Relieved to finally return to the Treehouse, the Team jumped off their bikes and threw them in their customary spot on the front lawn. Then they waited impatiently for Cheri to park her car.

"When I take driver's education, remind me to cover all the safety precautions with Cheri before I take my test," said Stick, grinning.

The Team laughed at Stick's comment.

"No doubt," laughed Runt. "You would get one hundred percent right, for sure."

"She is taking forever. Head back to the tree, and I'll meet you guys there," Tater yelled.

He ran across the street to Cheri's car, opened the door, grabbed her arm, helped her out and hurried her back to the tree.

"Cheri, this is kinda crazy, but do you think you could crawl inside the tree through that opening?" asked Tater, pointing to the small gap at the base on the backside of the tree.

"How can you get inside a tree, Tater?" she asked hesitantly.

"You can in this one," said Squeaks. She knelt at the opening, wriggled her body in and yelled, "See. Follow me."

Cheri tilted her head to the right and asked, "What in the world is this?"

"This is the final clue to Moroni's Treasure Map,

Cheri. Inside the tree are the hieroglyphs that led us to find the treasure," said Tater.

"I know this might be hard, but would you try to see if you can climb inside?" asked Butch.

Cheri, still confused, agreed. She slowly dropped to her knees and peered into the opening. She turned back to the boys and asked, "Are you sure it's safe?"

"I promise, Cheri," answered Tater.

Sliding her head inside the small opening in the tree, Cheri started rocking her body forward. She moved her arms to push herself further inside. As she maneuvered her body about half way through, she yelled back to the boys, "Oh my goodness! What is all of this?"

Five minutes passed before she finally pulled her legs through to the inside. Cautiously standing up and looking around, not a word left her mouth as she stared at the amazing hieroglyphs that covered the inside walls of the tree.

Running her fingers across the drawings carved into the wood, Cheri finally broke her silence. "Team," she whispered, "do you know what you have found here?"

"We found Moroni's Treasure, Cheri," replied Runt.

Turning her head quickly away from the drawings, she asked, "What? Where is it? What is it?"

"That's why we need you," said Squeaks, as she poked her head over a small ledge above Cheri.

"Why? If you found the treasure, why do you need me?" Cheri asked.

"We lost the treasure today, too," answered Red. "And...," he paused.

"And what?" questioned Cheri, sensing more to the story.

"And, Hero, Bubba, Bean and KP," replied Tater.

"What are you talking about, Team?" she asked.

Tater, sensing her anxiety, said, "Cheri, we found the treasure. It looks like a brass ball covered with small, delicate engravings, and it has two spindles inside. The ball has a small panel on the front — almost like a digital watch. It flashed the number 73 BC on it."

"Yes, go on," she said impatiently, holding her hands to her hips.

"The ball flashed that number three times. Then we saw a bright flash of light. The light was so bright that we all had to turn our heads and close our eyes. When we turned back, our teammates were gone, and so was the ball Hero was holding in his hands," he finished.

"We think the brass ball was the Liahona, but we're not positive. We hoped maybe the pictures carved in here would give us a clue to where the rest of our baseball Team might be," said Squeaks.

Gasping, Cheri placed her hand to her mouth. "I told you to be careful," she scolded. Who is missing?"

"We already told you, Cheri," replied Red.

"Well, tell me again," she said, scowling at him.

"Four are missing — Hero, Bubba, Bean and KP," replied Stick.

"I hope they are safe and we can find a way to bring them home," Cheri said quietly. "I warned you, Team, that this treasure could be dangerous."

"I was trying to keep everyone safe," muttered Tater,

as he dropped his head and looked at the floor. "I'm sorry."

"Oh, Tater, this is not your fault. We need to concentrate on getting them back. Now, let's see what all these writings say before your teammates get too far away. And let's pray these hieroglyphs give us the answers we need." Cheri turned around and said, "Does anyone else know what has happened?"

"No, you're the only one," answered Runt.

"We didn't think anyone else would believe us," said Stick. "Disappearing into thin air is not a very believable story."

"Let's leave it that way — at least until we translate these hieroglyphs. Then we'll decide if we can get them home before we have a bigger problem," Cheri said, as she looked around the area.

"Can you tell what any of the writings mean?" asked Butch anxiously.

"Let me look for a minute, Team," she replied.

Cheri pondered each and every picture for several minutes before moving on to the next. She never uttered more than, "Hum...Wow...Interesting." She slowly climbed up the interior of the tree, over ledges and gnarled bulges. She stopped abruptly where Hero had found the box that contained the Liahona. The anticipation of Cheri's translations mounted, until Red finally broke the uneasy silence.

"What? What Cheri? What is it?" Red quizzed, unable to wait any longer.

Slowly maneuvering her way back to the bottom of

the tree, Cheri said, "Well Team, I think you might be right. I think the ball you found was the Liahona. Everyone move in closer. Do you all see this picture?" she asked, pointing to a small drawing engraved on the wall.

"Yes," replied Red. "What about it?"

"I believe this is the ball you saw," she said. "Look at its perfectly round shape, intricate designs and beautiful workings. If we start reading from the bottom of the tree, the translation doesn't call the ball by name. But, as I read the hieroglyphs up a few ledges higher, the pictures show that this same ball was used to guide Lehi and Nephi in the wilderness."

"Scary!" said Squeaks, still watching from above.

"The Liahona isn't scary, Squeaks. But I think it could be frightening if you use the treasure without having all the information," replied Cheri.

"Like we just did," said Tater, in a somber voice.

"Like *the Team* did, Tater — not just you," reassured Cheri. "I believe the others can still come back if their knowledge of the Book of Mormon is strong."

"I sure hope Hero listened in Sunday School," said Stick.

"You know he did," replied Runt. "He is the smartest kid we all know! I know they are going to be all right."

"Cheri, do the hieroglyphs say anything else?" asked Tater. "Do they mention a way to bring them home?"

"Tater, the writings are clues. They need to be translated — like on your map. Let's start at the bottom and work our way up. We're going to need someone to write down these clues," she said smiling. "I think these clues will help all of you to understand more about what has happened, after you get them all figured out."

"I've got some paper and a pen in my backpack Cheri," offered Stick.

"Good, make sure you write everything down."

"Cheri, what are these characters around the picture?" Red interrupted.

"Well, if you look at the characters forming a circle around the ball," she said, rubbing her fingers across them, "they're actually several words."

"What do they say? Do they tell us how to get everyone back?" asked Squeaks, shaking with excitement.

"No, the words describe what is required to use the ball," she replied. "The hieroglyphs read *understanding, faith, diligence, heed,* and *service.*"

"What do they mean, Cheri?" asked Stick, writing everything down.

Cheri stopped translating, looked up at the Team and said, "I really think I should have translated these drawings before you opened the treasure. Then you would've known exactly what to expect with your discovery. But, let me give you my definition of those words — maybe that will help.

"*Understanding* is knowing and being familiar with the Book of Mormon. *Faith* means believing in the Lord. *Diligence* means working hard to achieve something or sticking to a task. The word *Heed* means listening to the still small voice and doing what it prompts you to do. And finally, *Service,* doing something for others, is what the Lord requires from you when using the Liahona."

"Those were some of the same words used in a scripture reference from the treasure hunt," stated Tater.

"Yes, Tater. I think you're right. Some of these words were used during your search for Moroni's Treasure," replied Cheri. "On the next ledge," she continued, as she climbed cautiously, "the drawings show a bright light followed by two pictures of the earth. An arrow starts at one picture of the earth and moves to the other," she explained, as she turned her head and carefully looked down to see the Team.

"What does it mean?" asked Stick.

"I think the picture represents traveling in time," replied Cheri casually. "And the word's *traveler of time* are written underneath the picture."

"As you serious?" asked Tater. "You reckon' our teammates have really traveled somewhere in time?"

"I believe so," she replied. "I told you before, I can't translate all of the writings. But what I do understand clearly shows time travel."

"How can that be?" asked Red. "I don't understand."

"Pay attention, Team. These hieroglyphs tell you what you are to do with the Liahona. To make it work properly, you must have faith. While you are serving Him, you need to be smart and do what He requires by listening to the Spirit."

"How do we know what to do?" asked Butch.

"I'm not sure," answered Cheri. "Maybe the picture on the next ledge will tell more."

"Well, get moving. We need to know how to get our teammates home," insisted Squeaks, smiling at Cheri.

Again, Cheri climbed higher looking for more answers for the Team.

Cheri remained quiet for several minutes before she said, "This set of hieroglyphs is a clue."

"Read them, quickly!" said Squeaks. "Maybe we can get everyone home by tonight."

Cheri smiled and said, "I don't think getting them home is going to be quite that easy."

"Tell me! Tell me! What does it say?" Squeaks pleaded.

"Okay, okay. Let me see here. Stick, get ready to write this down. Now then, the hieroglyphs read,

'As you travel in Alma 34:32, doing service for the Lord,

Your Words of Mormon 1:8 will be tested, your return the reward.

Take heed in the Lord's promptings, and remain 1 Nephi 3:16 in all things.

The Liahona will direct you, providing the Alma 9:26 you will need.

The Book of Mormon is your Mosiah 2:36, at your side, shows you the light.

Keep it with you as you Alma 37:41, setting back what is not right.'"

"What in the world?" asked Red bewildered. "More scriptures?"

"Looks that way, Red," said Runt. "We figured out the last clues. I know we can these, too."

"We'll have to figure out what they mean," said Stick.

"And quick."

"Cheri, why more clues?" asked Squeaks. "We've already found the treasure. Why doesn't the Lord tell us what to do?"

"Finding the treasure wasn't everything you needed to do, Squeaks. Have faith — maybe the clues from the scriptures will help you. Your teammates may need your knowledge of the Book of Mormon. I don't know, but in order to help your teammates, you will need to get this clue figured out."

"Are you serious? I'm not sure my knowledge of the Book of Mormon is that good. How would I ever know exactly what to do to correct a problem in an ancient land?" asked Butch.

"I guess the prophet wasn't kidding when he told us to read the scriptures every day, was he?" asked Cheri, with a grin. "We never know when we will need the information we learn from them — whether we use the scriptures in our daily lives or in doing work for the Lord," said Cheri.

"I wonder where our teammates are in the Book of Mormon," said Butch.

"I wonder if Hero's meeting great prophets — prophets we've read about and been taught about our entire lives," added Runt.

"Hey, wait. Tons of scary times with lots of wars happen in the Book of Mormon. Do you think they could be in the middle of a war, Cheri?" asked Squeaks, concerned again.

"They could be anywhere. But, I am sure the Lord

will take care of them," she answered.

"Before we start translating, are there any more clues up there, Cheri?" asked Tater.

"I saw one or two more writings a few feet higher on the tree. Give me a minute to get up there and see what else we've got," Cheri replied.

She again wiggled her way slowly to the next gnarled ledge, using every ounce of strength to steady herself. Then she read,

> "'Your travels will begin when you hold Helaman
>   5:8 in your hand.
> Be prepared to take a journey into a long 2
>   Nephi 25:17 land.
> Three flashes start your mission — your
>   adventure to the Mosiah 8:17.
> Without guidance from the 1 Nephi 3:7, your
>   journey will forever last.'"

"They could stay there forever?" exclaimed Squeaks, suddenly terrified.

"That seems to be a possibility," replied Butch. "But until we finish the clue, I'm not sure."

"How can we help them get home from wherever they are? Is there anything we can do?" Butch asked. "I don't want them to stay there forever."

"We have no way to know where they are, let alone help them get home," replied Red. "We can't talk to them if they're in the past."

"I think you're right, Red," Cheri replied. "I think this

is something they have to do on their own. Team, do you think your teammates were prepared to do what is going to be required of them?" she asked.

"Not a chance. How could they be?" said Stick. "This all happened so fast."

"I'm sure they will be able to fix the problem and get home quickly," said Butch, confident in their abilities. "They have an advantage."

"What advantage?" asked Squeaks.

"The Book of Mormon," replied Butch. "They should at least have an idea of what might be happening."

"Well, I'm not so sure," said Red. "The Book of Mormon is a fairly big book. I can't remember everything in it. Can you?"

"No, but the Lord will help them, right?" he asked. "The Liahona didn't only show direction, but it gave counsel from the Lord as well."

"Will the Liahona tell them what they have to do to get home?" asked Squeaks.

"I've got no idea," replied Tater. "Hopefully, they will know that the Lord can send them messages through the Liahona."

"If they don't figure out why they're there, they'll never figure out what to do to get home," added Stick.

"You're right, Stick," said Tater smiling. "But, I'm sure Bean will figure it out. Girls always seem to have the answers."

"Hey, what about the box that held the Liahona? Should I bring it down?" asked Butch.

"You better. When the rest of the Team gets home, we'll need a place to keep it safe," said Stick.

"Did you look at the hieroglyphs on the box, Cheri?" asked Red.

"No, I didn't see them," she responded.

"Maybe you better take a look at them. The writings could possibly provide some valuable information," said Butch.

"I'll be right there," said Cheri, as she finished carefully climbing to the bottom of the tree. "Let's have a look at the box, Team."

"What does it say?" asked Runt. "Anything new?"

"Well, it does have one more piece of information," Cheri replied.

"What is it?" asked Red.

"Instructions," Cheri replied.

"Instructions? What kind of instructions?" Red asked.

"Without finishing the clues, I can't be sure. But I would guess, based on what I can read, that the instructions will help get the Team home," she responded.

"What do they say? What do we have to do?" asked Squeaks.

"Not what we have to do, Squeaks," replied Cheri, "but what they have to do. Absolutely nothing can be done here at home to help them."

"Enough suspense, Cheri," said Runt. "We know we can't help them now. What do they have to do?"

Cheri began to read,

"'Once your Alma 37:41 is through, and you've
   completed the Jacob 2:10,
Then hold the Liahona, and you will travel
   straight back.
To the 2 Nephi 27:21 you have left, you will most
   definitely return.
With the Lord's Mosiah 2:17 finished, you will
   have no concern.
If the task is not complete, nowhere will you
   travel.
What's wrong must be put right, or your 1 Nephi
   9:2 will unravel.
Your time it is short; your journey only Mosiah
   13:18 of the Lord's days,
To fix what's gone wrong, or remain forever
   there to Mormon 8:26.'"

"We've got to finish these clues. At least then I will know what their chances are," said Squeaks, with a panicked expression on her face.

"Isn't there anything else we can do to help them?" asked Stick.

"No, we're gonna to have to wait here and keep our fingers crossed, Team," said Tater.

"You can pray for their safety and quick return," suggested Cheri.

"What do we tell Mom in the meantime?" asked Squeaks.

"Well, why don't we plan a sleepover for tonight in the Treehouse? Maybe by tomorrow, the four of them will have solved the problem. Hopefully they'll be home before your mom gets really suspicious," said Tater.

"Cheri, do you think that will be all right?" asked Red.

Quietly contemplating the question, Cheri climbed to the bottom of the tree. "One night, Team. Only one night. Then you will need to tell your parents what has happened here today. Okay?"

Tater slowly nodded in agreement.

"Now, Team, not a word about the treasure to anyone, other than your parents. They will know how to protect you from the thousands of people that would love to travel back in time. These same people would kill to take the Liahona from you. This is a special gift from the Lord. Protect it, and make sure you don't let Him down," Cheri insisted.

"We won't, Cheri," responded Tater. "But, you can't tell anyone either. This is our problem, and we will figure out how to fix it."

As Cheri began to climb out of the tree, she paused and said, "Good luck, Team. I know you will figure out what to do. Please let me know when your teammates return so I won't worry. Don't hesitate to call me if you need any more help. Remember to trust in the Lord." With that said, she turned and left the Team to contemplate their next move.

"Thanks, Cheri," Stick called after her.

The Team slowly climbed out the secret opening to the tree and waved to Cheri. They headed from the backyard into Hero and Bubba's kitchen, hoping to casually get permission for the night's sleepover. They really hoped that Mrs. M. would not realize Hero, Bubba, Bean and KP were missing.

Chapter Five

A slight breeze stirred, rattling the leaves on the palm fronds above Bean's tent. She awoke from her restless sleep with a start. Afraid to open her eyes, she gradually reached to her side and searched for the soft, cozy feeling of her favorite blanket. Not finding the velvet texture she had anticipated, she slowly took a deep breath, opened her eyes and hoped everything that had transpired the night before had been a terrifying dream. To her dismay, the nightmare continued. She looked around the inside of her dark prison. Scared and homesick, the events of the night before finally registered in her mind, and a tear trickled down her face.

"Stop that," she thought to herself. "You're stronger than this. Don't ever let them see you cry." She sat up and angrily wiped the tear from her face. She decided she needed to plan her escape. Looking around the interior of the tee-pee where she was being held, she saw only the blanket that she slept on, a small basket of fruit, a vase full of water, the moccasins the warrior had given to her the night before and the woman who had forced her to change her clothes.

"Where are my clothes and my backpack?" she wondered. Then she panicked when she realized the treasure that was inside her pack could possibly be her only way home. "Those warriors better not have done anything with our treasure," she thought.

Standing up from the floor, she quietly moved to the door of the tee-pee, being careful to not wake the woman. She slowly pulled the material, which was covered by palm leaves, to the side. The bright sun revealed the unfamiliar surroundings of the camp.

"This is going to be easy," she thought. "These leaves can't keep me locked in here."

As she peered through the slight opening, she recognized several objects that she had seen the night before. Twenty feet to the west, she saw the small path to the jungle that the warriors had used to bring her to the camp. The warrior's tee-pees circled the edge of the jungle.

Actually, Bean thought the tee-pees looked more like small huts. The frame of each one was made of bamboo sticks, with some kind of animal skin stretched between the sticks to form the ceiling and walls. This material was covered with leaves and foliage from the jungle — a tactic most likely used to keep the camp hidden.

In the middle of the camp was the fire pit where the warriors had danced and chanted all night. She could still feel the warmth from the burning embers. She watched as the smoke swirled around the wood and then floated in a small, shoestring line to the clouds in the sky above. As she continued peering around the camp, everything was still, except for a few warriors strategically patrolling around the perimeter.

"They must be the guards," she thought.

As she continued to scan the area, she saw guards encircling her tee-pee, though she could not tell exactly how many. Directly across camp on the other side of the campfire was another tee-pee that must have belonged to the leader. Several guards encircled it, and it was bigger than the other huts. Bean's tee-pee could fit only three people, but that tent was big enough to sleep six or eight.

"I'm sure he doesn't need that much room," she thought.

Bean carefully allowed the material she had pulled back to fall into place. She checked to make sure the woman guarding her was still asleep, then turned to crawl to the other side of the tee-pee for another view of the camp and her surroundings. As she took a step in the opposite direction, she stumbled on her new clothes and fell to the ground with a thud. She turned quickly to make sure she had not woken the woman in her tee-pee. She watched as the woman adjusted her head, pulled her legs to her stomach and stretched the animal skin blanket over her arms. Bean breathed a sigh of relief as she watched the woman continue to sleep.

"This dress is a huge pain," she thought, as she pulled the material out from under her knee. "I'm sure the warriors outside heard that noise. Why couldn't they have given me some pants or shorts? Why couldn't they have left me with my own clothes?" she asked herself.

Holding the dress above her knees with one hand, Bean crawled to the other side of her tent. She tried to separate the material and open a small hole at a seam where the animal skins had been sewn together. Unable to manipulate the seam, she pulled the material apart as hard as she could and grabbed the thread with her teeth. She gnawed on the thread for several minutes.

"Man," she thought. "What is this stuff? I have never felt thread this strong."

Unwilling to give up, she kept chewing on the thread, hoping she could cut through it. Finally, the thread gave way, allowing her to pull a hole in the seam about the size of a baseball. She then maneuvered the leaves covering the hole to the side and revealed more of the area outside.

To her surprise, one of the warriors was directly in front of her, guarding her tent. He was a large man — bigger than most of the other warriors. He looked a little older and seemed harmless. Although he remained quiet, Bean was sure he saw her small opening. As she looked beyond the warrior, she saw a beautiful waterfall in the distance. The water fell elegantly into a pool that had formed twenty-five feet below. Several women were washing clothes on the rocks and collecting water from the pool. She even saw two women fishing with spears.

Pulling the material together to look as though nothing had changed, Bean moved to yet another part of the tent. She stood about five feet two inches tall, and the window in the tent was a bit higher than her eye level. If she stood on her tippy-toes, she was barely able to see outside. She pushed back the animal skin flap that was covering the hole and discovered another warrior guarding her tee-pee.

The Lamanite warrior looked down at Bean, watching her try to see out of the window. Bean cringed as her eyes came in contact with his. He scowled at her as if to ask, "What are you doing?" She kept eye contact with him, not wanting him to think she was afraid. After a moment, she recognized the man. "That is the guy who captured me!" she thought.

Her restricted view of the area revealed a canopy fifteen feet long. Underneath the covering were three, five-foot-long tree logs, each with one side chiseled flat. Holding them up off the ground were two tree branches tied together with leather in the form of an X. One was placed on either end of the log. On the logs were rocks, sticks, leather, two small animals of some kind and, to her surprise, her backpack and clothes, as well as several pieces of flat metal. "I sure hope the treasure is still in my backpack," she thought. Beyond the canopy were several more tee-pees and hundreds of weapons she had only seen in Mr. Jensen's photographs.

"These warriors are not spies," she thought. "They

manufacture weapons. I've got to get out of here so I can warn someone."

Suddenly the warrior's voice broke the silence. "Stand back!" he commanded.

Thinking quickly, Bean said, "I have to go to the bathroom. Do you understand?"

"I do, and you will wait until the leader allows it."

"Ask him, then," she demanded. "I must go to the bathroom."

"He is sleeping, so you must wait."

"I can't wait," she replied.

She did not really need to go, but she wanted a better view of the camp.

"Then do what you must in your tent," the warrior responded, turning his face away from her view.

"You would have me go in here?" Bean asked, obviously disgusted.

"Or you must wait," the warrior said calmly. "You would already be dead if I had my way.

"Auuuhhhh," Bean said angrily, as she let go of the flap to close the window.

Spinning around, she headed back toward the animal-skin blanket she had laid on during the night. She was surprised she had not woken up the woman guarding her. No longer worried if she did, she reached down and angrily snatched the blanket of skin off the ground. Looking around the tee-pee for the best location to sit down, she noticed a small ray of sun shining through the window. She quickly walked over to the sunlight and sat down. She closed her eyes and let the ray of light shine right on her face. She had missed seeing the sun for the last several days and enjoyed the slight warmth it provided. Thinking of how rude the warrior was, she scowled at the guard through the window, although he could not see her.

"What an idiot," she thought. "I would never treat a prisoner that way!"

Opening her eyes, she leaned over and grabbed what she hoped was a mango from the bowl on the table. She pulled the blanket over her legs, which were cold from the chill in the air. Biting the skin of the mango with her teeth, she continued to stew over the rudeness of the warrior.

"I wonder what his name is. I bet he is one of the bad people talked about in the Book of Mormon," she thought, as she continued to peel her small breakfast.

"Guard, what is your name?" she yelled, not afraid of waking the woman.

"That is none of your concern," he responded.

"Yes, it is," she answered.

"Why?" he called.

"So I can tell my father the name of the man who wouldn't allow me to go to the bathroom," she answered, smiling to herself.

"I will tell you the name of the warrior who is going to kill you if you don't learn some manners," he replied heatedly.

"Coninihah, stop fighting with her," said another warrior. "She is only a child."

"A child? What are they talking about? I am not a child. I am thirteen — a teenager in my land," she thought angrily. "A child smart enough to learn your name," she yelled.

The warrior remained in silence for only a moment, before he ripped open the flap of her window.

"Do you see this spear, child?" he asked, holding it in the window for Bean to see. "This spear will kill you and your father if you don't remain quiet."

"We'll see about that," she responded, looking him directly in the eyes. "My father doesn't even live here."

"I know who your father is," he snapped back at her.

"Oh, yeah? Who is he, then?" she asked.

"Any child who is taught in the ways of our language, as well as your own, and who is well schooled, is the child of a prophet, judge or captain." He smirked at her, as if he knew everything about her.

"We will see about that," she replied, not wanting to tell them who she really was. At least for now, their assumptions were keeping her safe and alive.

"Shaliah, wake up!" shouted Coninihah.

"Yes," she answered, looking at the floor.

"Can you not control this child?" he barked, pointing at Bean.

"I'm sorry, Coninihah," she replied, still looking at the ground. "I thought she was asleep."

Coninihah angrily moved from the window back to his post, mumbling words Bean could not understand.

"The day is very early, child. Is there something you need?" the woman shyly whispered. "Do not bother the warriors."

"I need to not be called child," Bean answered sharply.

"I'm sorry, I don't know your name."

Bean watched the woman look at the ground and wondered why she spoke so meekly. "My name is Bean," she stated. "What is yours?"

"My name is Shaliah. Can I fetch you some water or another skin for warmth?"

Ignoring her question, Bean asked, "Why won't you look at me?"

"You know that I am not allowed to," she replied politely.

"Why?"

"I am not of noble birth, like you are," she answered.

"As a Lamanite woman, you have to be of noble birth to look at anyone?" questioned Bean.

"Not anyone — I may look at others like me. But I am not a Lamanite woman," she answered.

"Who are you then?" Bean asked, crawling closer toward her.

"I cannot say."

"Tell me!" Bean demanded, hoping her voice would intimidate the woman into telling her.

"I am a convert of Ammon. I became lost in the wilderness as we journeyed to meet Alma, and I was captured by the Lamanites," she whispered. "I would be killed if they knew I told you that."

Bean crawled over to the woman and lifted her chin to see her face. As a tear fell from her eye, Bean asked, "Have you ever tried to escape?"

"Several times, after I was first captured," she replied. "They took me to Antionum where thousands of

Lamanites live. I was with seven others, and we all tried to escape."

"What happened?"

"They hunted us down," she replied. "Five others got away, but three of us were caught."

"Where are the other two?" Bean asked.

"I don't know. They forced me to serve in the work camp until now," she whispered. "Now I help with the weapons."

"How long have you been a prisoner?" questioned Bean.

"The time of my birth has passed six times," she replied.

"Six years? Do you continue to believe in the word of Christ?" Bean asked.

"Yes, I pray in secret every night."

"If I am rescued, will you go with me?"

"Can you take me to my family and the people of Ammon?"

"We can try," Bean replied.

Shaliah slowly nodded her head and said, "I will go if the Lord provides a way. Now I will bring you some bread, Bean," she said smiling. "I will return."

Shaliah stood up, opened the cover of the tent and disappeared outside.

Bean sat silently contemplating her next move, sure she could devise a plan of escape. Thirsty, she picked up the vase and took a drink. She closed her eyes and tried to imagine the layout of the camp in her mind. Suddenly, she noticed the liquid she had swallowed was not water.

"What is this stuff?" she asked, yelling to the warrior, hoping to annoy him.

"Food," he answered. "Be grateful for it."

"I know it is food," she barked back. "What is in the vase, Coninihah?"

Irritated that she had learned his name, he ignored her request.

"I will scream as loud as I can and wake your leader if you don't tell me," she warned.

With no response from the soldier, Bean started to scream. She did not scream very loud, but loud enough to make the warrior nervous.

"Coconut milk," he responded. "Now be quiet."

The other two warriors posted at her tent snickered at how Bean was able to control Coninihah, which irritated him even more.

Quietly eating her mango and drinking her coconut milk, Bean pondered what she should do first.

"The trees in the forest — if I can get to the trees," she thought, "I could easily hide behind them. If I can get to the waterfall, I could hide there. Maybe I can figure out the treasure, if I could get to my backpack. The treasure may be my only chance. I wonder if Shaliah can get it."

Leaning her head back against the wall of her prison, Bean wondered where her friends were. "I hope they're okay," she thought. "No, I hope they rescue me. But they can't rescue me, at least not until I get my backpack and clothes. We won't be going home without the treasure. I have to get that before I can escape."

She knew where the warriors put her backpack,

although she was not quite sure how to get to it. She wished she had her Book of Mormon from inside to read about the events that were happening. Bean stood up quietly and pulled the window open one more time to see exactly how far away her pack was from the tent.

"I know the Book of Mormon well. If I knew the leader's name, maybe then I'd know exactly where I am. I'm sure Shaliah would know his name. Maybe I will ask her when she returns."

Bean then thought she might be able to trick the warrior into telling her. She sat down on the floor and devised a plan.

"Warrior," she called. "What is your leader's name?"

"Quiet," he replied. "I have had enough of your games."

"I will not be quiet," she snapped. "I will scream. Now tell me, what is his name?"

Watching his shadow move from the side of the teepee to the front, she grinned as the warrior pulled the animal skin aside.

"His name is Zerahemnah, child, but I'm sure you already know that. If you want to scream, go ahead and we will see what happens."

"Zerahemnah? Are you sure?" she gasped.

"Yes, I'm sure," he barked. "And you are right to fear him."

Remembering the name from the Book of Mormon, and knowing the events that were to happen she asked, "Have you been to war with Captain Moroni yet?"

"You know that answer child," he responded.

"I don't know. Tell me," she demanded, almost yelling.

"We are outside the city of Jershon," he answered. "As our mighty leader, Zerahemnah, said last night, we will meet with your father, one of the Captains of the Nephite Army, in three days. Only the war will not take place where your army can win. We are planning some surprises of our own for your people."

"So, you have not gone to war with the Captain yet?" she asked.

"Do you listen child?" he asked. He dropped the flap to her tent and said, "In three moons, thousands of Nephites will die."

"Where will the war be?" she asked, hoping he would tell her.

"I won't tell you that, so scream if you want, child," Coninihah responded. "I would love to see what Zerahemnah does with you."

"I am not a child," she replied angrily.

She sat and worried about what the Lamanites were planning. "Something isn't right. In three days? The bloodshed is so great the people have to throw the dead into the River Sidon," she thought. "I don't want to be here when that happens. I will most likely be one of the dead when Zerahemnah finds out that I'm not the daughter of a captain."

Her mind wandered through all of the events that had transpired over the last few days. Bean closed her eyes, and the stories she had read from the Book of Mormon vividly came to life.

"I hope the boys have found help," she thought, opening her eyes — not wanting to visualize war. "I am so tired. I've got to get some sleep."

She closed her eyes and prayed that she would not have to experience the nightmare of a war. She rolled over onto her side, on the dirt floor of her tee-pee, and fell asleep before her new friend returned.

Chapter Six

'Hero, Bubba, Squeaks and Team,' the note started:

'I've gone to the grocery store and have several other errands to run today. Boys, please watch your sister. Get your room cleaned and help Squeaks vacuum the living room.

Your cousin, Bear, is coming to visit. He will be here this afternoon. Watch for him, and play with him until I get home. I left burritos in the freezer for your dinner. You can warm them up when you get hungry.

Make sure the Team has permission for tonight's sleepover. I'll check in with you in a little while. Hope you're all having fun on your treasure hunt.

Love you, Mom.

Squeaks, breathed a big sigh of relief and then showed Tater the note.

"Mom's busy today. With her gone, hopefully we will have the time we need to find everyone. That takes care of Hero and Bubba," said Squeaks. "What about Bean and KP?"

"Someone needs to call their parents and tell them the Team is having a sleepover," suggested Red. "It's already noon, we better call soon."

"I think you should do it, Squeaks," said Tater. "Tell them your mom was planning on us sleeping over."

"I guess that would work," she replied.

Butch grabbed the phone and dialed Bean's number.

"Here you go," he said, as he handed her the phone.

"Hi, this is Squeaks — Hero and Bubba's little sister," she said.

"Hello, Squeaks," Bean's Mom replied. "How are you today?"

"Fine, thanks," she answered. "The Team asked me to call and tell you that our mom is planning on everyone staying for a sleepover. Is that okay?" she asked.

"Are you sleeping with them up in the Treehouse?" Bean's mom asked.

"Yep," she replied.

"Well," she said hesitating, "I guess that would be fine, then."

"Great," said Squeaks.

"Tell Bean she needs to come home early tomorrow. She's got some chores to do."

"Okay, I'll tell her," Squeaks replied. "Goodbye."

"Goodbye, Squeaks," she said.

"Oh, man. That was close!" said Squeaks, as she hung up the phone. "I'm not sure Bean's mom really wanted her to stay over tonight. She said Bean would have to go home early tomorrow."

"That's not good," said Tater.

"What are we going to do in the morning?" asked Stick.

"We'll worry about that later," replied Tater. "Let's take care of KP's mom first — one problem at a time," he said smiling.

"Are you ready for the next call, Squeaks?" asked Butch, as he dialed KP's number.

"I guess so," she answered, as she took the phone from Butch.

"Um, hello, this is Squeaks — Hero and Bubba's little sister," she said. "The Team asked me to call you and tell you that our mom is planning a sleepover for tonight. Would that be all right?"

"Well, I don't know, Squeaks," she answered. "KP has a lot of chores to do, and we would really like to see him every now and then at our house," answered his mom.

"Oh, okay," Squeaks said disappointedly. She suddenly felt sick to her stomach.

"Well, tell me what the plan is, Squeaks," KP's mom said.

"No plan, really. We're still working on our treasure hunt, and we think we are really close to finding it. We were hoping that sometime tomorrow we would finally find it after all of this hard work," she answered.

"What is the Team doing right now?" KP's mom asked.

"Searching for the treasure," Squeaks answered.

"Why aren't you with them?" she asked.

"Tater walked me home so we could call all of the Team's moms and get permission for a sleepover," Squeaks answered.

"Is everyone else staying?" she asked.

"Yes," Squeaks replied.

"Oh, all right. I guess he can stay over tonight, but tomorrow he will need to be home to get his things done," she stated firmly.

"I will tell him," Squeaks answered, with a big grin on her face. "Thanks."

"I appreciate your call, Squeaks," said KP's mom. "Bye."

"Bye," answered Squeaks, as she hung up the phone.

"What happened? Can he have a sleepover?" asked Runt.

"Yes," replied Squeaks. "Just barely! KP's mom wasn't really happy about it though. She wants KP home tomorrow to do chores, too."

"I guess we have one day to figure out what to do," said Red.

"I guess that's better than everyone going home right now," said Butch.

"What's next on our list of things to do?" asked Red.

"All of us better get permission from our parents," said Runt.

"And then we better straighten Hero and Bubba's room so that their mom doesn't get suspicious," suggested Tater.

"Or not allow us to have a sleepover," replied Runt.

"I don't want to clean their room. It's a pigsty," protested Squeaks.

"I don't want to either, Squeaks," said Stick. "It's not my mess."

"Stick, Squeaks, let's just get it done. Now is not the time to worry about how messy everything is," insisted Butch. "Besides, the sooner we get the room clean, the sooner we will be able to get up to the Treehouse and get the clues figured out."

"I know, but have you ever seen how Bubba puts away his clothes?" Squeaks asked.

"No," answered Butch.

"Well, I have seen him clean. He stuffs everything under his bed. If we don't pull it all out and clean up the mess, Mom will get really mad," explained Squeaks.

"I guess we better hurry before your mom gets home. If Hero and Bubba aren't here cleaning, she will want to know where they are," replied Red.

"Why is Bear coming over?" asked Tater.

"Oh, he's just coming to play for a few days," answered Squeaks.

"Good!" exclaimed Tater. "The Team will look bigger with one more person here."

"And the cleaning will go faster," said Stick, really not wanting to clean Hero and Bubba's room. "I have an idea. How about I start figuring out the clues and you guys clean the room?"

"Come on, Team. We need to get cleaning," said Runt. "And we all need to stick together."

"I'm sure it can't be that bad," said Butch. "We should be able to get everything cleaned pretty quickly," he said, as the Team walked through the door to Hero and Bubba's room.

"Oh, my goodness!" said Squeaks. "I think a bomb went off in here."

"I thought you were joking, Squeaks," said Red. "I never dreamed those guys would be this messy."

"I told you," she answered. "I'm not sure I've ever seen it quite this bad."

"Let's get started cleaning, or we're gonna be here forever," said Tater, as he pushed up his shirtsleeves and started to pick up the clothes.

"Where should I start?" asked Runt.

Tater took over and assigned everyone a job. "Squeaks, you climb under the bed and clear everything out. Runt, pull everything off the beds and then make them. Red, get a bag for trash from the kitchen and pickup all the garbage in here. Stick, clean up all the videos and CDs, and then put them in their cases on the shelf. Butch, carefully clean everything off the desks, dust it and then put everything back. Everyone make sure not to touch Hero's bug collection. He has been catching those bugs the entire summer, and I don't want any of them to get lost."

The Team scattered and quickly started on their assigned jobs.

"What about the dirty clothes?" asked Squeaks, poking her head out from underneath the bed.

"Make a pile outside the bedroom door," said Tater.

"What about all their shoes?" asked Red, as he had already found seven pairs.

"Where do they go, Squeaks?" asked Tater, as he continued to fold the clothes on the floor.

"In the closet," she yelled, still pushing stuff out from underneath the bed.

"They're going to owe us big time!" exclaimed Red, quickly filling his trash bag.

"How can you be this messy?" asked Stick, shaking his head.

"I told you it was a pigsty," responded Squeaks, as she crawled out from underneath the bed.

"And I bet all of our rooms are perfect," said Runt. "We never leave anything out."

"Not this bad," replied Tater. "My mom wouldn't be too happy if my room was this messy."

"With all of us cleaning up, it's not that bad," said Runt.

"That's because you're just making the bed, Runt," said Squeaks. "Try cleaning out from underneath the bed. Talk about stinky!"

"I'd rather be doing this than be lost somewhere in time," said Butch, as he carefully moved Hero's bug collection.

"I wonder exactly where they are," said Tater. "I hope those clues help us to get them home fast."

"Me, too," said Squeaks. "I hope they're okay."

"I'm sure Hero's taking care of them," said Stick. "But how scary would it be to not have any idea where you are."

"I think I'd be more scared of how I was dressed," said Butch.

"What do you mean?" asked Tater.

"They're not going to look like they belong there," he replied. "Watches, modern clothes, baseball caps, tennis shoes — nothing is going to look right!"

"I forgot about that," said Tater, pondering Butch's statement. "That could cause some trouble."

"I'm sure they traveled some place safe," replied Red.

"Oh yeah? Like where?" asked Squeaks.

"Like when Christ came," he answered. "That's probably a safe time. They had peace for over two hundred years or something like that."

"That would be so cool!" replied Red. "Can you imagine meeting Him?"

"I think I might be afraid," said Runt.

"Why?" asked Tater.

"I'm not sure I'm worthy to meet Him," Runt replied.

"No way. He would be so glad to see us," said Stick.

"You think so?" asked Runt.

"Yep, no matter what," replied Tater.

"And besides that, to live by His side for a few days would be amazing," added Stick. "You'd want to do everything right all the time."

Suddenly the doorbell rang, startling the Team.

"Is it your mom, Squeaks?" asked Runt, cleaning faster.

"She doesn't usually ring the door bell," answered Squeaks sarcastically.

"Quick, go see who it is," said Tater.

"Okay, okay," she replied, as they ran to answer the door.

"Hi, Bear. Come on in," said Squeaks, waving at his mom who was pulling out of the driveway.

"Hi, Squeaks," answered Bear. "Where are Hero and Bubba?" he asked, as he walked in the house toward their bedroom.

"They're not here right now," she answered hesitantly.

"What?" he replied. "You're mom said they'd be home. I came out here to see them, not you."

"Well, they're supposed to be home soon," said Squeaks. "Until then, you're stuck with us."

"So where are they?" he asked, a little confused.

"It's a long story," replied Tater. "Come help us. We've got a few more things to do, and then get up to the Treehouse before anyone gets home.

Bear, puzzled about what was going on, followed Tater and Squeaks back to Hero and Bubba's room where the rest of the Team was still cleaning.

"What are you guys doing?" asked Bear. "Why are you cleaning the boys' bedroom?"

"We have to," replied Squeaks, "or else our fun's gonna be over."

"What fun?" he asked.

"We've been searching for a treasure," she answered.

"I know," said Bear. "My mom told me. But I still don't understand why we're cleaning their room."

"It's a long story, Bear," said Tater. "We'll tell you everything when we get up to the Treehouse."

"Don't worry, Bear. Everything is worse than it seems," said Stick smiling.

As the Team finished the boys' room, it looked cleaner than Squeaks had ever seen.

"Okay, what else does the note say we need to do?" asked Tater.

"Do you want me to read it?" asked Squeaks, as she unfolded the piece of paper.

"Yes, quickly! We're running out of time," Tater replied.

"Hero, Bubba, Squeaks and Team," Squeaks started,

"I've gone to the grocery store and have several other errands to run today. Boys, please watch your sister. Get your room cleaned and help Squeaks vacuum the living room.

Your cousin, Bear, is coming to visit. He will be here this afternoon. Watch for him, and play with him until I get home. I left burritos in the freezer for dinner. You can warm them up when you get hungry.

Make sure the Team has permission for tonight's sleepover. I'll check in with you in a little while. Hope you're all having fun on your treasure hunt.

Love you, Mom."'

"Okay, we still need to vacuum the living room," said Runt.

"And pack up food for tonight," said Stick, holding his growling stomach. "We can't decipher clues without nourishment."

"That's right," Tater replied. "I'm hungry, too. Squeaks, you and Stick pack up supplies to take to the Treehouse. Runt and Butch, vacuum and straighten the living room. Bear, help Red and me carry the dishes and dirty clothes out of Hero and Bubba's room. As soon as we're all finished, let's get up to the Treehouse before anyone notices anything."

Everyone jumped into action.

"I still can't figure out why I am helping clean the house," said Bear. "I thought I came over to play."

"You will. We'll tell you everything when we're up in the Treehouse," replied Butch.

"I've got the clothes. You guys get the dishes, and I'll meet you in the kitchen," said Red, as he ran to the laundry room with an armful of dirty clothes.

When Tater, Red, Butch, Bear and Runt finished, they hurried to meet Squeaks and Stick in the kitchen. As they all gathered, Squeaks heard a noise that sent a chill down her spine.

Chapter Seven

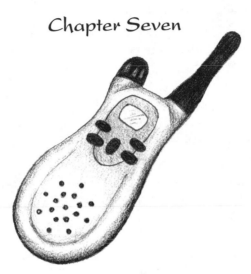

The loud, vibrating hum from the garage door lasted only a minute, but signaled the return of Mrs. M.

"OH, NO!" Squeaks exclaimed. "The garage door just opened."

"What does that mean?" asked Stick.

"Mom's home," she frantically replied. "What do we do now?"

"Let's get out of here, quick!" shouted Stick. "We finished the chores."

"No, we can't. If she sees us running with a huge bag of goodies, she'll figure we're up to something, and she'll come up to the Treehouse to find out what we're doing," Squeaks said.

"If we stay, she'll find out for sure Hero and Bubba are gone," said Runt.

"Then what do we do?" asked Butch.

"Why can't we stay here?" asked Bear, looking at the Team as though they were crazy. "And where exactly are Hero and Bubba? Is there a problem?"

"Tater, we've got to get Bear out of here until he knows what's happening," said Stick. "He could accidentally give away our secret and not even know it."

"You're right," replied Tater. "Here's the plan: Stick, take Bear and the food up to the Treehouse. Walk slowly so no one gets suspicious. Make sure we have a couple of Book of Mormons up there, explain to him what has happened, and then get back down here as quickly as you can."

"Bear, promise us now after Stick tells you what's going on, you won't tell anyone," insisted Runt. "This is a matter of life and death."

"I never tell any secrets," Bear answered.

"Stick and Bear, get moving," ordered Tater.

"Yeah, hurry back. The more Team members we have in here, the less likely she is to know that something is going on," said Red.

"What should the rest of us do?" asked Runt.

"I don't know. Let's sit at the kitchen table and act like nothing's going on," said Red.

"Then she'll really know something's up," replied Butch.

Squeaks knew what to do. She quickly grabbed a deck of cards, a bag of chips, salsa and two bags of candy.

The Team sat at the table pretending to play cards as casually as they could, waiting for Mom to enter the kitchen. Several long minutes passed, and still she had not come into the house.

"Where is she?" asked Runt, looking at the kitchen door.

"I don't know. Should I go look?" asked Squeaks. "She could be upstairs changing."

"No, that will look suspicious," said Tater. "Let's wait."

Minute after minute ticked away as the Team pretended to play a game, not even looking at the numbers on the cards. Positive Mom would ask to see Hero and Bubba, the Team sat nervously anticipating her entry. With their eyes stuck on the door, they continued to lay cards down on the table. When everyone had laid down every card they had, Squeaks quickly dealt them out again.

"Hey, guys," said Squeak's Dad, as he walked in the back door, causing Runt to jump in fright. "Oh, sorry Runt. I didn't mean to scare you," he said.

"Oh, we're not scared," said Tater.

"Well, that scared me!" said Runt, as he held his hand on his heart.

"So, what are you up to, Team?" he asked, walking to the sink and washing his hands.

"Uh, nothing really," Red answered. "Playing UNO."

"And getting ready to have a sleepover in the Treehouse," said Butch.

"I'm glad your getting good use out of that Treehouse," he replied, drying his hands.

"What are you doing, Dad?" asked Squeaks, trying to change the subject.

"Getting ready to meet your mom for dinner," he replied. He finished washing his hands, then quickly gathered his keys and cell phone. "And I am running late."

"What were you doing out back?" asked Squeaks.

"Mom said we're out of chicken scratch. I picked some up so the boys could take care of the chickens tonight," he replied. "Where are they, anyway?" he asked, looking around.

Squeaks, playing dumb, said, "Where's who?"

"The boys, Squeaks," he replied.

"Uh, they're in the Treehouse with Bear," she said. She laid down her card and yelled, "UNO!"

Looking down at his watch, Mr. M exclaimed, "Well, I'm late to meet your mom. Tell the boys to take care of the chickens, okay?"

"Okay, Dad, I'll tell them. Have fun at dinner," she said, smiling at him.

"Boy, you're acting funny tonight," he said. "Where's my hug goodbye?"

Squeaks quickly got up from her chair and walked over to him. She threw her arms around his neck and whispered, "Sorry, Dad. Everybody's watching."

Dad smiled and said, "Oh, I get it. You're too old to hug me in front of your friends."

"Right," she answered smiling.

"Okay, well have fun with the Team tonight," Dad said. "And be nice to your brothers."

"I will," Squeaks replied.

"Bye, Team," he hollered. He grabbed his tie and ran out the garage door.

As the Team listened to the garage door clang shut, they breathed a cautious sigh of relief.

"Whew!" said Butch. "That was too close."

"No kidding," said Red. "There's no way your mom would have left without talking to Hero and Bubba first."

The Team walked to the window and watched his blue truck drive away. They listened to the squealing of the tires as he rounded the corner and wondered how much time they were going to have to get the missing teammates home. As soon as the revving engine could no longer be heard, Tater turned to the Team and asked, "Do we have all the supplies we need to decipher the clues and enough treats to eat?"

"I think so," said Squeaks, as she walked over to the sliding glass door. "We packed enough snacks for three days."

"Good, let's get out of here then," suggested Tater. He turned to follow her outside.

Unexpectedly, a loud buzzzzzz sounded, startling the Team. Turning quickly to see where the noise came from, Tater tripped over the dog standing right behind him and landed with a loud thud on the floor.

"You all right, Tater?" asked Bear, as he returned with Stick to the kitchen.

"I think so," he replied.

"What in the world was that?" asked Stick.

"I don't know for sure," said Tater. "Squeaks, what was that buzzing noise?" he called to her.

"What buzzing noise?" she asked.

"The noise that sounded like a clothes dryer or

maybe an alarm clock," he explained.

"I don't know," she answered, walking back into the house. "I didn't hear anything."

"Maybe it was nothing," Tater said, as he turned to leave the house again. "Did anyone else hear the buzz?"

"Yeah, Tater. I heard it, too," replied Bear.

"The sound was probably the clothes dryer," suggested Runt. "Come on already. Let's go. We've got a lot of work to do!"

As the Team turned to leave the house for the second time, the buzzing noise sounded again. The noise echoed through the empty kitchen.

"There, Squeaks," said Runt. "That buzz — did you hear it?"

"Oh, that's Mom's walkie-talkie," Squeaks replied. "Sometimes other people cross over to our channel and we hear a buzz or voices talking," she said calmly, walking over to turn it off. "The volume must be turned up loud. I don't ever remember it echoing quite this loud before."

"Wait a minute," said Butch. "Leave that alone."

"Yeah, don't turn it off. Didn't Hero have the walkie-talkie from the Treehouse in his backpack?" asked Red.

"Yes, he did," squealed Squeaks. "Do you think it could be them?"

"Yeah, maybe Hero is trying to call us. Grab it, quickly!" yelled Red excitedly.

As Butch, Runt and Squeaks raced through the kitchen to retrieve to walkie-talkie, the loud buzzzzzz rang out again. Squeaks grabbed hold of Butch's shirt and jumped on his back trying to slow him down. Runt climbed under the table so no one could catch him.

"Get off me, Squeaks!" demanded Butch, trying to pull her off his back.

"No! Let me get it," cried Squeaks. "This is my house."

"Oh, give me a break, Squeaks," replied Butch. "We spend almost the same amount of time here as you do."

As the teammates reached the cradle for the walkie-talkie, it was nowhere to be found.

"Where is it?" asked Runt, the first to the cradle.

"It's not here," Butch replied, lifting up some papers and moving them around.

Looking around the kitchen frantically, they could not locate the walkie-talkie anywhere. Red, who had been watching the three look around, held up his hand and asked, "Is this what you are looking for?"

"Hey, give it here," said Runt. "Where did you find that?"

"Oh, no, I live here — I get to answer it," shrieked Squeaks, kicking the laundry out of her way as she ran.

Laughing because of all of the commotion in the room, Tater stood up from the table, walked over to Red, grabbed the walkie-talkie out of his hand and said, "Don't get your hopes up. The buzz was probably a false alarm. I don't reckon' there's any way walkie-talkies can work through time."

Tater looked at the object in his hand and wondered if he should try to call the others, or just place the walkie-talkie back into the cradle. As he looked at his teammates, he could feel their excitement. He knew if he did not at least try, their disappointment would be devastating.

"Come on, Tater. We have to at least try!" exclaimed Squeaks, with a tearful expression on her face.

"But realistically, what kind of walkie-talkie could communicate through time?" asked Red seriously.

"At least try to talk to them, Tater," said Runt, as he watched the commotion inside the kitchen. "There's a lot you could tell them that might help their situation."

"You're right. We'd be able to tell them what we've learned so far," replied Tater.

"Which isn't very much," said Red, "but I guess it's at least something."

"And once we get the clues translated, we can tell them what they need to do to get home," said Squeaks, smiling.

"That's true. We could tell them about the clues," said Stick. "And besides, trying to call them won't hurt anything."

Tater looked apprehensively for the VOLUME knob. Locating it, he turned the volume up as high as it would go. He switched to the Team's top-secret channel, walked over to the kitchen table, pulled out a chair and sat down. Crossing his fingers tightly in his lap, he took a deep breath and pushed the TALK button.

"Hero! Hero! Is that you?" he asked anxiously.

Releasing the button, he prayed for the four lost members of the Team to answer.

Chapter Eight

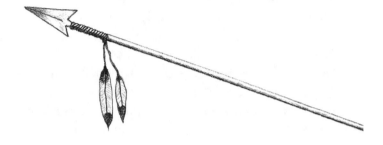

"Who's there?" demanded Comonti. The Nephite warrior held his spear across his body with both hands, and he searched the area very carefully. Unable to locate where the noise had come from, he tightened his grip on the spear and swung it in the air wildly. "Show yourself, now!" he insisted in his deep voice, pretending he was fighting in a battle.

The young warrior stood only two feet away from the boys. The five-foot by five-foot make-shift hideout Hero, Bubba and KP had built during the night, using bamboo branches and various leaves from the jungle, would give them little protection from a direct hit of the warrior's spear. The boys were paralyzed with fear as the warrior continued to swing his spear. He moved closer and closer to their location, knocking the foliage down as he searched for the noise.

"It's the walkie-talkie," Bubba mouthed to Hero, afraid to utter a sound.

Hero nodded his head.

Afraid that Tater's booming voice would sound again and give away their position, Bubba mouthed the question, "Hero, what do you want me to do?"

Hero shook his head, held up his hand and whispered, "Wait, don't do anything."

Hero quietly pulled the small metal tab and unzipped his backpack. As he shuffled the contents around, he cringed every time they made noise. At last, he located the walkie-talkie. He slowly turned the VOLUME button, one click at a time, toward the OFF position. As the last click sounded, the boys breathed an anxious sigh of relief.

Suddenly, the warrior's spear broke through the boys' hideout, scaring Bubba half to death. KP jumped toward him, covering his mouth to keep him from screaming.

"SHHHH! Don't move. He doesn't know we're in here," KP whispered.

Bubba's terrified eyes looked up at KP. He nodded his head and remained quiet.

Finding nothing, the young warrior turned a different direction and continued scouting through the surrounding area. Suddenly, a cat-sized tamandua fell down out of the hanging canopy tree, frightening the teenager. He fell back and gasped in fear.

"Ridiculous anteater! Go back up into the trees. You shouldn't be down here!" he snarled at the animal.

"Comonti?" a girl's voice hollered in the distance. "Where are you?"

"I'm over here, Kalia," he growled.

"What's the matter?" she asked, as she reached her brother, who was still sitting on the ground.

"That," Comonti answered angrily, pointing to the small animal.

"Don't they usually stay up in the trees?" she asked.

"They're supposed to," Comonti barked. "I almost killed the dumb thing."

Kalia smiled. "Did it scare you, mighty warrior?" she snickered, as she grabbed his hand and pulled him from the ground.

Comonti glared at her and said, "I'm not scared."

"You look scared," she flippantly answered, as she brushed the dirt off her hand.

"No, I don't!" he bellowed, holding up his spear. "I was making sure you were safe from Zerahemnah's army. You know we're too far from the city, and we'd be in big trouble if anyone knew."

Kalia knew she was breaking the rules — especially now. Captain Moroni's defenses had kept the Lamanites from taking over the city of Jershon, but even so, someone had entered the city and stolen the records of the people of Ammon. Since then, no one was allowed outside the city gates.

"And we'd be in more trouble if Captain Moroni knew," Kalia interrupted.

"Did you hear that?" whispered Bubba.

"Yeah, Captain Moroni," replied Hero in a low voice.

"He's here, and they know him. I guess that warrior last night was right."

"This is bad. We've got to get out of here," whispered KP. "We're in the middle of the war years from the Book of Alma in the Book of Mormon. Have you ever read them?"

Hero held his finger up to his mouth and quietly whispered, "Shhhh."

"Well," whispered Bubba, "these are really bad times. I don't want to be here!"

"I hear voices, Comonti. Someone is watching us," Kalia whispered, nervously looking around. "I can feel it."

"No, don't worry. I thought I heard them, too, but I think it's the tamandua you hear," he answered. He looked over at the noisy animal, chewing frantically on a log filled with Leaf Cutter Ants.

"I'm not sure. I don't like this," Kalia answered, still cautiously looking around the area. "I don't want to be captured. Let's get out of here."

"Then quit wasting time, and find your silly flowers before we get caught," Comonti answered.

"My flowers? You wanted to help, too," she snapped.

"Come on, Kalia. You don't really think I wanted to pick flowers, do you?" Comonti asked.

"You told me you did," she replied angrily.

"I didn't want to get into trouble when my little sister got captured," Comonti teased, as he patted the top of her head.

"Stop it, Comonti. I could have done this by myself. I didn't need you! Besides, you know the flowers will help Mom to feel better," Kalia said.

"I know, Kalia. You could've done it yourself. Let's just hurry and get the flowers, so we can go back to the city," Comonti answered softly.

Frustrated, Kalia angrily knelt next to the boys' hideout. She gathered beautiful yellow orchids, brightly colored, feather-shaped flowers, and large green leaves that resembled fans — enough to fill her arms. Hero intently watched her every move, from inside the hideout, through a small break in the leaves that the young warrior had created earlier with his spear. Afraid to move with the girl so close, Hero remained perfectly still and tried to breathe silently.

Kalia could sense that someone was close by. Several times, she paused from collecting the flowers to glance around the area.

"Comonti, are you sure no one is out here?" she nervously asked.

"I'm sure. Why?" he asked.

"I don't know. I thought I could..." she began.

"Did you see something?" he asked.

"No, I... I'm not sure," she answered.

"What is it?" Comonti insisted, as he walked toward the boys' hideout.

"I can't explain why, but I feel like someone is watching us," she replied.

"There's a good chance we could run into Zerahemnah's soldiers, Kalia. We should get out of here. I'm not sure I feel very good about being here," Comonti answered.

He stood and glanced over towards where the boys were hiding.

"Comonti!" Kalia cried.

He turned back to see Kalia's collection of flowers scattered all over the ground. A chill shot up his spine, and he quickly rushed to her side.

"Are you all right?" he asked.

She nodded.

"What happened?" he asked.

"I don't know. The flowers just blew out of my hands," Kalia answered.

"Do you have what you need?" he asked, as he picked up the flowers she had dropped.

Again, she nodded. Comonti stood up, handed Kalia the flowers and turned toward the city.

"Finally, slowpoke! Come on. Let's go, before something gets us!" he teased.

Kalia scrunched up her nose and scowled at her brother. "Wait for me!" she yelled. "Don't leave me here!"

Comonti ran fast and was quickly out of sight. Kalia ran after her brother, trying desperately to catch a glimpse of him. She continued running as fast as she could toward the city, pushing back her feelings that someone was following her. Suddenly, someone reached up, grabbed her arm and pulled her to the ground.

※

As the boys watched the two teenagers disappear toward the city, the excitement grew inside the hideout.

"Can you believe this?" KP asked. "They know Captain Moroni. I guess that confirms we are in Book of Mormon time."

"I thought we had confirmed that last night," said Hero, looking at KP oddly.

"I was hoping I had just dreamed about those crazy warriors last night," said KP, grinning.

"Should we try to follow those kids to the city?" asked Bubba.

"Why would we try to follow them? We might get caught," KP said. "I thought we were trying not to get caught."

"They seemed nice enough. Besides, they seemed to be on the Lord's side. They live in the city with Captain Moroni," said Bubba.

"That's true. Being on the Lord's side is a good thing," answered KP.

"Why were they so worried about the jungle?" asked Bubba. "They seemed really nervous to be out here."

"Maybe they're worried because they were told not to go outside the city walls," replied KP.

"Hello? Do either of you remember the scary dancing and drums beating all night long?" asked Hero.

"Oh, yeah," said KP. "I was hoping all of that was a bad dream, too."

"I don't think so," Hero answered.

"Hero, do you know who Zerahemnah was?" asked Bubba.

"Yes, Bubba. I have read the Book of Mormon and listened to the CD *Righteous Warriors*."

"I wonder if the camp leader we saw last night was Zerahemnah," Bubba said, contemplating the man's appearance. Deep lines crossed his forehead as he tried to remember exactly what the leader looked like.

"Do you think so?" asked KP.

"If it was Zerahemnah, we are in some serious trouble," replied Bubba.

"We need to stay close together," suggested Hero.

"I think we should try to follow those two kids," said Bubba. "I think they might be able to lead us back to the camp where we might be able to find some answers. Maybe someone from the city will even help us save Bean."

"Is that a good idea?" asked KP. "At least here we are hidden and safe."

"We can't stay here forever. Besides, we don't know if we'll be safe here for long," answered Hero. "Anyway, we have to rescue Bean."

"And I could really use some food. I'm starving," chimed in Bubba.

"Should we try to call the Team back?" asked KP.

"We should, but I'm afraid if we do, we'll lose those two kids," answered Hero. "I'm not sure that voice we thought we heard wasn't just our imagination anyway."

"Oh, okay," said Bubba. "But I'm kinda afraid of following those teenagers we saw."

"We'll be all right. I can't imagine those kids would hurt us," replied Hero.

The boys slowly pulled back several palm leaves and crawled through the dense bushes into the small clearing. Scouting the area in the light for the first time, they could see tons of trees everywhere. The jungle was so wet; they could see moisture collecting on the leaves of the bushes that surrounded them. The tamandua that had frightened the warrior was still on the ground, eating ants. Moss covered the tree trunks and animal noises filled the area.

"Which way did they go?" asked KP. "I didn't see."

"That way," said Bubba, pointing eastward toward the small city they had seen in the distance the night before.

"Let's go find them," said KP, as he started moving quickly through the trees.

"Wait, KP! Wait!" shouted Hero. "I said we need to stay together."

✺

"What are you doing, Comonti?" Kalia yelled. "You scared me, you dimwit."

"Quiet, Kalia," replied Comonti.

"Why?" she asked.

"We are being followed," he replied, staring back in the direction they had come.

"By whom?" she asked. "Don't try to scare me. You already told me no one was out here," she said, as she started to stand up.

"I'm not trying to scare you. Now get down here before they see you!" Comonti demanded. "I'm serious — someone is following us."

Kalia realized Comonti was not joking. She knelt down behind the thick brush to hide with her brother. Within minutes, a strange, fair-haired boy appeared.

Comonti grasped his spear firmly, motioned for Kalia to stay there and crept through the undergrowth of a fig tree. As the fair-haired boy maneuvered his way through the trees and vines, Comonti quickly positioned himself to attack. Carefully watching the boy's movements, Comonti took aim and waited for the boy to pass. As the boy passed him, Comonti stood up and screamed, "Aye, yi, yi, yi, yi!" Then he hurled his spear toward the boy.

Startled by the noise, KP turned just in time to see a spear flying toward his head. He instinctively threw his body sideways to escape the path of the spear, but he was too late. He felt a sharp pain, and he knew he had been hit.

"You got him! You got him, Comonti!" squealed Kalia excitedly. "Good job."

"Captain Moroni will be pleased," Comonti boasted.

"Are you really going to tell him you broke his orders and came into the jungle?" Kalia asked, as the two cautiously approached the boy.

"I hadn't thought about that. He will be angry, won't he?" Comonti asked.

"Yes, he will!" she replied. "Maybe this boy is a spy, and Captain Moroni will be glad we captured him. Hey, I know, maybe he's the one who stole Ammon's records. Let's interrogate him and find out who he is and why he was following us."

"Interrogate? Where did you learn that word?" Comonti asked, smiling.

"Don't make fun of me, Comonti," Kalia snapped, as they reached KP's side.

Comonti reached to pull the spear out of KP's arm. "Who are you?" Comonti demanded.

KP was afraid to say anything. As Comonti removed

the spear, KP realized it had only grazed his arm and pierced his sleeve, pinning him to a tree.

"Who are you?" Comonti demanded again.

"A friend," KP quietly answered.

Not satisfied with his answer, Comonti held the spear to KP's chin and again demanded, "Who are you?"

"My name is KP," he nervously replied. "I really am a friend."

Suddenly Hero came rustling through the leaves into the opening where KP was being held captive. Comonti and Kalia quickly stepped into the shadow behind KP to hide themselves. Comonti held KP's arm with one hand and pressed his spear firmly into KP's back with the other.

"Don't say a word," Comonti whispered.

"Where are you going all alone? What are you thinking? This isn't like being back home, KP," Hero scolded. He leaned over, placed his hands on his knees, trying to catch his breath. "You've got to be careful out here," he finished.

KP softly muttered, "Sorry, Hero."

"No problem," Hero panted. "Let's stay together from now on — especially in this area."

KP stood motionless. Hero did not notice the terrified expression on KP's face.

"Nice move, KP," said Bubba, as he finally caught up to the others. "What are you trying to do — get us all caught?"

"Yeah, that really was a good one, KP," chimed in Hero.

The young warrior suddenly stepped out from behind the shadows.

"Quiet!" yelled Comonti. "Who are you?"

Hero shook his head and said, "I told you the jungle wasn't safe, KP."

"Talk only to me," the warrior instructed. "Tell me who you are, now," he insisted.

"You'd never believe us," Bubba said.

"What are these clothes they are wearing, Comonti?" asked Kalia, as she touched KP's arm. "I have never seen anything like these before."

"Stay away from him, Kalia!" he yelled. "They could be spies. Now, for the last time before I kill all of you, who are you?" Comonti demanded.

"We are time travelers," replied Hero, trying to keep the young warrior calm.

"Impossible," Comonti replied.

"I said you wouldn't believe us," Bubba said.

"From where?" he asked, looking over at Bubba.

Hero started to answer, only to have Comonti yell, "Not you, him. From where do you come?" he asked, pointing to Bubba.

Realizing he had upset the warrior, Bubba answered, "We are from the future."

"How did you get here?" Comonti questioned.

"We don't know," Bubba replied.

"We believe the Lord sent us," said KP.

"Do you believe in the Lord?" asked Kalia excitedly.

"We do," he replied.

"Have you seen Him? Have you talked with Him?" she eagerly quizzed. "We have been waiting for Him to come."

"No, we haven't met Him," answered Hero. We have

faith that He does exist and that He has sent us here to your time."

"Why?" Comonti asked, as he slightly relaxed the pressure of the spear in KP's back. "Why would he send you here?"

"We don't know," Bubba replied.

"I don't believe you," Comonti said angrily. "You are trying to trick us and take us captive back to your leader, Zerahemnah."

"No, we're not," replied KP, feeling the sharp point of the spear in his back once again.

"Have you come to kill Captain Moroni?" Comonti asked. "I will not let you do that."

"No, we have not!" Bubba exclaimed. "He is one of my favorite people. Has Zerahemnah's army attacked yet?"

"How do you know about Zerahemnah?" asked Comonti suspiciously. "You must be part of his army."

"No, we're not. In the future, the Lord has given us the Book of Mormon," replied Hero.

"The Book of Mormon? What is that?" asked Comonti.

"It is a record of your time," answered Bubba. "The book tells us all about people like Zerahemnah, Captain Moroni, Alma and others."

"I don't believe you," insisted Comonti. "You are trying to trick us. How would you have a record of our time?"

"From the Lord," replied KP, trying to move away from the sharp point of Comonti's spear.

"Why would the Lord give you our records? We don't believe you," Kalia said. "Those records are for people like us."

"We are people like you," replied Hero. "We believe in Jesus Christ."

"We can prove it," said Bubba.

"How?" Comonti asked suspiciously. "How can you prove it?"

"We have a copy of the Book of Mormon with us," replied Bubba.

"Let me see it then," insisted Comonti.

Bubba, who was carrying Hero's backpack, quickly opened the pack and started to rummage through the contents.

"It's not here, Hero," Bubba said nervously.

"What do you mean? The Book of Mormon has to be in my backpack," Hero declared. "Look again, Bubba. Empty the entire thing."

Bubba picked up the pack and dumped the contents on the ground. Sifting through the items, Bubba found a sweatshirt, some rope, a little food, a water bottle, the walkie-talkie, a flashlight and batteries, a few pens, some change, and Moroni's Treasure Map.

"It's not here!" he exclaimed.

"It has to be here!" cried Hero. He grabbed the pack from Bubba and started searching through it himself.

"You are spies — I knew it," declared Comonti. "I will take you to Captain Moroni, and he can decide if you will die."

Comonti grabbed KP's arm and held the spear to his back. Then he ordered Hero and Bubba to stand up.

"Wait, I know it's here," Bubba said.

Hero frantically continued to search through all the

pockets of his pack. "KP, do you have one?" he asked.

KP, looking at Comonti for permission to pull his pack from his shoulder, was relieved when Comonti nodded his head in approval. He took his pack, quickly unzipped it and searched through the contents. Moments later, he yelled, "I have it. It's here, Hero."

He held up the book for everyone to see. Relieved, Hero took the book from KP, breathed a sigh of relief and walked toward Comonti.

"Here, let me show you the Book of Mormon," Hero said.

Chapter Nine

Comonti apprehensively took the Book of Mormon from Hero. He inspected every detail of the exterior. The rough, blue leather and stamped gold writing were clearly nothing he had ever seen before. Sure he could determine what the book was made of, he held it up to his nose and smelled the cover and inside pages, but neither smelled familiar to him. Noticing the small writing printed on the thin pages, he slid his finger over a page to feel the rough grooves of engraved writing — like the records of his day. Surprised by the smooth feeling, he quickly picked up his finger and turned the page, accidentally tearing the corner of the paper.

Shocked by the torn paper, he slammed the book closed and said, "What is this material? I have never seen anything like it before."

"It is what we call paper," answered Hero, taking the book out of Comonti's hand and opening it slowly. "This is what we write on in the future."

"And what about this?" Comonti asked, pointing to the blue leather. "What animal did this come from?"

"Cow," answered Hero.

"You have blue cows?" he asked, with an odd look on his face.

"No, not blue cows," answered Bubba smiling. "The leather from cows has been dyed blue."

"Why?" asked Kalia, scrunching up her nose.

"In the future, leather is dyed all sorts of colors," said KP.

"We dye things to give people a choice of colors to pick from," Hero explained.

Comonti again took the book from Hero. He turned it over and over in his hands. Finally, he laid the book on the ground and opened it again. He sat down next to it and cautiously turned one page at a time, looking at the many rows of unfamiliar writing.

He looked skeptically at Hero and said, "This is not reformed Egyptian or Hebrew. How am I to know what is written?"

"The book is written in the English language. Can't you read it?" asked KP.

"No, I can't understand anything written here. What language is English?" he asked. "These symbols don't mean anything to me."

Kalia, wanting to see the writings for herself, slid the book around to where she could see it better. Gazing upon the writings, she too slid her finger down the page and was surprised at the delicate texture.

"I have never seen these strange symbols, and I have learned to write Egyptian and Hebrew," Kalia said. "Can you read them?" she asked, looking up to Bubba.

"Yes, I can read the symbols. But aren't these symbols in the same language as you are speaking?" Bubba asked, puzzled that the two could not read the words.

"No, we are speaking the same language as you are — Egyptian — not this language," said Comonti, still skeptical of the book.

Confused, Bubba looked over to Hero. "Why can they understand us, but not the writing?" he asked.

"I don't know. Maybe the Lord doesn't want them to read what happens in the future," he replied.

"I hadn't thought about that," said Bubba.

"I'm sure He doesn't," agreed KP. "I wonder if we're even supposed to talk to anyone here."

Bubba shrugged his shoulders and said, "I don't know."

Comonti suddenly jumped to his feet. He grabbed the handle of his spear and shrieked, "Quiet! No more of this. This book says nothing. Captain Moroni can deal with you."

"And he won't put up with your trickery," chimed in Kalia, acting as though she knew Captain Moroni personally.

Shocked by Comonti's sudden actions, the boys moved closer together.

"I promise, we're not tricking you," said KP.

"In fact, one of our friends was captured by warriors in the jungle last night," added Hero, pointing his arm toward the enemy camp. "We have to find a way to get her back. Without her, we cannot go home."

"How can I believe you?" asked Comonti. "Nothing you have said makes any sense."

"We can show you. The camp where they are holding her is this way," Bubba said, pointing back in the direction they had come.

"I won't go deeper into the jungle. I will already be in trouble for traveling this far," responded Comonti. "Besides, I am not convinced that you're not warriors from that camp. You are probably the thieves who stole the records of Ammon."

Kalia, intrigued by what the boys had said, asked, "Is your friend a girl?"

"Yes, she is," answered KP, "and I'm sure she is scared."

Kalia stood, contemplating the thought of a girl being held captive by the savages who her father often battled. She could not shake the images of the warriors' frightening appearance. The thought of their shaved heads, large rings hanging from their ears, and colors painted in stripes all over their bodies, gave her chills.

"We can't leave a girl out there, Comonti," Kalia protested. "They will hurt her or maybe kill her. And I am sure they are scaring her. They scare me."

"This could be a trap, Kalia," barked Comonti. "What if these boys are Lamanites and fighting for Zerahemnah? Then we will certainly be captured. At least right now they are our prisoners," he said, aiming the point of his spear at the boys.

"They don't look like warriors, Comonti. I have never seen these clothes before, nor these things on their backs. I've never seen the thing they call *paper* or their *colored leather*. Maybe they are telling the truth. Maybe they are from the future," Kalia reasoned.

"Can we take that chance?" Comonti asked apprehensively.

"Our father would never turn his back on a Nephite or a follower of Christ," she replied.

"Are they followers of Christ?" questioned Comonti, looking over at the boys.

"We are," said Hero. "I was baptized when I was eight. I attend church every Sunday, and I'm even starting Seminary this year," he added nervously.

"What are all those things?" asked Comonti. "I pray to the Lord everyday, and I follow the teachings of the Prophet Alma. Do you do any of that?"

"The prophet in our day is Gordon B. Hinckley," said KP. "I try to follow his teachings and I pray every day."

"The scriptures the Lord gave us from the records of your time help us in our time. We try to read these scriptures often. I can read to you some of the scriptures the Lord gave us about your day," offered Hero. "Would you believe us then?"

"If they are true teachings of the Lord of Alma and the other prophets, I will feel the Spirit He sends," Comonti replied.

"Which verses should I read, Bubba?" asked Hero.

"Read to him the events that are happening right now," Bubba replied. "You will need to start reading in Alma 43."

Hero agreed. He reached out toward the Book of Mormon and gently took the scriptures from Comonti's hand. He quickly flipped through the pages, searching for the right chapter. Finding what he was looking for, he looked toward Comonti and asked, "May I start?"

"I'm not sure what good this will do you," he replied, turning his back toward Hero.

Hero looked down at the scriptures and read, "Alma, Chapter Forty-Three. Then he asked, "Comonti, may I start?"

With his back still toward Hero, Comonti reluctantly nodded his head once in agreement.

"I will read you the chapter headings. When I read something you want to hear more about, stop me, and I will read you the entire section, okay?"

Again Comonti nodded once in agreement.

Hero looked over to Bubba nervously and asked, "Alma, Chapter Forty-Three, right?"

Bubba answered, "I'm sure that is the chapter that discusses the beginning of the war with Zerahemnah."

Hero looked down at his scriptures and started reading.

"Alma, Chapter Forty-Three, chapter heading, 'Alma and his sons preach the word — The Zoramites and other Nephite dissenters become Lamanites — The Lamanites come against the Nephites in war — Moroni arms the Nephites with defensive armor — The Lord reveals to Alma the strategy of the Lamanites — The Nephites defend their homes, liberties, families, and religion — The armies of Moroni and Lehi surround the Lamanites.'"

Kalia had remained quiet for several minutes. Finally, unable to wait any longer, she stomped over to Comonti. She placed her hands on her hips and said, "Comonti, this book talks about Father. These boys wouldn't know this information if they were Lamanites."

"Quiet, Kalia," said Comonti, with his back still turned to her.

"No! Comonti, I believe these boys. They are not from our time!" she yelled. "We need to help them, and you know it. If you aren't going to help them, then I will. You can explain to Father what happened and why you didn't help them."

Kalia turned to the boys and motioned for them to gather their things. She immediately started walking further into the jungle. Shocked at her actions, Comonti still had not moved. Hero slowly stood up, placed the Book of Mormon in his pack, zipped it closed and stared at Comonti. Finally, he turned toward the cries of KP and Bubba calling for him to follow them.

"I'll be right there," he quietly answered. "Wait one minute." Turning back toward Comonti, Hero grabbed his shoulder and anxiously asked, "Are you coming with us?"

Comonti turned, looked at Hero and said, "The Spirit spoke to me."

"And?" asked Hero.

Watching Kalia walk further into the jungle, he breathed out a heavy sigh, picked up his spear and said, "Come on. Let's go see if we can find your friend."

Hero and Comonti walked swiftly to catch up with the others.

"Stay behind me and be quiet. I will protect you," said Comonti.

Smiling, Kalia said, "You sound like Father."

"He's going to be so mad when he finds out we have been out here, Kalia — even if other Nephites or friends are in trouble."

"He will be proud of you, Comonti. You are doing the right thing," she said. "And if the information they have keeps our father safe, we need to help them."

Comonti looked over to the boys and said, "The Spirit of the Lord is strong with you. Show me the way to your friend."

"She is this way," replied Bubba, running west and away from the city.

Knowing better than to run, Comonti watched as Bubba struggled to maneuver through the jungle. The lush greenery of trees, vines and foliage, worked together to trap the food the jungle wildlife needed to survive, and the plants had succeeded again at claiming their prey.

"I'm stuck again," yelled Bubba. "Help me!"

Hero shook his head as he walked toward Bubba. "You've got to be more careful," he warned, as he pulled the vines from Bubba's leg.

"You cannot run in the jungle," Comonti added. "You must move quietly and watch your surroundings carefully. Many dangers besides Lamanites exist here."

"That is true," agreed Kalia. "A lot of the animals in the jungle can be dangerous, but none as deadly as the jaguar."

"Jaguars?" asked Bubba nervously.

"It's daytime, Bubba. I'm sure you'll be fine," replied Hero.

"I'm worried, Hero. I haven't had the best luck here. So far, I've sat in a pile of Fire Ants, walked through a poisonous spider web, and been caught in the jungle vines — twice now. With my luck, I'm sure I will come face to face with a jaguar next."

"Don't worry," said Kalia. "I will protect you."

Bubba smiled, as he looked down at the confident Nephite girl. He shook his head and maneuvered his way cautiously behind Comonti. Walking five feet behind him, Bubba took hold of Kalia's hand and said, "All right, will you please protect me?"

Everyone laughed — even Comonti who had shown no sense of humor until now. Kalia proudly showed the boys Forest Cucumbers that would make them sick and Bromeliad vines that were filled with water. They could be cut open and used for drinking water. She identified the Strangler Fig vines that Bubba continued to get caught in, and the Liana vines that were strong enough to swing on. And she showed them her favorite tree — the Cocoa Tree.

After they had walked for approximately thirty minutes, Comonti suddenly sensed danger. Stopping abruptly in his tracks, he quickly squatted down to his knees and motioned for everyone else to do the same.

Comonti quietly whispered, "We are close to a Lamanite camp. Be quiet, and move slowly."

"How can you tell?" whispered KP.

"Look, in the distance, over the Parkia Tree," he replied. "I can see a wisp of smoke."

"Parkia tree? What does that look like?" asked Hero, squinting to see the smoke.

"The tree in the distance with the red flowers that are closed," said Kalia, pointing at the tree.

"Okay, I see it," said Bubba.

"Follow me," Comonti said, as he cautiously moved toward the smoke.

"What are your names, anyway?" Comonti asked.

They each responded in turn.

"Hero."

"Bubba."

"KP."

"Those are odd names," he replied.

"Not for our times," said Hero.

"What is the girl's name?" whispered Kalia.

"Bean," Bubba replied.

"Bean? What kind of name is that?" Kalia asked.

"That's the name we call her," answered KP. "You will like her, Kalia. She's a lot like you."

Kalia smiled tenderly. "How did she get caught by those warriors?"

"I sat on a hill of ants," replied Bubba.

"Fire Ants?" interrupted Kalia. "On purpose?"

"Yes, they were Fire Ants. No, not on purpose."

"Why?"

"We'd been running for close to an hour and I was almost ready to pass out. We sat down to rest in the grass, and my luck helped me to pick the spot where the ants lived," Bubba replied.

"How many times were you bitten?" she asked.

"I don't know for sure," he said. "A lot."

"When did this happen?" she asked.

"Late last night."

"Is your skin burning?" she asked.

"Yes, I can hardly stand it. I feel like I'm on fire," he replied.

"Comonti, he needs mud," said Kalia. "He might have a reaction."

"We can find some on the way back," Comonti replied, continuing further into the jungle. "If we are going to rescue this girl, we better get moving. Father is not going to be happy about all of this."

"Who is your father, Comonti?" asked Bubba, struggling to keep pace with his new friend.

"Lehi."

"Lehi — as in the Captain of a Nephite Army?" asked Bubba.

"He is not a Captain," replied Comonti. "But we hope he will be soon."

"Yes, he will. He's a great man," replied Bubba.

"Yes, he is," answered Comonti. "But, please don't tell me the future."

"Why? I thought you would be very interested," said Hero.

"I am, but I worry enough about my father and mother. If I knew that my father was going to be injured or killed, I'm not sure I would let him go to battle again," replied Comonti.

Comonti, Kalia and the boys swiftly maneuvered through the trees, vines and dense brush to the same area where the boys had watched the warriors the night before. Locating the camp, they spotted a few warriors along the perimeter who seemed to be sleeping. Bean was nowhere in sight, and neither was the warrior who spoke the night before.

Surprised at how quiet the camp was, Comonti said, "The Lord helps us today. I have never seen a camp with warriors who are asleep this late in the morning."

"I think Bean is in one of those tents," said Bubba, pointing to the camp.

"I didn't realize our enemies were so close, Comonti," said Kalia.

"I guess Father had a good reason for telling us not to go into the jungle," replied Comonti.

"Any ideas on how we might get in and save her?" asked KP. "Do you think they are still keeping her here?"

"Yes, she is here, and I'm sure she is all right," said Comonti.

"How do you know?" asked Hero.

"I have never seen the Lamanites post three guards on a prisoner. The leader must really think she is valuable."

"Can you see her?" asked Kalia, trying to get a better view.

"No," replied Comonti. "I can't see her yet."

"I can't either," said KP.

"Look at those two tents, Hero," Comonti said, pointing beyond the fire.

"I see them," Hero replied.

"The tent on the right must be for the leader of this camp, and the tent on the left is for the prisoner," he explained.

"Are you sure?" asked Hero.

"Your friend is in the one on the west side. Can you see the three guards?" he asked.

"Yes."

"A guard is never to stand within three feet of the leader's tent. Can you see that the warriors on the left are touching the sides of the tee-pee? That is the tent she is in."

"How do you know this?" asked KP.

"My father has taught me well," he replied.

"Do you think we will have any luck freeing her?" asked KP.

"No, not a chance," said Comonti.

"Why?" asked Bubba.

"You tell me," said Comonti, turning to the boys. He had a stern look on his face. "What happened here last night?"

"I told you," replied Hero. "We were in the jungle, heading toward the lights of your city. Bubba was attacked by hundreds of Fire Ants. While we were helping him, Bean was kidnapped."

"What happened after that?"

"Well, we followed them until we got here. Then we watched them do some kind of ritual dance."

"Yes, then what?"

"The leader came out of the tent with Bean. He said that she was a Nephite captain's daughter, and that they would use her to win the upcoming war. He said they would demand their land back before they gave the girl to Captain Moroni," said Hero.

"She is not a captain's daughter," said Kalia.

"I know that, but they don't," replied Hero.

"This could be bad. We must tell my father immediately," warned Comonti. "And we must get out of this jungle as quickly as we can."

"Why?" asked KP.

"Because Zerahemnah will be watching closely for our soldiers to come rescue her," he replied.

"Zerahemnah?" asked Bubba. "Do you think he really is the leader here?"

"Possibly," answered Comonti.

"The Nephite army doesn't even know she exists," said KP.

"Yes, but as you said, Zerahemnah does know she exists, and he believes that she is a captain's daughter. We must tell our father so that he can warn Captain Moroni."

"What do we do about Bean?" asked Hero.

"They will not allow anything to happen to her," said Comonti. "If they did, Captain Moroni would not bargain with them."

"So we leave her here?" asked Bubba.

"Yes, for now," replied Comonti. "We must go quickly. Follow me, and stay close."

"I'm afraid to leave her here," said Bubba. "Can we at least wait until we see that she is alive?"

"By that time, the entire camp will be awake, creating a bigger chance for us to be caught," replied Comonti. The Lord has provided a way for us to get home while they are still sleeping, so we must go."

"Come on, Bubba. Listen to Comonti," said Kalia. "He is very smart when it comes to matters of war."

Bubba agreed tentatively and forced a smile across his face. "No running ahead this time, KP," he teased.

"Don't worry. I'm staying with the guy who has the spear," KP responded, standing right behind Comonti.

Comonti silently led the way through the jungle. He carefully maneuvered every stick and rock, knowing that even the smallest noise could trigger an attack or capture from the army of warriors hiding in the jungle. He stopped only once to collect mud for Bubba's ant bites. He led his sister and the boys back within the safe walls of the city where Captain Moroni was busy training his men to fight in battle. With Comonti leading the way, the return to the city walls took forty-five minutes from where Bean was being held captive. As they reached the city, Comonti held up his spear.

"Wait here," he instructed. You do not look like you belong within the city. I will go find my father and bring him to you."

"Why can't we go with you?" asked KP.

"Important records were stolen yesterday, and I am afraid people in the city might believe you stole them," he replied. "When you are dressed like one of us, no one will suspect you."

"What do you want me to do, Comonti?" asked Kalia.

"Father will want them to change their clothes. Run to the market, and see what you can find. Remember to get shoes as well."

"How do you want me to pay?" she asked.

"Have the storekeepers put the clothes on Father's account, and I will tell him later."

"Hero, keep your friends hidden in these trees," said Comonti, as he pointed to an area thick with bushes and leaves. "Be careful, because we have guards surrounding our city. Security has been tightened because the precious records are missing."

Hero agreed. The boys watched as their two new friends headed toward the city walls. Hero, KP and Bubba sat nervously in the jungle, watching and listening to the commotion of the city.

"Look," said KP, pointing to the bridge that led into the city. "Those people are not wearing loincloths like the warriors back in the jungle."

"I think that most of the Nephites wore modest clothing — not loincloths," replied Bubba.

"I guess I'd never really paid attention," said Hero. "When I think of Nephites and Lamanites, I have always assumed they all wore loincloths."

"That's just because of pictures you've seen in church," said Bubba.

"Hero!" yelled KP excitedly.

"Quiet, KP. What?" asked Hero, nervously looking around.

"I just remembered," he replied.

"Remembered what?" Hero asked.

"Back in the jungle — the walkie-talkie rang remember?"

"I completely forgot," said Hero.

"Get it out, quick," shrieked Bubba, excited at the prospect of talking to the Team back home.

"Guys, I'm sure it was nothing," said Hero. "Think about it — a walkie-talkie could never cross through time."

"What if it did?" KP responded, unsure it was possible.

"It has to work," said Bubba. "I heard Tater's bellowing voice, and so did Comonti, remember?"

"I think we all wanted to hear, Tater," said Hero. "But I'm not sure we really did."

"You may be right, but what do we have to lose?" responded Bubba. "Come on. Let's check it out, anyway."

Hero rummaged through his backpack and pulled out the black clear-tone Motorola, Model 1000 walkie-talkie. It had 240 channels and a seven-mile range. He smiled and said, "Don't get your hopes up, guys. There's no way this walkie-talkie could be anywhere within seven miles of our Treehouse."

He slowly turned the small black knob to the ON position. He gently pushed the TALK button and quietly whispered, "Tater, Stick, any of your guys there?"

Nothing. No response came from home.

"See, I told you guys. They can't hear us."

"What if Mom answers? What are we going to say?" asked Bubba.

"I don't know," responded Hero. "I'm not sure she even knows anything about what has happened."

"Come on, guys. Try again," demanded KP.

Hero smiled up at KP, who was now anxiously hovering over him.

"Tater, Stick, Squeaks. Is anyone there?" Hero asked again, this time speaking louder.

Again, silence. The boys heard only static. Waiting for a moment, Hero held the walkie-talkie up for everyone to hear.

"I guess we are too far out of range," Hero said.

As Hero started to turn off the walkie-talkie, Bubba heard a faint voice for a split second.

"Wait! Turn that back on," demanded Bubba. "I think I heard something."

Hero turned up the volume, and the boys listened intently for several minutes. No other sound was heard.

"Come on, guys. No one's there," insisted Hero.

"What channel are you using?" asked KP.

"Channel Fourteen, Substation A. Why?"

"When we use the walkie-talkie for Team chatter only, so that your mom can't hear, we use Channel Twenty-One, remember?" KP asked.

"That's right. I forgot," said Hero. "Let's try one more time on that channel."

"Hurry, Hero," said Bubba. "Maybe they have been trying to talk to us for hours now."

Hero, still skeptical, quickly turned to Channel Twenty-One. As he reached the station, the static was worse than normal, and the boys quickly turned down the volume.

"We're going to get caught if we're not careful," said Hero. "Maybe we should try this later, after we are settled in the city."

"Try, one more time," prodded KP. "Please?"

Hero smiled, nodded his head and twisted the black knob until the sound was completely turned off. He cancelled Substation A on the walkie-talkie and slowly turned up the volume.

"Hero, Hero. Can anyone here me?" the voice

boomed. "Hello? Hello? Anyone out there?"

"Squeaks, is that you?" asked Hero, shocked at the voice on the other side. He slowly moved the mouthpiece closer to his face.

"Hero, I knew you could hear me," she answered. "Where are you? Are you safe? What are you doing? What is going on?" she demanded, as tears welled up in her eyes.

"One question at a time, Squeaks," Hero answered. We are okay, but I don't know for sure if we are safe," he replied. "We're trying to figure out what is going on right now."

"Have you figured out why you are there?" she asked.

"Are we supposed to?" Hero whispered. "Do you know why we are here?"

"Cheri came and translated all of the writings in the Treehouse. They tell us all about the Liahona," she said through the static.

"So, the treasure is the Liahona, for sure?" he asked.

"Yep," Squeaks said proudly. "I was so worried about you. I'm glad you are alive."

"Squeaks, is Tater with you?" Hero asked.

"Yes," she replied, as she handed Tater the walkie-talkie.

"Hey, Hero. How are you guys?" Tater asked.

"Tater, I don't have much time. Is everything okay there?"

"Yes, so far. No one even knows you are gone yet, except Cheri," Tater replied. "But, you haven't been gone very long yet."

"Very long? We've been gone for eighteen hours, at least," answered Hero.

"What are you talking about, Hero?" Tater asked. "You have only been gone for a few hours."

"Tater, we disappeared yesterday, late afternoon," replied Hero. "Didn't we?"

"Not according to my watch, Hero. You have only been gone a few hours," said Tater, looking at his watch. "In fact, you've been gone four hours and thirty-seven minutes — give or take a few.

"What's going on then?" Hero asked. "We have been in this land for at least eighteen hours now."

"I don't know," Tater replied. "Nothin' has been easy since we found this map."

"Maybe time is different here. I don't know, but I don't have time to figure that out right now," said Hero. "I've got to be quiet, or we could be captured at any minute. Now, tell me what Cheri said when she translated everything."

"Okay," replied Tater, relieved to know his friends were all right. "First, tell me exactly how this walkie-talkie thing is working through time?" he asked, baffled at how it was possible to get a signal that worked.

"Tater, we'll figure that out later," answered Hero. "Tell me what is going on with the Liahona."

"Well," started Tater through heavier static. "Che.. cam. and translated the writings. She s..d, th.. wri... were clu.. lik. th. lst t.m. We need to trans.... th cle in ord.. for y.u to co.. hme, you mu.. figu... out w.o is dan..r a.. sav. thm."

"Wait, Tater. Wait!" yelled Hero. "Repeat that. What did Cheri say we have to do to come home? I couldn't understand anything."

"Her., are y.u the..?" asked Tater. "We w.l hav. to fig... ou. wh. t.. c.u. is and dan... and sav. th..."

Suddenly, the signal and the static on the walkie-talkie went silent.

"Hero, we're losing the signal! Try again," Bubba said frantically. "Try again."

"Try shaking it or something," suggested KP. "Maybe even hit it on the ground."

"No way, KP," said Bubba. "Just shake it."

"I am. I am," replied Hero. "Tater, are you there? Tater, are you there?" he asked, almost yelling.

"Did the batteries go dead?" asked KP.

"No, the batteries are fine," said Hero, still fiddling with all the switches. "We've lost the signal."

"I guess we're lucky we heard that much," said Bubba, disappointed they did not get more information. "We never should've had a signal. These walkie-talkies don't have this kind of range!"

"You better save the battery," said KP.

Hero turned off the walkie-talkie, and he placed it in his backpack. Whispering to each other ideas about how the walkie-talkie could have possibly worked through time, the boys waited eagerly for Comonti and Kalia to return. Suddenly, in the distance, Hero heard whispering. He motioned to Bubba and KP to be quiet, and then he strained to hear what was being said.

"Who is it?" whispered KP.

"Shhhh," replied Hero. "I don't know. I can't see them."

As the voices moved closer, the boys heard only part of the conversation.

"Moroni will never figure out that I took the records," he whispered, in a gruff, confident voice.

"How do you know that?" another voice asked.

"I have been his trusted messenger for a long time. He will never suspect me."

"I hope you're right. Zerahemnah is not prepared to battle the Nephites until our men meet with the other warriors in three days."

"Keep quiet. Our plan will be complete later tonight at our meeting with Moroni," the gruff voice replied. "We may take the city of Manti without Moroni even knowing."

The boys tried desperately to see the two men. They watched carefully as the men moved further into the jungle, straining to hear every word spoken.

Frightened, and uncertain about what they had heard, the boys quietly waited for Comonti to return.

Chapter Ten

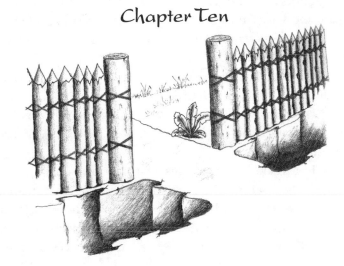

The sound of approaching footsteps frightened Hero. He was suddenly afraid the men they heard talking earlier were returning. He prayed the footsteps would continue past their hideout. "Maybe they are Nephite warriors returning from battle or guards patrolling the area," he hoped. Little by little, the heavy footsteps moved closer to the boys' position. Then they stopped abruptly — directly in front of Hero, Bubba and KP.

Bubba looked at Hero and whispered, "Who is it?"

"Should we run?" KP quietly asked.

Hero shook his head. He placed his finger to his lips and whispered, "Shhhhh."

"Hero," a young voice called. "Hero, it is I, Comonti. Where are you?"

A flood of relief raced through Hero's body when he heard the voice. Pushing aside the enormous palm leaves that kept the boys hidden, they were relieved to see their new friend, Comonti.

Hero quickly jumped to his feet and said, "Comonti, I was afraid you wouldn't return."

"I'm sorry to have taken so long, Hero, but I had to convince my father to come," he said, as he stepped to his left.

He revealed a large, muscular man, standing behind him. As Hero stared silently at the man, he noticed that his calves were nearly as big as Bubba's chest. The muscles in his arms were well defined. "He could easily be the strongest man I have ever seen," thought Hero, overwhelmed by his sheer size.

Comonti's father stood at least six-feet tall, had premature gray, wavy hair that fell just below his ears, piercing brown eyes and tanned skin. He wore two leather bands around his right arm. He had a wheat-colored shirt, which had straps that went over both shoulders, and a long, knee-length skirt with long shorts underneath. With his sword hanging on his left side and a machete tucked into the sash around his waist, he was the most intimidating man the boys had ever seen.

"Hero, Bubba and KP, this is my father, Lehi," said Comonti, pointing to the large man. "He is the leader of a Nephite army."

Lehi watched the boys silently for several uncomfortably tense minutes. The scowl on his face drove deep lines at the sides of his eyes and above his nose. Finally breaking the awkward silence with a deep, overpowering voice, he asked, "Who are you boys? What vile trickery are you playing on my son?"

Looking directly in Lehi's eyes, Hero quickly responded, "No trickery, Sir. We have come from another time."

"Another time. How is this possible?" he demanded. "I do not have time for games."

"We aren't sure how it's possible. We found a treasure of the Lord's that unexpectedly brought us here to this time," replied Bubba.

"Where is this 'treasure' you speak of?" asked Lehi.

"Our friend, who was captured by the warriors while we were in the jungle, has it with her," KP replied.

"A girl? You let a girl keep your treasure?" Lehi asked.

"Yes, Sir, we did," answered Hero.

"Tell him of that book, Hero," interrupted Comonti. "Give him the one you showed me."

"We also have with us a record given to the people of our time from the Lord. It is called the Book of Mormon," replied Hero, "and is a record of the people and events in your day."

"How did you get this record?" asked Lehi.

"The record was given to a man named Joseph Smith, Jr. by the Angel Moroni. Joseph translated the record with the Lord's guidance, and then he published the book in the year One Thousand, Eight Hundred Thirty A.D.," answered Bubba.

"One Thousand, Eight Hundred Thirty A.D.," said

Lehi. "What does A.D. mean?"

"The year One Thousand, Eight Hundred Thirty Annus Domini, in the year of our Lord," replied KP.

"Annus Domini?" he asked, looking puzzled.

"The year the Savior was born, people began to count forward starting at the number one," replied Hero.

"Do you know what year we live in now, boys?" he asked skeptically.

"Yes," answered Bubba. "If the book we read as the Word of God is correct, the year, according to our records, is either the seventeenth or eighteenth year of the reign of the judges, or approximately 73 or 74 B.C.," answered Bubba confidently.

"B.C. What does that mean?" asked Lehi.

"B.C. stands for the years before Christ came to the earth," explained KP.

"We do not know exactly when the Lord will come," replied Lehi. "How could you possibly know this?"

"We know because we come from the future," Hero replied, "after the Lord has already come."

"How many years until the Lord comes here?" asked Lehi.

"About seventy-four," answered Hero.

"Did you meet him when he came to your time?" Lehi asked, somewhat intrigued.

"No, he came one thousand, nine hundred ninety years before I was born," Hero answered.

"Does the girl have the record you speak of as well?" Lehi asked.

"No, I have it here," answered Hero. He pulled off his

backpack and fumbled through it, searching for the Book of Mormon.

Hero handed the book to Lehi, and then watched as Lehi inspected it closely. Lehi ran his finger across the cover's rough texture, marveled at the thin paper pages and was astonished at the smooth writing. The boys quietly watched as he turned page after page, looking for anything he could understand.

Slamming the book closed, he asked, "Why should I believe you? Everything you speak of makes no sense. I can't believe these writings are from our Lord or that he would send children traveling back in time."

"We believe the Lord has sent us here to help," replied KP.

"How can you help us?" Lehi asked, puzzled.

"We know that the Lamanites are taking up arms against you right now," replied Bubba. "We can help with preparations for that war and give you information you could use to be victorious in the battle."

Lehi stood motionless, thinking for several minutes. Then he said, "The Spirit of the Lord resides with Captain Moroni. We will speak to him about what you say. If you are spies for Zerahemnah, then Captain Moroni will know. Follow me."

As Lehi turned toward the city, he motioned for the boys to follow.

"Wait! What about our friend?" questioned KP.

"We will tend to her later," Lehi answered.

"No, first," begged Bubba.

"No, you will advise Captain Moroni of the things you

know — of your book and your captured friend — before I put any of my men in any danger looking for her," Lehi firmly declared. "Now follow me!"

With no other choice, the boys knew they had to do as they were told. They hastily retrieved their backpacks and followed closely behind Lehi.

Clouds had covered what little sun penetrated the jungle, and the air was becoming cold. Following in his giant footsteps, the three boys crossed a narrow path toward the gateway of the city. On both sides of the path, the boys observed a moat that encircled the entire city. The moat was approximately fifty feet wide. The water was murky in the shadows of the afternoon. But Hero was sure he saw a crocodile floating like a log on the surface, and then he watched it quickly dive to the bottom as the boys passed.

"Hey guys, this is Captain Moroni's defensive earthwork," said Bubba. "The Book of Mormon talks about it several times."

"What is defensive earthwork?" asked Hero.

"The moat, twenty-foot tall fence, and everything done to offer more protection for the people," Bubba answered.

"Good thing you know so much about this time in the Book of Mormon, Bubba," said KP.

"I can't believe Captain Moroni is still in the city," declared Bubba, smiling. "I thought he would've already moved his army to the city of Manti."

"I can't wait to meet him," said Hero. "I'm glad he hasn't left yet."

"Me, too," said KP.

Inside the city, the boys saw a network of small buildings leading to one large building in the center of town. Trees were plentiful, and small houses, which resembled cottages, were scattered throughout the area. They were petite, with only one open room or two small rooms inside. They were constructed from tree timbers, and a muddy paste filled up any holes.

As the boys continued to follow Lehi, Kalia came running up with new clothes from the market.

Lehi watched as she ran toward the men. "Are you involved in this too, Kalia?" asked Lehi angrily. "I expected you to make better choices," he said.

"Yes, Father," she replied. "I am afraid it's my fault that Comonti was in the jungle. He came to protect me."

"Can anyone tell me why you two chose to disobey your father?" he asked.

"I wanted to gather flowers for Mother," Kalia answered. "She is in so much pain."

"Was that a good enough reason to ignore my requests?" he asked.

"No, but we did find one of the Lamanite camps," she replied, hoping the information might help shield her from her father's wrath.

"We have spies to do that, Kalia," he responded heatedly. "The jungle is not a place for you right now. Do you realize you could have been captured or killed?"

"I'm sorry, Father," she said, trying to soothe her father's anger.

"I'm not sure that is good enough," he replied. "You

two are both in serious trouble. The jungle is too danger-ous right now. Do not leave the defenses of the city again. Do you understand?" he asked angrily.

"Yes, Father," they both quietly replied.

"What's this city's name?" asked KP.

"Don't you know, travelers of time?" Lehi warily asked, testing their knowledge.

"If our scriptures are correct, we can't be far from the River Sidon," replied Bubba confidently. "Has the battle at Jershon taken place yet?" he asked.

"Which battle?"

"The battle where Moroni has the men in the army wear armor for the first time," replied Bubba.

"That's right. He has the men wear clothes that are sewn together and filled with sand. In addition, he has the men use head, arm and chest armor. The Lamanites are so scared, they leave and regroup for an attack somewhere else," said Hero.

"That's right, Hero," said Bubba. "So has the battle happened yet, Lehi?"

"Yes, last week," he replied.

"Has Captain Moroni sent messengers to the Prophet Alma yet," questioned Bubba.

"Not to my knowledge," Lehi replied, with a puzzled look on his face. "But I do not know everything Moroni does."

"Then we are in the city of Jershon, but we will soon be heading to the city of Manti," replied Bubba.

"Why?" asked Lehi.

"Because the messengers will bring news from the

prophet about the strategies of the Lamanites," he replied. "So, are we in the city of Jershon? Am I right?" Bubba asked.

"Yes, but I don't believe that the army will be leaving anytime soon," Lehi responded.

Quietly pondering what Bubba was saying, Lehi took the clothes from Kalia and handed them to the boys. "Follow Comonti and Kalia to our home. Move quickly, and change your clothes — you do not look like Nephites in what you are wearing. I am worried the people might mistake you for the thieves that stole the records of the people of Ammon. Go quickly, and I will meet you back there shortly. I must hurry if we are to speak with Captain Moroni today. He leaves for the jungle very soon. Speak to no one."

He turned to his son and said, "Comonti, draw no attention to yourselves as you travel through the city. Stay at home until I return. Do you understand?"

"Yes, Father," Comonti, replied.

Lehi turned and departed quickly into the city, which was bustling with people. They watched as he maneuvered his way through the crowds, politely shaking hands and greeting the citizens. Worried about what Captain Moroni would say, they watched nervously until Lehi could no longer be seen.

"Where's he going?" asked KP.

"To find Captain Moroni," Comonti answered, turning and heading for his home.

"This is so cool," said KP. "I never believed that we would be talking with men from the Book of Mormon — men that were faithful and cool."

"Stay focused, KP. Now is not the time to get an autograph," teased Bubba.

Following Comonti to a modest cottage hidden in the canopy of fig trees, the boys scurried inside. The interior of the home was beautiful. On the wall hung stunning tapestries. Several rugs adorned the floor in the main room and beautiful pottery decorated the family room. A small room to the east had an animal skin hanging over the opening. Comonti and Kalia's mother was rocking a baby by the fireplace when they entered.

"Mother, these our new friends, Hero, Bubba and KP. Father has asked us to stay here until he returns," said Comonti.

"Nice to meet you, boys," she answered softly. "Comonti and Kalia, you have chores. I need the figs picked from the tree today, or they will go bad. We cannot afford to waste the food the Lord sends to us."

"Yes, Mother," replied Comonti.

"Are you feeling any better today?" Kalia asked, concerned about the pain on her mother's face.

"I'm trying to feel better," she replied, swallowing hard. "Now get to work," she said smiling.

Comonti showed the boys into the small bedroom and said, "Change in here. When you are finished, meet us outside so we won't bother mother. She is not feeling well again today."

The boys nodded in agreement. Comonti then released his grip on the fur hanging in the doorway, allowing it to fall back into place. Quickly separating the pile of clothes Kalia had given them, they each slipped on a baggy, gunnysack-style shirt and short pants.

"Hey, these aren't pants — they're capris," said KP, holding them up to his waist. "Only girls wear capris."

"I think the men wear these and the girls wear dresses here, KP," replied Hero. "Don't worry. You'll still look cool."

Distressed, KP slowly pulled the capris on and tied them low on his waist, hoping to make them a bit longer.

"You're boxers can't hang out here, KP," said Hero. "We're not in the twenty-first century. No one here cares how you look."

"I'm sure some people here judge you based on your clothes," he replied.

"Well, what's the saying?" said Bubba. "Beggars can't be choosers, and right now, we are beggars!"

Laughing, Hero smiled and said, "Come on, guys. Let's hurry."

"What should I do with my shoes and clothes from home?" asked Bubba.

"Put them in your backpack," answered Hero.

The boys quickly folded their clothes and placed them in the bottom of their packs, along with their tennis shoes and socks.

"I'm not really good at making strap-on sandals work," said KP, as he grappled with tying them.

"I guess these two straps go in between your big and second toe. Then you probably pull these straps around behind the heel and tie them in a bow," suggested Bubba.

"Sounds good to me," replied Hero. "I guess maybe this sash ties around the waist?"

"Looks right to me," said KP, already tying his.

"Let's go," suggested Hero, as he grabbed his pack. He threw it over his shoulder and headed into the family room.

The smell of food from the kitchen made Bubba salivate. The boys were absolutely starving.

"Thank you, Mrs. Lehi," Hero said, as he moved toward the door.

"Have you boys had anything to eat today?" she asked.

"Not very much," answered Bubba, holding his stomach.

"I thought not," she replied. "Here are some turkey strips, wheat nuggets and figs to hold you over until dinner."

"Thank you so much," said Bubba, smiling from ear to ear.

"Can we help you with anything?" asked Hero, noticing she was in some pain.

"No thanks," she replied. "Now hurry outside. Comonti is waiting for you."

"May I hold your baby?" Hero asked, hoping to help.

"Do you know how?" she replied, surprised at his offer.

"Yes, I have a little sister at home," he answered smiling. "I can even change a diaper."

"That is impressive, Hero. If you could hold her for just a few minutes, that would be a great help," she said, handing the baby to Hero. "Please be very careful with her."

Hero took the baby, smiled and nodded. As Hero, the baby and the boys turned to walk outside, Hero noticed Mrs. Lehi reach down and rub her leg. He watched as a tear slowly rolled down her cheek. Once outside, the boys quickly found Kalia and Comonti in the fig tree, pulling the abundant fruit off the limbs.

"Why is you mother in pain, Comonti?" asked Hero.

"She traveled into the jungle, and her leg was scratched several times by a Lamanite trap, I think," he replied. "She has a bad wound, and her leg is not getting better."

"A Lamanite trap?" asked Bubba. "What is that?"

"The Lamanites carve tree branches into sharp points. Then the branches are dipped into poison from the Dart Frog," he replied.

"A frog?" asked KP, obviously shocked. "Are frogs poisonous?"

"Yes, we have several poisonous animals in the jungle, so you must be very careful not to touch any," warned Comonti.

"How did she come into contact with the poisonous branches?" asked Bubba.

"The Lamanites, knowing Nephite women and children pick fruit and flowers, laced the poisonous branches in with the branches of a Gongora Orchid growing at the base of a Cocoa tree. She was lucky that only one of the spikes scratched her leg."

"When did that happen?" asked Hero.

"About twenty-one days ago," he answered.

"How bad is it?" asked Hero.

"I'm not sure. I know she's getting sicker every day, and that she has less and less energy," he replied. "The poison must have been very strong."

"Some days she can't even move, or she drags her leg behind her," interrupted Kalia.

"I bet she has an infection," said Hero.

"A what?" asked Comonti.

"An infection," replied Hero. "She may die if she doesn't get rid of it."

"Die?" Kalia gasped.

"She could, if the infection goes untreated," he replied.

"What can we do for her?" Kalia asked nervously. "How can we treat the wound?"

"I will need to look at it," replied Hero, turning toward the house. "I don't know everything, but I'm sure I can spot an infection."

"She will not let you without Father here," said Comonti. "I'm surprised she's letting you hold the baby. She doesn't allow anyone, let alone boys, to hold the baby. She must be feeling really bad today."

"How old is the baby?" asked Bubba, holding her hand.

"She is seven full moons," replied Kalia.

"How old, Hero?" asked Bubba.

"I guess she means seven months," Hero replied.

"Look at her hair," said KP, pulling the blanket from her face. "She's beautiful. What's her name?"

"Her name is Isabelle," Kalia answered. "I wonder if Mother's too weak to hold Isabelle today. Maybe that's why she let you hold her."

"I thought she might get better, but now I don't

know," said Comonti. "I hope Father can help her. If something happens to Mother, I believe Father will leave the army."

"What?" asked Hero, confused at Comonti's remarks.

"I heard them talking last night," he replied. "Mother asked Father to leave the army and protect his children if anything happened to her."

"What did Lehi say?" asked Bubba.

"He told Mother that he would leave the army if anything happened."

Considering what Comonti said, Hero, Bubba and KP sat in the cool grass and watched Kalia maneuver her way to the top of the fig tree. Comonti caught the fruit as she threw it down. Playing with the baby and gazing at the beautiful scenery, the boys enjoyed their unfamiliar surroundings for the first time. The grass was a vibrant green, and the flowers were very colorful. Everything seemed 'cleaner' than at home.

"Why are only a few cottages around here?" asked KP. "We saw many more closer to the market."

"Our father teaches the warriors how to fight in battle on the open land over there," said Kalia, pointing to the north. "Captain Moroni leaves the field open for training."

"When do they have training?" asked Hero.

"Every morning at sunrise," Comonti answered. "Would you like to attend one morning?" he asked.

"To train?" questioned Bubba, concerned at the possibility of physical pain.

"Yes, to train for battle," he responded.

"I...I'm not so sure," Bubba replied apprehensively.

"I'm gonna check out the surrounding area," interrupted Hero. "Would that be all right?"

"Don't leave the yard until Father returns home," Comonti insisted. "He would be very angry with me for disobeying him twice today."

Hero agreed. He picked up the baby and said, "I will be right back."

As he maneuvered through the open fields, he saw several small rock paths and large boulders that dotted the field. As he glanced toward the city, he could see that Lehi's home sat on the crest of a small hill. From there, he was able to get a complete view of the area. Intrigued by his surrounding, he was amazed at how civilized this ancient city functioned.

He watched as the aqueduct, or waterways, brought in clean, fresh water from the river. The ducts were about three feet wide and three feet deep. They ran above ground, circling the city and then cutting straight through the center of town. As the aqueduct passed every cottage, a small trench, one foot deep and one foot wide, worked its way to every kitchen, bringing water to every cottage.

Hero could see that each cottage had a garden. He could see corn, peas, tomatoes, and even fruit and vegetables he did not recognize. Continuing his search, Hero watched as the downtown streets of the city bustled with people. Vendors sold their hand-made jewelry, clothes and shoes. Others sold food. Some danced around and played music to earn money.

"This is almost like being home," thought Hero warmly. "Oh, who am I kidding? There are no baseball games, no skateboards or bicycles, no television and definitely no internet here. In fact, I would love to play a Gameboy or something."

Suddenly, a stray arrow whizzed past his head, abruptly ending his peaceful daydreams.

Chapter Eleven

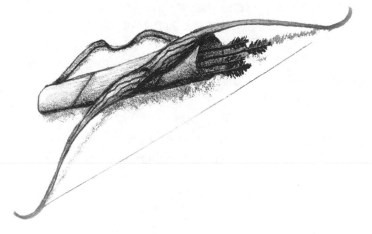

Ducking for cover, he yelled, "What's going on? I have a baby here."

"Sorry," shrieked a young girl, hurrying to make sure no one was hurt. She was not much taller than Bean. She had shiny, almost-black eyes that sparkled at everyone she met. And she had the longest, dark-brown hair Hero had ever seen.

"No problem," responded Hero, as he picked up the arrow and handed it back to the girl. "What are you doing shooting arrows anyway?" Hero asked curiously.

"Practicing, so that I can fight in Captain Moroni's army someday," she answered.

"Are girls allowed to fight?" he asked.

"Not usually, but then I'm not any girl," she answered.

"What do you mean?" he asked, puzzled.

"Well, I thought about cutting my hair and dressing like a boy. But then I figured, if Captain Moroni needs extra warriors to guard the city, he will know to look for me, and I will be ready," she said confidently.

Hero smirked and asked, "Do you think he will?"

"No, not really. But I can still hope. I am every bit as good as you are at shooting an arrow," she replied.

"No way!" Hero replied, smiling. "I'm positive you're a much better shot than I am."

Delighted by Hero's words, she smiled. "My name is Annah," she said. "What is your name?"

"My name is Hero."

"That is an odd name. I have never heard it before," she replied.

"I am from the North," he explained.

"Oooohh."

"Is that bad?" Hero asked.

"No," she quickly replied. "It's not bad. No one really knows much about the people from the North. You're young to have a baby already," she said, changing the subject.

"She's not mine," answered Hero assuredly. "I'm only fourteen."

"I am fourteen also," Annah replied. "If this is not your baby, then to whom does she belong? Or did you just take her?" she asked, smiling at Hero.

"This is Isabelle. She's the daughter of Lehi," Hero answered.

"The army trainer?" she asked. "Is he here?"

"Not right now," replied Hero. "But he will be back soon."

"I must leave. I will be in trouble if I am caught practicing," she replied, turning quickly to leave.

"No, wait," replied Hero. "Don't go."

Annah paused for a moment, turned and asked, "Why?"

"What if I can get permission from Lehi for you to practice here?" he asked.

"Can you do that?" she asked excitedly. "Do you really think you can?"

"Well, it can't hurt to ask," Hero replied. "Follow me."

As the two walked back to Lehi's home, Hero asked, "So, where do you live?"

"I live alone, not far from here, over on the other side of the waterway," she replied, pointing west to cottages in the distance.

"What? Why do you live alone? Where are your father and mother?"

"My father was killed in battle when I was very young. My mother was taken captive in the jungle as my people traveled with Alma to this city."

"Who takes care of you then?"

"I was eight when my mom was taken. I've lived with friends until recently, when they left with Alma to travel to another city. Now I live alone in their home," she replied quietly.

"Why didn't you go with them?" Hero asked.

"My mother will come for me," she replied confidently. "She knows I am here."

"How will she know where to look?" Hero asked. "Did she know where you were heading when she was captured?"

"The Lord will guide her to me. I am sure of it," she answered. "Now where are we going?"

Hero, sensing that she wanted to change the subject, pointed to Lehi's home not far in the distance and said, "There's the commander's home. Let me introduce you to his wife and family."

The two hurried toward the fig tree where Comonti and Kalia had been picking the fruit. Bubba and KP were asleep in the grass when Hero returned.

"Hey, everyone. This is my new friend, Annah," he called.

Bubba lifted his head and sleepily said, "Nice to meet you," as he held up his hand, ready to shake.

Not sure what that meant, Annah looked at Hero and shrugged.

"Bubba, they don't shake hands here, Goof," said Hero, pushing his hand away.

"Sorry, nice to meet you, Annah," Bubba said, standing up slowly.

Annah smiled and waved.

"And this is KP," introduced Hero, as KP looked up and smiled.

Again, Annah smiled and waved.

Comonti and Kalia returned with empty baskets to gather the figs they had picked. Comonti raced over to the stranger and asked, "Who are you?"

"Annah," she replied. "And you?"

"Comonti," he answered.

"Do you live in the city?" asked Kalia.

"Yes, north of here, next to the waterways," she replied. "And your name?"

"Oh, sorry. I'm Annah," she replied.

"I have not seen you in the city before," said Comonti.

"I live among the people of Ammon," she answered.

"Didn't the people of Ammon leave with Alma to the city of Mulek a couple of weeks ago?"

"Yes, two weeks ago," she replied.

"Why didn't you go?" Comonti asked.

"I am waiting for my mother to meet me here," she replied with a smile.

"Oh, will you go to Mulek when she returns?"

"Hopefully," she replied.

"So, where is she? When will she be back?" Comonti asked, as he picked up the basket and headed for the fig tree.

"I don't know," she replied.

"Why?" asked Kalia.

"My mother was captured in the jungle as we traveled to Jershon. She has been held captive for six years now."

"Are you serious?" asked KP, finally awake and paying attention to the conversation.

"Is she alive?" asked Bubba.

"I hope so," Annah replied. "I believe she is somewhere with the Lamanites."

"I'm sorry you don't have your mother right now," said Kalia sadly. "I would hate to be without mine."

The momentary silence was broken when the baby

suddenly screamed. Hero tried unsuccessfully for several minutes to console her. He sang to her, rocked her in his arms, and even checked her diaper, but nothing seemed to work. Annah watched impatiently as Hero struggled with the baby. Unable to wait any longer, she asked, "May I please hold her?"

"Sure," he replied grateful for the help. "My arms are killing."

Annah took Isabelle from Hero's arms. Cradling her tightly, she sang a song none of the boys had ever heard before. Quickly settling her down, Annah said, "She's hungry. We need to take her to her mother."

"That's probably a good idea," replied Comonti, as he continued to pick up figs. "Mother's probably worried about her."

Hero and Annah turned and quietly headed for the house with Isabelle. Hero knocked twice, opened the front door and hollered for Mrs. Lehi as he entered. Hearing no response, they moved into the kitchen and called to her again. Still they heard no reply.

"I wonder where she went," Hero said "She wasn't feeling well enough to travel very far." Hero walked back to the front door and called, "Comonti, did your mother leave?"

"No," he replied, as he stopped picking up the figs. "She's not in the house?" he asked.

"Not unless she's in her room," called Hero. "I didn't look in there."

Immediately concerned about his mother, Comonti dropped the figs he was collecting and raced toward the house. As he entered, he called with a loud voice, "Mother! Mother, are you in here?"

Still no response came. Comonti ran to the small room and threw aside the skin covering the door. He instantly spotted her, lying in a heap on the floor.

Panicked, he screamed, "Mother!" and quickly ran to her side.

Kalia heard the screaming from the field and ran toward the house. KP and Bubba following right behind her.

"What's the matter?" Kalia yelled, as she entered the room.

She watched in disbelief as Hero and Comonti carried her mother to the rug in the main room. Comonti tried desperately to revive her as Hero tried to figure out what was wrong.

"Her head is on fire," Hero said, as he laid his hand on her brow.

"What does Mom do for that, Hero?" asked Bubba, nervously watching from the door.

"Oh man, I'm not a doctor, and I don't know everything she does. I can only remember a few things," he replied. "Annah, give Isabelle to Bubba and help me please. KP, run to the ditch and retrieve a bucket of water, quickly. Kalia, collect some rags or towels. Comonti, do you know where your father might be?"

Comonti, completely in shock, did not immediately respond.

"Comonti!" screamed Hero, "Do you know where you father is?"

Looking over at Hero, Comonti asked, "Is she alive?"

Feeling her neck with his finger for a pulse, Hero replied, "Yes, but I need you to get your father quickly. Go as fast as you can."

Comonti jumped to his feet, looked down at Hero and said, "Please don't let her die."

"Comonti, go now. There's no time to waste. Run as fast as you can, and get your father, now!"

Comonti turned to the door and raced toward the city, terrified at the thought that his mother might not be alive when he returned home. He ran past the beautiful buildings in the center of town, through the market place and straight to the government plaza. He hoped his father would be there with Captain Moroni.

KP ran in the door with the bucket, spilling water everywhere, and Kalia had found some rags. Annah quickly doused the rags in the water and handed them to Hero. He grabbed them and frantically placed them on Mrs. Lehi's burning head. Then he rifled through his pack looking for some ibuprofen. Finding it quickly, he hoped the tablets would help to bring her fever down. Annah watched as Hero dripped water on her lips, trying to get fluid into her body. As he frantically tried to help her, he noticed blood soaking through her clothes, right above her knee.

"Kalia, come here quickly," he yelled.

"How can I help?" she asked nervously.

"Slide her dress to the side so I can see her knee," he instructed, pointing to the blood.

Kalia slid the dress over to reveal a gash that was a couple inches long and approximately one-half inch wide.

The wound was not unmanageable in size, but was oozing blood and yellowish-green goo. Kalia gasped in horror when she saw the wound.

Annah was also shocked by what she saw, but she held her composure. She placed her hand on Kalia's shoulder and said, "Don't worry, Hero will help her."

"Kalia, I need more rags, cloths, anything. Annah, find a chair, stool, basket or something I can place her leg on." Hero knew he had to raise her leg above her heart immediately.

Annah thought quickly and remembered the baskets Comonti had been using to collect figs. She ran outside to find one lying on its side. In the commotion, it had been knocked over and fruit was scattered everywhere. She snatched the basket, finished dumping out its contents and raced back into the house.

"Will this work?" she asked, holding up the basket.

"Yes, it's perfect," Hero replied, as he grabbed it from her hands.

He placed the bucket upside down and slipped it under Mrs. Lehi's knee, bringing her leg about twelve inches off the ground. Hero then grabbed the rags Kalia was holding and dipped them in the bucket of water.

"Kalia, Annah, help. She's too hot. We need to bring her temperature down immediately."

Neither girl was sure what to do, so KP jumped in and started placing wet rags all over Mrs. Lehi's body. He covered her arms, legs, head, and everywhere he could think to put a cold rag. But her body was still too hot.

"More water, KP, quickly," insisted Hero, pushing the bucket toward him.

Without a word, KP jumped to his feet and raced outside, returning moments later with another bucket of water. Hero knew the rags were not cooling her body enough to make a difference. He took the bucket from KP and sprinkled the water all over Mrs. Lehi's body, soaking her clothes.

"I need a cup or something she can drink from," said Hero.

Kalia grabbed one and Hero poured the remainder of the water from the bucket into the cup. He again tossed the bucket to KP to refill.

Hero tried to revive Mrs. Lehi enough to get her to drink. He dripped water onto her swollen, dry lips. Suddenly Lehi burst through the door, startling Kalia so badly she screamed.

"What are you doing?" Lehi demanded, seeing his unconscious wife soaked and covered with wet rags.

"Her body is on fire," replied Hero. "We have to reduce the heat, or she may never wake up. Help me!"

Lehi fell to the floor and grabbed the rag from her head. He dipped it into the bucket of cool water KP had just placed on the ground.

"We have to get this medicine in her," said Hero. He held down her bottom lip to drip water into her mouth.

"Why is her leg raised?" asked Comonti, watching from the doorway.

"KP, explain it to him, please. Lehi, help me to get her to swallow. Rub her neck softly, up and down," ordered Hero.

Lehi watched as Hero demonstrated. Then gently

picked up her head and softly rubbed the front of her neck up and down, trying to prompt her swallowing reflex. Several tense minutes passed as she lay lifelessly on the ground.

"I felt something," Lehi said, breaking the silence.

"Stop rubbing, and hold her head up slightly," Hero replied. He placed the cup to her lips and gently poured the water into her mouth. Watching closely to make sure she was breathing, he motioned for Lehi to start again. Suddenly she gasped and swallowed the water. She was still unconscious, so Hero tried again. This time, he placed the ibuprofen tablets inside her mouth. Then he poured just enough water from the cup to fill her mouth. Again he motioned for Lehi to gently rub. She gasped for breath and swallowed the water.

"What was that?" asked Lehi, tenderly holding his wife's burning body.

"Medicine from the future," he replied. "I only hope it works."

"Can it help her?" he asked.

"Yes, it will help her, but it won't fix the problem."

"What's the matter? Why is she not getting better," Lehi asked.

"Comonti told me she was scratched by a poisonous tree branch. Is that true?"

Lehi shook his head.

"What happened?" asked Hero, pulling away the rag that covered the cut above her knee.

"She needed some wood for the house to keep Isabelle warm. I was protecting the city and the children were away, so no one was here to help her. She tried to chop wood out back, but the blade slipped over the log when she swung, landing on her leg," he explained. "She did not want the children to worry, so she told them she wasn't feeling well because of a poisonous scratch. Is there anything we can do?"

"Yes, if only I had some super glue, antibiotic cream, and possibly a tetanus shot," Hero muttered, shaking his head.

"Hey, I think I might have some super glue," offered Bubba. "I never cleaned all of my school stuff out of my backpack."

"That's a start, Bubba. Check, will you?" asked Hero.

Bubba handed Annah the baby and ran outside to find his pack that was lying in the weeds by the fig tree. He grabbed the handle and ran quickly back into the house. Dropping on one knee, he turned the pack to face him, unzipped the front pocket and pulled out his pencil bag from class. Through the clear plastic, he spotted the small tube. Excited he declared, "Yep, I've got some. Sorry, I don't have antibiotic cream. I think Bean has it in the first aid kit."

Hero smiled and said, "What don't you have in there, Bubba?"

"Hey, I also have the bag of medicine from the school nurse. I was supposed to give it to Mom when school got out, but I forgot."

"What medicines are in there?" Hero asked hopefully.

"I don't know for sure — it's the medicine I had to take after my ear surgery. There might be something we can use," he answered, holding out the bag for Hero to see.

"Check for me, will you?" asked Hero, still tending to Mrs. Lehi.

Bubba unfolded the white paper bag, opened it and dumped the contents on the floor. He sorted through the pile and said, "Okay, I have a box of allergy tablets, a bottle of acetaminophen pills, lip balm, two throat lozenges, ear drops and a bottle of antibiotic tablets. Will any of that help?" asked Bubba.

"Really? Antibiotic tablets? Those could help. Let me see the bottle," Hero said, holding out his hand. "What did you need these pills for?" he asked.

"My ears. Mom gave the school nurse this stuff in case I needed any during the day. We didn't want to take the chance that my eardrum might burst, remember?" Bubba asked.

"I remember the surgery, but I didn't know Mom had all this stuff at school for you. Bless your messed up ears, Bubba. You may have just saved Mrs. Lehi's life."

Hero pulled the rag from Mrs. Lehi's head and placed the backside of his hand on her forehead. "She's cooling some. I think that's a good sign. Lehi, we should try to wake her again."

Lehi gently rubbed her face and called her name several times, but received little response. He continued softly talking to her, but her eyes remained shut. Hero knew she needed something more abrupt to wake her up, so he grabbed her hand and slapped it hard.

"Mrs. Lehi, wake up!" he shouted.

"Her name is Loriah," Lehi said softly.

She smiled softly without opening her eyes and weakly whispered, "Lehi, is Isabelle all right?"

Lehi pulled her close and said, "I thought you were gone, my love."

"I'm not going anywhere," she replied, slowly opening her eyes to see her husband and children. "Sorry to have scared you all. What happened?"

"You passed out and fell in a heap on the floor," answered Comonti.

Hero let out a sigh of relief and sat back against the wall. "Loriah, you scared me," he said, dropping his head into his hands.

She smiled lovingly at Hero and said, "Thank you for watching Isabelle." She slowly pulled her foot off the basket and tried to stand up.

"Oh no! You're not going anywhere," Hero instructed. "Please lie still. Lehi, we have to fix that cut."

"Loriah, stop and listen. This boy saved your life," Lehi tenderly said.

"I must wash the clothes, prepare the figs, fix dinner and take care of the children. I cannot lie here," she stubbornly replied. "I'm feeling better. I will be fine."

"Mother, you are not fine. Let him help you," pleaded Comonti.

"You will lie on the sleeping mat," said Lehi, "and you will listen to his counsel."

"But, I have things to do. Who will help me?"

"I will," offered Annah.

"So will I, Mother," added Kalia.

Loriah looked up at the young girl holding Isabelle

and asked, "Who are you, my child?"

Before she could answer, Hero interrupted and told Lehi and Loriah about Annah.

"Until my mother returns home, I can help," Annah said.

Loriah smiled and said, "Lehi, I would love for this beautiful girl to stay and be part of our family until her own mother returns."

"Annah, are you the girl who wishes to be part of the army?" asked Lehi.

"Yes, I practice everyday," she replied, holding her head high.

"Well, I have seen you practicing, and you are a very good shot," Lehi said. "Would you be willing to put down your bow and arrow, and live here with my family for a while?"

"Would you be willing to call upon me if your army ever needed my help?" she asked.

Lehi smiled and turned to Loriah who was looking sternly at Lehi. Understanding the meaning in her eyes, Lehi replied, "Only if there's no other choice. All right?"

Jumping with excitement inside, her voice squeaked as she answered, "All right."

"Comonti," called Lehi. "Help me carry your mother into our room. Be careful of her leg."

Comonti, Hero and Lehi moved Loriah into the small room and laid her on the soft straw bed, which was covered with animal skins. KP carried in the bucket of water and placed it close to her side. Hero and Lehi then cleaned the wound the best they could, as Loriah tried desperately to control the tears running down her face from the pain.

Hero showed Lehi how to close the wound quickly and explained the opening was a little large to glue, but felt it was their only option. Lehi held the wound closed tightly, just as Hero had shown him, while Hero quickly glued the skin together.

Lehi got a drop of super glue in between his fingers and panicked when he could not pull them apart. Loriah laughed, as his eyes grew bigger and bigger, while he tried unsuccessfully to pull them apart. Hero smiled too, as he showed Lehi how to separate his fingers.

Hero then placed several skins behind Loriah's back to make sitting more comfortable, and again placed the basket under her right leg. When he was finished, he read to her the instructions on the bottle of antibiotics that Bubba had brought, and he explained to her how it would help her to get better. Hero poured the tablets into his hand and counted them carefully.

"Twenty-one. Good," he said. "You have enough medicine for seven days. Loriah, you are about the same size as Bubba, so I think it's all right to follow the directions on the bottle. According to the instructions, you must take one tablet three times a day, until they are all gone, okay?"

Loriah looked at Hero and said, "I owe my life to you, son."

Hero beamed from ear to ear and answered, "No, only to the Lord. He must have sent me here to help you. I need to tell you one more thing, Loriah. This medicine will help to fight your fever. Do you know what that is?" Hero asked, as he showed her the ibuprofen tablets.

She shook her head.

"A fever is when your body is too hot," he replied. "Take one when you feel hot or your leg hurts badly. Also, my mom always tells us to drink a lot of water when we are sick, so try to drink often."

Grateful for the help, a tear streamed down her cheek. Hero smiled at her. Then he stood and left Loriah and Lehi alone together.

"Good job, Hero!" said Bubba, as he walked into the family room. "I couldn't have done that."

"Yeah, me neither. My heart was racing, and I was only watching. I must have spilled half of the water I carried to the house," added KP.

Annah, still holding the baby, smiled and asked, "So, you are from the future — not the North? No wonder your names are strange!"

"I didn't think you would believe me if I told you we were from the future," Hero replied, smiling shyly.

Lehi walked out of the room, pulling the animal skin across the opening. He strode over to Hero, put both arms around him and swung him in a circle. "Thank you, Hero," he whispered. "Thank you, everyone."

When he was back on the ground, Hero took hold of his head with both hands and tried to stop the room from spinning.

"Annah," said Lehi, "I think the Lord sent you to our home. Thank you for being willing to help us."

She smiled and said, "I'm glad to help. I was lonely all by myself."

"Well, you won't be lonely anymore — not with

Comonti, Kalia and Isabelle around," Lehi replied. He grabbed Comonti and Kalia and hugged them tightly.

"Father, stop," begged Comonti, embarrassed by the attention.

"Are you two okay if Annah lives with us for a while?" Lehi asked.

"A new big sister? You bet," replied Kalia, running to hug her.

Comonti nodded his head in agreement.

"Annah, Loriah is ready for the baby. Would you take her in? I have to leave with all the boys for a while. Can you keep an eye on all of my girls while I am gone?"

Annah, excited to be part of a family, grinned with excitement. "Yes!" she exclaimed.

Lehi motioned for the boys to follow and walked briskly outside. "We need to journey quickly if we are to meet Captain Moroni on time."

Chapter Twelve

The boys struggled to keep up with Lehi and Comonti as they moved hastily westward through the maze of cottages and buildings in the city. Hero wished they had time to look at the buildings, which were described in the Book of Mormon. He stumbled three times as he gazed at the beautiful stonework and detailed hieroglyphics carved in each stone, rather than watching where he was running. They finally reached the outermost walls of the city. Hidden in a small grove of trees was a quaint, but run-down cottage. Lehi stopped the boys outside the fence surrounding the cottage and motioned for them to wait.

Grateful for a chance to catch their breath, they stared at Captain Moroni's home. The cottage had smoke rising from a small stack on the south side of the roof, which was crumbling and in desperate need of repair. A small, odd-shaped opening, used as a window, faced the garden to the west. The fence that surrounded the house was broken, and in some areas was non-existent. A dozen chickens were scattered around the yard, and at least twenty or more eggs laid in the grass. The only part of the yard somewhat manicured was the area where beautiful flowers grew, just outside the front door of the cottage. Lehi quickly rushed inside and closed the door tightly.

Moments later, Lehi poked his head out the front door of the cottage and motioned for the boys to join him. Excited to finally meet Captain Moroni, they hurried through the broken gate and followed the small stone walkway to the cottage door. Stepping into the dark room, several awkward moments passed as the boys waited for their eyes to adjust to the darkness. Finally able to focus, they observed the interior of the cottage and its humble contents.

They noticed one small, motionless rocking chair next to a tiny fireplace. The fire inside the hearth was small and the burning embers cast an almost non-existent light. On the floor in front of the fire was a beautiful hand-woven rug that covered nearly the entire area. A tattered hammock, which looked unusable, stretched between two walls. They saw one small table next to the tiny window that overlooked the garden. The small table also served as the kitchen counter and washbasin.

As they continued to examine their surroundings, KP whispered, "There are no signs of life here — no food, clothes, mess, nothing."

"Where's Captain Moroni?" asked Bubba. "I thought we were meeting him."

Hero shrugged his shoulders and whispered, "I don't know."

Lehi closed the front door, making the small home even darker. He took five steps from the door to the table. He picked up a wooden plank and quickly placed it into the window's opening. Once the room was completely dark, Lehi shuffled across the floor from the kitchen to the fireplace. Suddenly, a loud creak broke the silence, as Lehi grabbed the tassels of the hand-woven rug in front of the fireplace. The boys were surprised to see a heavy door attached to the rug and a secret passageway concealed underneath.

"Come boys," Lehi ordered. "Climb down the ladder."

Afraid of what might lie ahead, Hero asked, "Where are we going?"

"And where's Captain Moroni?" asked KP.

"All will be revealed in time," responded Lehi. "Climb down this ladder to the room below. When you reach the bottom, wait quietly for me."

Bubba went first, struggling in the darkness to find the steps of the rough wooden ladder. Afraid of falling, he slid his hands down the splintered handrail, holding back a scream as a large sliver pierced his thumb. "Where are we going, Lehi?" he asked, as he shook his hand wildly, hoping that the pain would stop.

"Quiet, Son. You will understand soon," he replied.

After struggling down the remainder of the ladder, Bubba waited patiently in the darkness for Hero, KP and Comonti to join him.

"Where are we, Hero?" asked Bubba, as he pulled the sliver from his sore thumb.

"I don't know, Bubba," Hero answered. "Hang in there. I doubt Lehi would put us in any danger."

As the boys waited restlessly, Lehi pulled the door to the secret tunnel closed, leaving the room above quiet and undisturbed. The boys tried not to panic as the remaining light disappeared.

"Father, I can't see anything," Comonti said nervously.

"See with your faith, Son," was all Lehi whispered, as he moved across the dirt floor and fumbled with a small wooden torch. A flash splashed light across the tunnel, and for the first time the boys could see their surroundings.

"Where are we?" asked KP, looking down a small, narrow tunnel. "I really don't like dark or enclosed places."

"We're in a secret, underground tunnel that leads to the jungle outside the city walls," Lehi answered.

"What?" asked KP. "Why?"

"I've heard of these tunnels in stories before," Comonti interrupted excitedly. "You mean they really exist?"

Lehi forged quietly through the dimly lit tunnel, leaving Comonti's question unanswered. The torch he carried cast shadows on the walls and ground, playing tricks on the boys' eyes. The ground was uneven, and in many areas, was very difficult to move across. The boys crossed the rough terrain, at times on their hands and knees, as they struggled toward the jungle.

"Stories?" asked Bubba. "What stories have you heard?"

"I've heard stories about these tunnels since I was a child, but I never believed they were true," Comonti replied He could not wait to tell Kalia.

"Quiet now," insisted Lehi. "We must be cautious as we travel to where Captain Moroni is waiting. And Comonti, you can tell no one of these tunnels; the city's safety depends on your silence."

Noticeably disappointed, Comonti asked, "Not even Kalia, Father?"

"No, Son. No one can learn of these tunnels," he replied. "Many of Moroni's most trusted men do not know of these tunnels."

"Lehi, why would Captain Moroni be waiting for us in these tunnels?" asked KP.

Lehi was bothered by all the questions, but could tell the boys were nervous. "These are secret tunnels that were built to save our people in times of war — to be used if the enemy was able to break down our defenses and enter the city. A maze of tunnels runs underneath the city. They were designed and built by Captain Moroni. If you have been taught how to follow them, and which turns to take, they will lead you to the middle of the jungle, where you can hide from those who desire to kill you," he explained. "Now be quiet. No more questions. We will be meeting with Captain Moroni shortly. Follow me and stay close.

These tunnels can be very confusing."

Lehi continued moving through the tunnel. Having traversed a hundred yards of difficult terrain, the tunnel suddenly split in five different directions. Lehi opted for the third tunnel from their right. As they entered the opening, the ground immediately dropped four feet in elevation, and continued down an additional ten feet before the path leveled out. Two hundred yards further through the tunnel, the boys took a sharp turn to the left and ran directly into a dead-end.

"What now, Father?" asked Comonti. "I think we've chosen the wrong way."

Quietly moving ahead of the boys, Lehi reached the muddy wall. He looked over his shoulder at the boys and smiled as he stretched his hand to a rope above his head.

"This is where we go now," he said boldly. "Comonti, come here. You'll go first. Climb the rope, and wait for me at the top."

Lehi hoisted Comonti as far up the rope as he could, and then he waited for his son to reach the top. Then he called for Hero, Bubba and finally KP to follow. Once they had all shimmied up the rope, Lehi grabbed the end and climbed the ten feet to the top where the boys were waiting.

"I never expected that," said Bubba. "I would have seen the dead-end and turned around."

"Captain Moroni is a very smart man with his defensive earthwork," replied Lehi. "Come, we must hurry."

The boys quietly followed Lehi's lead for nearly one hundred fifty yards before encountering another split in the tunnel, which divided into another three legs. Lehi chose the tunnel to the north and continued in silence.

"How much longer, Father?" asked Comonti.

"Not far now," he whispered. "Stay quiet. We're almost there."

The tunnel began to narrow rapidly, forcing Lehi and the boys to again crawl on their hands and knees. As they followed the tunnel, the dirt turned to mud — almost like thick quicksand.

"What's happening?" asked Hero.

"I can hardly move through this stuff," complained KP.

"Boys, keep moving. This mud is caused by ground water," said Lehi.

"Ground water?" asked Comonti.

"The river is not far from here," replied Lehi. "Now, be quiet. We're deep in Lamanite territory."

Lehi took every step with great caution. He held the torch up as high as possible, watching closely for any hidden danger, as he and the boys moved slowly through the thick, gooey mud. Bubba was sure the mud was going to pull his sandals from his feet at any moment. He was grateful they were strapped on tight. About fifteen feet in the distance, the tunnel took a sharp turn north and opened up again.

"We will continue from here without light," said Lehi, as he doused the flame in the watery mud.

"Why?" Comonti asked anxiously.

"The fire and smoke from the torch can be seen from outside if it remains lit," he whispered.

"From where?" asked Hero.

"We are not far from the opening into the jungle," he

answered, as quietly as his commanding voice allowed. "Once we round the corner ahead, the opening is only twenty yards away."

Grateful to be standing and not crawling, the boys held one hand against the gooey dirt walls and trudged slowly toward the turn of the tunnel. As they rounded the turn, they noticed a tiny ray of light in the distance. Excited to see something other than darkness, they hurried toward the opening.

Suddenly, something struck Lehi from behind and knocked him to the ground with a thud.

"Father," cried Comonti, as he watched the dark shadow turn toward his voice.

"Lehi! Comonti! What's happening?" yelled KP.

Comonti screamed, "Watch out, KP!" as the dark figure moved closer.

"We're Nephites," said Hero, hoping that the stranger would stop attacking.

"Good," the crackly voice returned. "I don't care who you are. A few less Nephites would be fine."

"Quiet, Hero," said Bubba. "Don't make this worse."

The commotion in the tunnel was frantic, and the lack of light made fighting the assailant almost impossible. The muddy ground only added to the boys' frustration as they tried to fend off Lehi's attacker.

"Where is he?" yelled Comonti, still anxious about the condition of his father.

"I can't see him," replied Hero, as he turned wildly in circles.

Moments later, Hero received a well-placed strike to

his backside. The force of the blow sent his small, ninety-pound body flying violently through the air.

"Uuugggghhhh," he yelled, as he hit the wall hard and fell unconscious into a heap on the muddy floor.

"Hero! Hero!" called Bubba. "Are you all right?"

Hearing no response from Hero, Bubba cautiously crawled toward his brother's limp body that lay motionless on the ground.

"Where is he?" yelled Comonti, reeling from the unknown attacker.

KP screamed and jumped onto the attacker's back. "I've got him!" he yelled. "I've got him! Help me, quick!"

"Where?" shrieked Comonti. "Where are you?"

"Right here!" he muttered, as the assailant slammed KP's back multiple times into the muddy wall. KP's adrenalin was pumping, and his hold on the soldier was strong. KP knew the warrior had been trained well. He grabbed KP's arm and pulled one finger at a time as he peeled KP's hand from around his neck. Frightened, KP fought with all his might to keep his grip on the assailant. KP knew if the attacker removed him from his back, his life would be in danger. He tried to strengthen his grasp as the attacker thrashed around the cave, furiously slamming KP against anything he could. Several tense minutes of fighting passed until his attacker's strength was spent. The choke-hold KP had seen on television wrestling and used on the attacker had finally worked. The warrior passed out and sank to the ground.

"Bubba, is Hero all right?" asked KP, as he pulled his backpack off and opened the largest pocket. He retrieved some rope and tied the stranger's arms behind his back and his feet together so the assailant could not run. Moments after KP had the attacker tied up, he regained consciousness and struggled frantically for his freedom.

"Hold still. You're not going anywhere!" shouted KP.

"Looks like Hero's been knocked out," Bubba said to KP.

"Comonti, how about Lehi? Is he all right?" asked KP.

"I think he was hit on his head with a club. I see a little blood, but I think he's going to be okay," he answered, as he shook his father, hoping to revive him.

The prisoner smiled as he watched the boys struggle to awaken Lehi and Hero.

"Don't ever pretend to be Nephites again," said the prisoner. "I am one of Captain Moroni's best soldiers. He will rescue me," he added confidently.

"If my brother doesn't wake up soon, you're gonna hope someone rescues you," replied Bubba, scowling at the attacker.

"Who are you a soldier for?" asked KP.

"The great Captain Moroni," he replied proudly.

"We are on our way to meet with him," said Comonti. "Why did you attack us?"

"These are secret tunnels," said the attacker. "No one uses these tunnels without Captain Moroni's permission. No one was to be in here."

"Are you crazy? Couldn't you have asked before you attacked us?" questioned KP.

"Do you know you've harmed the great warrior, Lehi. He also serves Captain Moroni," said Bubba.

"I don't believe you," replied the attacker. "You would say anything to have me release you."

"Release us?" shrieked KP. "It's you who is tied up."

"Quit wasting your time with him, KP," said Bubba. "Let's move Hero and Lehi outside into the light. Maybe then we will be able revive them."

Comonti, unable to lift his father, took hold of his arms and pulled him the remaining fifteen yards to the opening. Bubba did the same with Hero. KP grabbed the ropes that bound the attacker's arms and feet, and forced him to the opening of the tunnel.

Bubba was afraid that Hero had been unconscious for too long. He worried that something might really be wrong with him. He softly tapped the side of Hero's face and repeated his name several times. Countless minutes passed, and Bubba's nervousness increased.

Finally Hero yelled, "Stop it, please. My head is pounding, and I don't need you to make it worse by hitting me." Hero tried to sit up, but the pain from the blow increased. "Oh man, my head is killing me. What happened?"

"You were attacked Hero. Are you all right?"

"I hurt everywhere, but I think I'm okay," he answered slowly.

Following Bubba's example, Comonti started to tap his father on the face, repeating his name several times. Lehi regained consciousness moments later.

"What's happened here?" he asked, as he opened his eyes and saw his son's face.

"We were attacked," Comonti replied.

"By whom?" asked Lehi, holding his head with both

hands, as he reeled from the pain.

"This soldier," replied KP, pushing the man into Lehi's sight.

"Who are you, Son?" asked Lehi, still unable to focus on the man's face.

"I am a soldier for Captain Moroni," he replied boldly. "And a good one."

"Why did you attack us?" Lehi asked.

"Captain Moroni didn't tell me of any one using these tunnels today," he replied. "You should not be in them."

Lehi shook his head back and forth slowly and said, "You better take us to him, Son. You're going to have some explaining to do."

"I'd never take men I believe to be working for Zerahemnah to meet the captain," he replied. "I know you would try to kill him. With the Lord's help and guidance, we will defeat your armies."

Tired of the boy's chatter, Lehi stood slowly. He grabbed the prisoner by the shirt and said, "Do you know who I am?"

"No," the attacker replied.

"Well, you should," stated Comonti.

Lehi looked over to his son and motioned for him to be quiet. "Then we will take you to meet the great Captain Moroni, and we will see who is lying."

Bubba helped Hero to his feet, while Lehi continued to hold his head with both hands. The boys and the prisoner followed Lehi as he cautiously entered the jungle. He led the way to the secret meeting location of Captain Moroni.

"He's going to owe me for this one," said Lehi, smiling. "My head is dancing with stars."

"Mine, too," agreed Hero. "I wish I could lie down and get some sleep."

"Hang in there, Little Captain," answered Lehi. "We will be there shortly."

The wall of trees, vines and bushes formed a perfect hiding place, right in the middle of the jungle. The hideout was approximately fifteen feet around and was large enough for only a handful of men.

"Lehi, my friend. I am glad to see you," called a quiet voice from inside the hideout.

"Thank you, Captain," Lehi softly answered. "I'm lucky to be here."

"Come into the cover quickly, before you are spotted and our hideout is discovered," Moroni said.

Everyone quickly scurried inside the hideout, ready and excited to meet the great and noble Captain Moroni. As the Team gazed upon the man, they were surprised at how young he looked. He was tall and slender, with dark hair. His eyebrows were thick and bushy, and his smile penetrated the boys' very souls. As the boys gazed upon his face, his eyes seemed to glow with righteousness.

"Was your journey safe?" asked Captain Moroni.

"Yes, it was fine," replied Lehi, as a trickle of blood dripped down the side of his head.

"What happened here?" he asked, looking to Lehi's son.

"Your warrior mistook us for the enemy," Comonti replied.

"We are fine," said Lehi. "He was protecting you, Captain."

"Pahoran, what have you done here?" asked Captain Moroni.

"I was protecting the tunnels, as you asked," he replied confidently.

"Did you not get my message that Lehi would be coming through today?" he asked.

"No, I did not," answered the soldier, a little more timidly.

"Are you hurt, Lehi?" asked Moroni.

"I am fine — just dazed for a moment," Lehi answered. "I wish we could teach all of our men to fight like this warrior did," said Lehi, as he placed his arm on Pahoran's shoulder. "Comonti, untie this soldier," Lehi said.

"Yes, Father," replied Comonti. He swiftly untied KP's ropes.

"Are you sure you're all right?" asked Captain Moroni.

"Yes, Moroni," insisted Lehi. "Is Pahoran the son of Nephihah?"

"Yes, he is," answered Captain Moroni.

"I know your father, Son," stated Lehi. "He would be very proud of you."

"I'm sorry to have hurt you," said Pahoran. "I was protecting our tunnels."

"I know, Pahoran," replied Lehi. "You have nothing to worry about. Continue to serve the Lord in righteousness." Turning to Captain Moroni, Lehi said, "Now, these are the boys I spoke of earlier today." He pointed toward Hero, Bubba and KP.

Captain Moroni looked on the boys and asked, "Where have you come from?"

"We're from the future. We're from the year Two Thousand Four A.D." answered Hero, still holding his head and steadying his wobbly legs.

"When I was a boy," said Moroni, "I heard stories of another man who claimed to travel back in time. Are you from the same time?"

"He lived one hundred years before us, we believe," answered Hero, with his eyes half closed from the pain. "We believe his name was Ole."

"Yes, Ole. That is correct. That is the name I've heard stories about. What happened to him?" he asked. "No one has seen him in many years."

"We're not sure," stated KP. "We believe he was killed."

"Tell me your names," demanded Moroni.

"I'm Hero."

"I'm Bubba."

"And I am KP."

"You are very young. Why would the Lord send children with a message?" he asked.

"We have no message from the Lord," answered Hero. "And we aren't much younger than you are."

Moroni smiled and asked, "How old are you, boys?"

"Thirteen and fourteen," said Hero. "And you are twenty-five?"

"Yes, twenty-five today," Captain Moroni answered. "You must be my birthday gift from the Lord. Now tell me, why has he sent you here?"

"We don't know yet," answered Bubba. "We believe

we are here to help you win the upcoming war."

"We can use all the help we can get. We are fewer in numbers than the Lamanites," replied Moroni.

"I don't think we are here to help fight," stated Hero. "I believe we are here to give you information we have learned from the Book of Mormon."

"How can you give me information that I don't already know?" he asked.

"We have a book of records called the Book of Mormon that gives us knowledge about you and the wars," Hero explained.

"Have you sent spies to the Prophet Alma yet?" asked Bubba, not looking at Captain Moroni, but peering through a small opening in the impenetrable trees.

"I have. They should bring me word any minute," replied Moroni. "That is why I had Lehi bring you to meet me here. You can listen to what they say, and then you can tell me if they bring the words from the prophet."

"I can read you the words from the prophet before they bring them to you," offered Hero. He unzipped his backpack and searched for the Book of Mormon.

"You can read to me while I watch for them," Moroni suggested, as he peered through another spy hole. "Oh, here they come now."

Bubba whispered, "Hero, look in the distance. Doesn't that look like the warrior who captured Bean?" He quickly turned away from the small hole before the warrior could see him.

"What?" asked Hero, as he looked through the trees to see the man Bubba was talking about.

"One of the two men, twenty yards in the distance?" asked Captain Moroni.

"I believe so," said Hero. "I think Bubba is right. He is one of the men who captured our friend, and she is being held prisoner by a Lamanite camp right outside the city."

Moroni gazed through the leaves and said, "No, you must be mistaken, Son. That is Coninihah — one of my most trustworthy spies. He has been traveling for two days to meet with the Prophet Alma."

"I am not mistaken, Captain. He is the warrior who took our friend," said KP, now seeing for himself. "If he sees us, all of our lives might be in danger."

"Lehi, quickly take these boys out the back. Hide them, and don't let them be seen," said Captain Moroni. "Let us see if they are correct."

"Comonti, boys, follow me," Lehi demanded, as he turned and maneuvered through the thick bushes. Outside the brush and trees of Moroni's hideout, they searched for a place to quickly hide. "Comonti, do you have your knife?"

"Yes, Father," he answered.

Lehi quickly cut several palm tree branches and laid them against a bush. Then Lehi directed the boys to be still and stay quiet.

"Comonti, remain here with these boys. I will return to the hideout and be back for you all shortly," said Lehi. "Don't say a word."

"Yes, Father," Comonti answered, quickly climbing behind the branches.

Hero, Bubba, KP and Comonti silently hid in the bushes, waiting nervously for Lehi to return.

Chapter Thirteen

"Why would a Lamanite be spying for Captain Moroni?" questioned Bubba suspiciously.

"I have no idea," replied Hero. "Maybe he's not a Lamanite."

"He has to be. I know he was one of the warriors who stole Bean. I'm sure of it," whispered Bubba. "I saw him with my own eyes being honored by the Lamanite leader." "Do you think he could be a double agent?" asked KP.

"Double agent?" questioned Comonti, not understanding the words.

"Yeah, he pretends to be a Nephite, but secretively he's really a Lamanite," Bubba explained.

"Oooohh, I get it," he replied.

"Why would Moroni have this spy go to the prophet for guidance from the Lord?" asked KP. "Wouldn't he know?"

"Well, do you remember in the scriptures when Moroni sends out spies to see what the Lamanites are doing? He sends those same spies to Alma for guidance from the Lord. Alma then revealed the strategies of the Lamanites to the spies, who in turn gave the information to Moroni," Bubba quietly explained.

"Yeah, I remember," answered Hero.

"Well, what if these spies of Moroni's aren't really spying for him?" asked KP.

"What do you mean?" questioned Hero.

"Yeah, what if they're really Nephites who became wicked and are actually warriors for the Lamanite leader Zerahemnah? By pretending to still be Nephites maybe they have deceived Moroni," said Bubba.

"Then Moroni's life is in danger," interrupted Comonti, still keeping watch.

"And everything in the Book of Mormon would change," added Hero.

"Do you think the Lord sent us to this time in the Book of Mormon — to perhaps stop this spy from carrying out whatever is his plan?" asked KP, with an excited expression on his face.

"Possibly," replied Hero.

"Maybe stopping the spy is the service we are to perform for the Lord," suggested Bubba. "Maybe this is why we have to have a strong foundation of the scriptures."

"That makes lots of sense to me," answered Hero smiling, as he contemplated what Bubba had suggested.

Comonti fidgeted nervously, pulling the leaves of the hideout to the side. He hoped to catch a glimpse of the warrior who was possibly a traitor.

"Do you know how many Nephite lives could be lost in battle if Captain Moroni has traitors working against him?" Comonti asked nervously. "Thousands could be killed, including women and children — people like my mother and sisters."

"Don't worry, Comonti," answered Bubba. "We're going to tell Moroni what we know from the Book of Mormon."

"How will that help?" he snapped.

"The Book of Mormon is a record of what happened in your time," he answered. "If the events aren't happening the way they should, we can help to change them so they do."

"How will that help me?" he asked. "I don't know what the future holds for my family."

"I know that under Moroni's command, the Nephite armies protect their families, rights and liberties," answered KP.

"Maybe those spies are trying to kill Captain Moroni right now," Comonti said anxiously.

"Are you kidding? With the great leader Lehi with him?" replied Hero, attempting to calm Comonti's nerves. "There's no way."

"Should we go check on them?" asked Bubba.

"No!" said Comonti. "My father said to wait."

Sitting quietly, afraid to move but hoping for the best, the boys waited. Twenty minutes, then thirty passed as they huddled together in silence, with no word from Lehi. Unexpectedly, a heavy rain began to fall. With no way to move and no covering over them, they sat in the pouring rain and watched as the drops of water hit the warm ground and immediately condensed into clouds of rising steam. The rain in the jungle was unpredictable, typically lasting just a few minutes. Even though this time the rain lasted only five short minutes, the boys were completely drenched. Waiting an additional twenty minutes, the boys were quickly losing patience.

Unable to remain quiet any longer, Bubba broke the silence and said, "Do you think they're dead?"

"Dead?" asked Comonti. "What do you mean?"

"I mean, we have been sitting here so long now, that both Captain Moroni and your father could be in big trouble," he replied.

"Bubba's right. We need to check on them," said Hero. "We should've heard something by now."

"I don't want to sit here without doing something any longer," said KP. "We've got to at least check to see if they're all right."

Nervous to disobey his father's wishes again, Comonti asked, "Bubba, are you absolutely positive the warrior you saw was the one who captured your friend?"

"Yes," answered Bubba confidently.

"We have to be careful. I don't want anyone to see us. We need to stay hidden as much as possible. Hurry, follow me, quietly," said Comonti.

Moving the palm leaves, he climbed out of the bush on his hands and knees and headed toward where his father and Captain Moroni were meeting with the two spies. The boys maneuvered the twenty yards toward Moroni's hideout on their hands and knees. The leaves on the bushes were wet, and every time the boys bumped them, they dumped more water. As the boys neared Moroni's hideout, they could hear several voices. Unable to determine exactly what they were saying, the boys inched closer and closer.

"Hero, do you hear that voice?" asked Bubba.

"Yeah."

"Isn't that the same voice we heard talking about records outside the city walls when we were waiting for Comonti to return?"

Hero listened carefully for several minutes.

"That is what he said," insisted one of the voices. "Look, here is his seal."

"No, I cannot accompany you back to the city right now. I have other spies depending on me to come back," said another voice.

"You're right. I'm sure of it, Bubba," Hero finally replied.

"What are they talking about?" whispered Bubba.

"I can't tell," answered Hero.

"Shhhhh," mouthed KP, holding up one finger to his lips.

Comonti noticed a small patch of reed and grasses, just large enough to create a tiny hiding place. Once inside, he poked his head out and motioned for everyone to follow. Slithering like snakes, they crawled into the tall grasses and listened to every word being spoken.

> "Thank you for your loyal service, Coninihah,"
> said Captain Moroni. "Without you, we would
> have no idea that the Lamanites are sending
> warriors toward the Prophet Alma and the city
> of Mulek."
> "Captain, serving with you has been a pleasure,"
> answered the strong, confident voice. "Will you
> be leading the army to Mulek?" he asked.
> "Yes," Moroni replied.
> "We must hurry. Our time here has been long,
> and there's much danger," said another voice.
> "We must return to our posts."
> "You're right," replied Moroni. "The Lamanite
> strategy is clear. I will meet up with you in two
> days as we journey together toward Mulek.
> Now, hurry and tell the rest of our brothers the
> plan."

Hearing the subtle slap of hands, Bubba assumed Moroni had reached out to shake the men's hands.

"Be safe, men," Moroni's voice called softly. "And may the Lord be with you."

The rapid shuffle of the two men frightened the boys, as the men scurried through the grasses and off into the distance. Comonti, sure that Moroni was still alive, breathed a little easier.

"Now I need to hear my father's voice," he thought.

"I think you're right, Bubba," whispered KP. "Those are the warriors who we heard outside the city."

As the rustling sounds of the men disappeared into the jungle, the men from inside Moroni's hideout finally began to speak. The boys listened intently to every word.

"Do you think they were telling the truth?" asked Lehi.

"What do you think, my brother?" asked Moroni.

"Not one word," he answered frankly.

"I fear we have a traitor in our midst," he answered solemnly. "I wonder when his heart changed."

"Moroni, you must not blame yourself," Lehi said compassionately. "I am grateful those boys recognized him."

"Yes, I would have believed every word he spoke. I had no idea of Coninihah's unfaithfulness until I looked into his eyes just now. Also, I believe Alma's seal has been altered." Moroni paused a moment before he continued. "Many lives have been saved because those boys recognized him," he replied. "Tell me more of these boys. Are they trustworthy?"

"I believe they are," Lehi replied. "They bring with them a book, and claim it is our father's fathers' book of records. The records are similar to those that have been stolen from the city, but they are sacred records from all the prophets."

"Go and retrieve the boys, Lehi," requested Moroni. "I wish to know what they have to say. I need to know if what Coninihah said has any truth or not." Lehi turned to gather the boys when Moroni continued, "Lehi, in my heart I believe the men I have trusted for years have stolen the people of Ammon's records. Now, how do we get the records back?"

"The Lord will provide a way," Lehi replied, as he turned and left the hideout.

Hurriedly, the four boys jumped out of the grasses and raced back to the place Lehi had told them to wait. They had barely slid into the bush and pulled the leaves into place, when Lehi climbed out of Moroni's hideout, heading straight for them. Moments later, Lehi pulled back the palm fronds and said, "Moroni would like to speak with you now."

Trying not to look winded, the boys silently nodded their heads in agreement. They quickly followed Lehi back toward Captain Moroni. As they walked, KP suddenly noticed a bright red blob with shiny silver straps ahead of them. Frantically looking over his shoulder, he could see he was no longer wearing his backpack. Not sure what to do, he softly tapped Hero on the shoulder and pointed to his pack in the grasses ahead.

"I was sitting on it before we ran back," KP mouthed.

Hero shook his head and whispered, "What do we do?"

Comonti, watching the two silently communicate, understood exactly what had happened.

"Follow my father. I will retrieve the bag," he whispered.

They quietly followed Lehi ten yards further toward Moroni, praying Lehi had not noticed the pack.

As Lehi pulled back the reeds and grasses, he introduced the boys. "Moroni, here are the boys — Hero, Bubba and KP."

Comonti retrieved KP's backpack and quietly sneaked in unnoticed, just before Moroni started speaking.

"Thank you for reminding me of their names, Lehi. Boys, I need to know what information you bring," he started. "Coninihah has met with the Prophet Alma. His message to me is to prepare for battle again here in Jershon. Zerahemnah is fortifying his armies, and half of them will attack here. The other half of his army is moving on to Mulek. Most of our soldiers will need to be sent there to reinforce the small army already defending its boundaries."

"That's a lie," interrupted Bubba.

"How do you know that?" Moroni asked sternly.

"He is the warrior from the Lamanite camp who was honored for capturing our friend," started Hero. "The leader of that camp said he would be preparing to meet you in battle in three days. At that time, he planned to trade our friend for the return of the Lamanite lands. The leader of the Lamanites believes our friend is the daughter of a Nephite captain. They plan to use her as a tool to gain your surrender, and then they plan to destroy the Nephites."

"How do you know that the Lamanites are not going to attack the city of Mulek or Jershon again?" he demanded. "I have trusted this spy for nearly two years. He has never given me bad information."

"I'm sure Lehi has told you that we're from the future. In that time, we study the records of your time," answered

Bubba, as he pulled off his backpack and found the scriptures inside. "Moroni, let me read to you what Alma actually advised your spies."

Bubba opened his scriptures and flipped to Alma 43:23. "'But it came to pass, as soon as they had departed into the wilderness Moroni sent spies into the wilderness to watch their camp; and Moroni, also knowing of the prophecies of Alma, sent certain men unto him, desiring him that he should inquire of the Lord whither the armies of the Nephites should go to defend themselves against the Lamanites.' Do you want me to go on?" Bubba asked.

"Do the writings you have tell me what the prophecies of Alma were?" asked Moroni, intently listening to every word.

"Yes, they do."

"Please continue, Bubba," said Moroni.

"Verse 24: 'And it came to pass that the word of the Lord came unto Alma, and Alma informed the messengers of Moroni that the armies of the Lamanites were marching round about in the wilderness, that they might come over into the land of Manti, that they might commence an attack upon the weaker part of the people. And those messengers went and delivered the message unto Moroni.'"

"I believe that I need to send additional messengers to Alma," announced Moroni. "Hero, Bubba, KP and Comonti, I need you to travel to the Prophet Alma and inquire of him again the intent of the Lamanites, and whither the Nephites should go to defend themselves. Alma has accompanied the people of Ammon to the city of Mulek until the fighting at Jershon is over. Then they plan to return here, having kept their covenant not to take up arms against their brethren. I wish for you to travel to Alma and return with his correct prophesies."

"Father, may I go?" asked Comonti excitedly.

"If Moroni needs you, I will honor his request," replied Lehi.

"Will you travel to Alma and return to me with his prophecies about what will take place?" Moroni asked the boys.

"Yes, we will," replied Hero, watching KP and Bubba nod. "But how will you know we are telling the truth? We have already told you what our records say."

"The same way I knew my messenger was lying," he replied. "Alma will send with you his written prophesies on a small brass plate carved with a personal mark — his seal. Return the seal from Alma unaltered. Then I will know you are telling me the truth."

"When should we leave, and how do we get there?" asked Bubba, excited to meet Alma.

"Leave today, but first travel back to the city and collect supplies. After you have done that, Lehi will take you to where your journey begins and direct you how to reach the city of Mulek."

"Once we reach Mulek, how will we find the prophet?" asked KP.

"The Lord will provide a way," Moroni answered, "if you are truly here to do his work." Pausing, he turned to Lehi and said, "Lehi, my friend, return these boys to the city and help them prepare for their journey."

Lehi nodded and swiftly maneuvered back into the open jungle. "Come boys. We have been here too long and we are no longer safe."

Without a word of goodbye, Moroni and Pahoran departed. As the boys turned around to wave, they were already gone. Disappointed, they turned back to Lehi, only to catch a glimpse of him far in the distance. Knowing they could not yell, they hurried to catch up with him. Lehi spoke few words on the return trip home. They followed the same path back to the city of Jershon. They were scared but hopeful they would be able to find the city of Mulek, locate Alma, receive his personal seal and return it to Moroni quickly — hopefully without any difficulties. Anxious to start their journey, the boys hurried toward Lehi's home to collect the supplies they would need for their trip.

Chapter Fourteen

Stuffing their packs with the food from Loriah's kitchen, the boys were anxious for their journey. Hero never thought Captain Moroni would choose them to travel through the dangerous jungle to retrieve the Prophet Alma's prophecies. But short of men, time, and in need of someone he could trust, Moroni allowed the boys to go. Lehi waited apprehensively for the boys to meet him at the edge of the city. Unsure about allowing them to go on the journey, he silently prayed for the Lord to watch over them as they traveled through Lamanite infested lands. As he watched the boys approach, his anxiety mounted.

He hugged Comonti tenderly and said, "Be careful, Son. Hurry home."

"I will, Father. We'll be fine," he answered. He wiped a tear from his eye, pretending to brush his hair back off his face.

Lehi stood very tall next to Bubba. Lehi reached out and hugged him, smashing Bubba's face into his chest. The same hug followed for Hero and KP.

Finally, Lehi stepped back and announced, "The path to Mulek is difficult. You must climb the mountain and then cross the river before reaching the city."

"We can do it, Father. Don't worry," said Comonti.

"Son, there will be many obstacles. Don't think this journey will be easy," he warned. "You must be cautious, and always anticipate danger nearby."

"Okay, Father. We will," he replied.

"We will, Lehi," added Hero, pulling Comonti's arm. "We have to go. Captain Moroni said the journey would take at least a half-day's walk."

"And without the Prophet Alma's blessing, he will not leave for Manti," answered Lehi. "Hurry, you must return quickly."

Lehi watched with a heavy heart as the boys ran outside the safety of the walls of Jershon toward the treacherous jungle that led the way to Mulek.

The journey to Mulek seemed different than anything the boys had seen so far. Although the jungle had been green and lush in the valley, the path they now followed up the mountain became dense with foliage that completely blocked any sun from shining its warm rays through the canopy. Animal life appeared more abundant, as lizards and snakes slithered furiously around their feet. Monkeys were everywhere, screeching louder the higher they climbed. Several iguanas lazily perched themselves on fallen trees, blending in with scenery, and startling the boys when they abruptly moved.

The boys cautiously and apprehensively followed the path into the mountains. Watching their surroundings closely, they jumped at every unfamiliar noise.

"I can't believe how loud the animals are up here," said KP.

"Yeah, I don't remember them being so loud in the valley," said Bubba softly.

"They stay higher in the mountains for added protection and ample food," explained Comonti, noticing a dark cloud floating overhead. "We need to move faster. This cloud is going to burst any minute."

"Burst?" asked KP.

"Start raining," replied Bubba. "Duh."

Suddenly the clouds in the sky seemed to burst open and dump humongous drops of water right on top of their heads. The water continued to pour longer than any of the other storms since the boys had arrived. After more than an hour of torrential rain, water was gushing down the path, making the walk up the steep incline even more difficult. The rain soaked everything they owned. As they reached the crest of the mountain, the water was puddled six inches deep.

Bubba hated to be cold and wet. Trying to stay out of the water as much as possible, he walked along the outer edge of the path that overlooked the valley. Afraid of heights, he held on to the tree branches that lined the path. As he grabbed the next branch, a large bird surprised him with a loud 'squawk'. Bubba looked up to see a beautiful yellow, red and blue toucan with an enormous beak.

"Hey, look at that," he called excitedly.

"What?" asked Hero, trying to see where Bubba was pointing.

"Everybody come here. Quick!" yelled Bubba. "There's a toucan hiding behind this branch," he said, pulling the branch down as far as he could, trying to let everyone see.

Hero, KP and Comonti moved closer to the edge of the trail to see the bird. Suddenly, the dirt on the edge of the path crumbled underneath their feet. In the blink of an eye, the boys disappeared off the ledge.

They slid uncontrollably down the mountain. Carried quickly by the mud and rain, they were unable to determine the direction they traveled. They hit trees and bushes with their bodies, tearing some out of the ground by the roots. KP screamed with all his might as the mud and water splashed over his head, covering his face so that he could not see where he was going. Bubba hit every dirt mound with a thud, creating a path for everyone to follow. As he continued sliding down the hill, he bounced off a mound of palm trees and moaned in pain. Hero, directly behind Bubba, bounced from side to side, grunting as he hit bushes and rocks.

The ride lasted approximately three full minutes and covered more than two hundred yards. Then KP shot off the mountain's ledge. Hurled violently in the air, he fell ten feet and splashed into a muddy stream below. KP's, flying technique was quickly tried without success by Bubba, Hero and Comonti, the only boy screaming in delight as he slid down the mountainside.

"Waaaaahhooooo!" yelled Comonti, as he landed in the stream. "That was great!"

Hero wiped the mud from his eyes and blinked several times to clear the dirt. Still struggling to see, he squinted hard and located Comonti and Bubba in the distance.

"Where is KP?" he called.

"I can hardly see," replied Bubba. "I don't know."

"He's got to be close," replied Comonti, as he stood up and searched the area.

"Here he is!" exclaimed Bubba, as he crawled to the edge of the stream.

"Are you okay, KP?" Bubba asked.

KP coughed violently for several seconds before he could answer. Finally, he said in a shaky voice, "I'm okay — I think."

The boys stood up and tried to determine where they had finally landed. The rain stopped as abruptly as it had begun.

"How did that happen?" asked Bubba.

"Storms like that happen all the time. The rain here soaks the ground, and occasionally the dirt gives way," explained Comonti. "I've never gotten to ride a mud slide before. Wasn't that fun?"

"Fun?" asked KP. "I'm glad to be alive."

"Was the ride really that bad?" Comonti asked.

Smiling, the boys had to agree that the ride, though scary, was a lot of fun.

"But I'm sure gonna be sore tomorrow," complained Bubba, rubbing his backside.

"Sliding down the mountain was almost like the drop of a roller coaster. The car climbs to the highest point, pauses just a moment, and then falls as fast as it can," said Hero, making the motion of a roller coaster car with his hands. "I think we should name that slide down the hill, 'Extreme Water Slide: Nephite Edition'," he suggested smiling.

The boys laughed as they crawled out of the ravine and onto the jungle bank. Hero and Bubba sat on a dead tree log, while Comonti and KP lay in the wet grass trying to catch their breath.

"I wonder what's gonna happen next?" asked KP. "I'm not sure my heart can handle much more."

"You should know better than asking that question, KP," warned Bubba nervously.

"Don't be superstitious, Bubba," said Hero. "Everything will be fine."

The words had barely left Hero's mouth when an arrow whizzed by their heads, hitting the tree behind him. Startled by the arrow flying by their heads, Hero and Bubba quickly climbed over the log and hid.

"What was that?" asked KP, who had been lying on his back with his eyes closed.

"An arrow," replied Bubba. "You two better get behind something."

"Who's shooting at us?" asked Hero.

"Probably Lamanite warriors. My father said many are

in this area, and we were screaming pretty loudly," Comonti said.

"What do we do?" asked KP, afraid to move.

"I will count to three," answered Hero, "and then you two move as quickly as you can behind this log. Okay?"

"Okay," replied KP and Comonti.

Hero began, "Ready? One, two, three."

Both boys hurriedly jumped behind the safety of the old log.

"Any idea where they are?" asked Bubba.

"I haven't seen them yet," replied Hero. "I wonder how many warriors are out there."

A voice from the distance yelled, "You're trespassing on our land. The punishment for trespassers is death."

Without warning, several furious screams sounded an attack, as ten more arrows flew all around the four boys.

"We've got to get out of here," said Hero. "Now!"

Comonti sat up and peered over the log to see a dozen or more Lamanite warriors running at them.

"Come on! Follow me! Hurry!" he yelled, as he jumped to his feet and ran through the tall grasses and reeds.

Pulling his machete from his waistband, Comonti started slashing everything in sight. He knew they had to escape the warriors who were following not far behind them.

"Any idea where we are?" Hero asked, following closely behind Comonti.

"Not really. I've never been this far away without my father," he responded.

"Don't worry. We can escape," said Hero confidently.

The boys hacked their way through more than fifty yards of grasses. Comonti swung his machete one last time to reveal the edge of a cliff. With nowhere to go, the boys stood on the edge of the cliff and scanned the area. They soon realized they were standing on one side of a cliff, and approximately thirty feet away was another cliff, with a seventy-five foot drop to jagged rocks in between.

"Oh man! You've got to be kidding. Where do we go from here?" asked KP, as he looked over his shoulder, sure the attacking warriors were getting closer. He knew they had only a minute or two before the warriors attacked.

Unsure what to do, the boys quickly checked both directions along the cliff's edge. They saw nothing that could help them — no bridge, no escape, nowhere to go. They were doomed for sure. Bubba, who was afraid of heights, held on to the thickest vine he could find. He closed his eyes as tightly as he could and waited for Hero to find an escape route. Comonti and Hero were desperately trying to find somewhere they could hide until the warriors were gone. As Hero ran by Bubba, he accidentally knocked him off the edge of the cliff. Bubba was headed straight for the rocks below.

Afraid to open his eyes, but too nervous to keep them closed, Bubba screamed as he peeked at the scenery fifty yards underneath his feet. "Aaaaahhhhhhhhhhhhhhhhh-hhhhhhhhhhhhhhhhhhhhhhhhhhhhhhhhhhhhhhhhhhhhhhhh-hhh!" Gulping in more air he continued screaming, "Aaaaaahhhhhhhhhhhhhhhhhhhhhh," with all his might. The vine he was holding on to swung across the gorge to the cliff on the other side. As he reached the edge of the other cliff, he did not want to swing back over the gorge. So, Bubba instinctively released his grip on the vine and dropped onto the ground with a thud.

As he landed, he grunted, "Uuugghhh! Ouch!"

Bubba opened his eyes wide and fell to his side, grateful to be back on land. He held his chest, as he tried to calm the rapid beating of his heart.

Comonti, Hero and KP watched in disbelief as Bubba safely landed on the other cliff. Hero nervously called, "Bubba, Bubba, are you all right?"

After several tense moments passed in silence, Bubba answered.

"I made it! I'm all right," he yelled, trying hard to smile at Hero, KP and Comonti. "Hurry! You can do it. Don't let the warriors get you. I don't want to be over here by myself."

With the warriors' screams close in the distance, the fear of being captured was more frightening than jumping. So, the boys grabbed vines and jumped together. Comonti calmly rode his vine to the other side, lifting his legs barely high enough to clear the cliff. KP watched Comonti's landing. He also lifted his feet and legs as he reached the other side — just high enough to clear the cliff's wall. Hero, however, did not. With a thump, he crashed into the side of the mountain. Though he was in tremendous pain, he knew if he let go of the vine, he would fall to his death below.

"Pull me up! Pull me up!" he yelled, as several arrows slammed into the rock wall all around him.

Bubba reached over the edge as far as he dared, stretching his hand out for Hero to take hold.

Hero stretched with all his might. He wiggled his body wildly, attempting to grab Bubba's hand. But Bubba's arm was just out of his reach.

"I can't reach!" he shouted, terrified he was going to be hit in the back at any moment with a Lamanite arrow.

Comonti and KP urged Hero to try again. Hero took a deep breath, closed his eyes for only a moment, reached up as high as he could on the vine, and pulled with all his might. He tried desperately to reach the outstretched arms of his brother.

"Come on. You can do it!" Bubba urged. "You're almost there."

With one last stretch, Hero's hand finally caught hold of Bubba's.

"I've got him. Help me!" Bubba yelled, as he pulled as hard as he could.

With Comonti and KP's help, Hero was over the top in no time. He lay on the ground gasping for breath.

As they stood looking at Hero, Bubba let out a terrifying scream.

Falling back, he squealed, "I've been hit! I've been hit!"

Comonti quickly grabbed Bubba's arm and dragged him on his stomach into the shelter of the trees. Once the boys were in the protection of the trees, Hero saw the arrow sticking out of his brother's left shoulder.

"What do we do?" he asked. "Do I grab hold and pull it out?"

Comonti, familiar with arrows and the damage they

can cause if they are pulled out, held his hand up to stop Hero. "No, wait. We need to see how deep it has gone first," Comonti warned.

Comonti inspected the wound without disrupting the arrow, but was unable to get a close look because of the pack on Bubba's back.

"Can we get this thing off?" Comonti asked.

Hero pulled Bubba's right arm through the strap and carefully tried to maneuver the pack over the arrow to free the left arm. Surprisingly, he found that the backpack itself was attached to Bubba's back by the arrow. Hero gently pulled up Bubba's shirt to examine the damage to his shoulder. But with every movement, the arrow tore deeper into the skin, bringing blood to the surface of Bubba's shoulder.

"The arrow has pierced your pack and is only scratching your skin, Bubba," reported Hero. Tremendously relieved, Hero grabbed Bubba's pack and lifted it off, taking the pain-causing arrow as well.

"The arrow only caused a small wound, Bubba," said Hero, as he lifted Bubba's shirt for a better look.

"Then why is my back stinging so badly?" he asked, trying to reach back and rub the painful area.

"The Lamanites often dip the heads of their arrows in poison," said Comonti. "We need to hurry to the city of Mulek as fast as we can. The people there will know what to do for him."

"Poison?" asked Bubba, panicking. "Will it kill me?"

"It could," Comonti replied quietly. "We need to find the city quickly."

"How do we find the city?" asked KP. "We have no idea where we are! After the 'Extreme Water Slide: Nephite Edition' and the 'Swinging Vine of Terror', I'm pretty sure we're lost!"

"Let's be calm! We can't help Bubba if we freak out," replied Hero. "Comonti, do you know where we might find any water?"

Unsure exactly why Hero needed water, Comonti grabbed a Liana vine and cut it open. "There is water in these vines," he said, as he handed the vines to Hero.

"Good. Bubba where is your hackey sack?" asked Hero.

"Why?" asked Bubba.

"Bub, where is it?"

"In the small pocket inside my pack," he answered.

"KP, get the hackey sack for me, and get Bubba's allergy pills from inside his pack."

KP moved without saying a word. Hero pulled the vines over to Bubba's back and began to pour water over the wound. KP found the hackey sack and handed it to Hero, then continued to look for the allergy pills. Hero took the hackey sack and forcefully rubbed its rough outer edge across Bubba's cut.

"What are you doing?" Bubba screamed in pain.

"Getting rid of the poison. Hang in there."

As Hero poured the rest of the water from the vine on Bubba's back, he noticed a bright red rash.

"Did you find that allergy medicine, KP?" asked Hero.

"Yes, here you go," KP, replied.

"My allergies are all right, Hero. Why do I need this?"

Bubba asked, holding the bright blue pill.

"I hope the antihistamine will fight the effects of the poison," he replied. "Kind of like a bee sting."

Bubba swallowed the medicine and lay in the grass, trying to cope with the pain.

"Lehi said we'd need to climb the mountain and then cross the river, right?" asked Hero, looking over their location.

"Right," answered Comonti.

"Well, we climbed the mountain and slid down the other side. Then we crazily leaped off the edge of the cliff and 'Tarzaned' to the other side of the river. So, I think we could be fairly close."

"You're right," agreed Bubba. "I bet we're close," he said, cringing in pain.

"We've got to keep moving," said Comonti. "My best guess is we need to head northwest from here. Should we get going?"

Everyone agreed.

As Bubba leaned over to pick up his backpack, Hero watched him grimace in pain.

"Let me get that for you," he offered, grabbing the pack from Bubba's hands. "I'll carry it until we get to the city. Okay?"

Bubba managed a small smile. "Thanks, Hero."

The boys moved northwest through the jungle, following Comonti as he cut a path through the greenery with his machete. The boys knew they had to reach the city, where they could get help for Bubba and find the Prophet Alma.

Chapter Fifteen

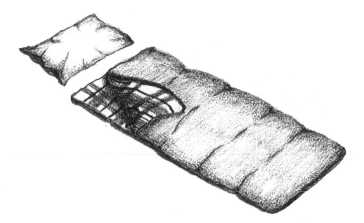

Back home, Tater hurried everyone from the kitchen to the Treehouse, anxious and excited to decipher the scriptures and finish the clues Cheri had translated for them. Holding the ladder steady, he watched as Squeaks, Stick, Runt, Butch, Red and Bear climbed to the top. When Tater reached the top, he pulled up the ladder so the Team would not have any unexpected adult visitors. They rolled out their sleeping bags in a circle, placed a bag of goodies in the middle and got ready to work.

"Is everyone as excited as I am?" asked Squeaks, holding up her shaking hand.

"How do you think we got through to them?" asked a perplexed Runt.

"I bet the Lord needs us to tell them what they have to do to get home," reasoned Butch. "That is why they heard us call."

"If that's true, then we better get to work. We have a lot to do," added Tater.

"I have my scriptures ready," said Squeaks, holding them up for everyone to see.

"I'm not sure I quite understand what we are doing now," admitted Bear, with a puzzled expression on his face. "Where did you get the clues from, and how are they going to help the other teammates?"

"We'll have to show you later where they came from. But Cheri, the librarian, translated the clues for us," replied Tater.

"If they have been translated, then why do you need to do anything with them?" asked Bear.

"Sorry, Bear. Let us show you. Butch, do you have the translations?" asked Tater.

"Yes, would you like me to read the first one?"

Tater nodded his head, and Butch began,

"As you travel in Alma 34:32, doing service for the Lord,
Your Words of Mormon 1:8 will be tested; your return is the reward.
Take heed in the Lord's promptings, and remain 1 Nephi 3:16 in all things.
The Liahona will direct you, providing the Alma

9:26 you will need.
The Book of Mormon is your Mosiah 2:36, at
your side shows you the light.
Keep it with you as you Alma 37:41, setting back
what is not right.'"

"Do you understand now Bear?" asked Tater.

Bear nodded his head and said, "I sure do."

"I wish Bean was here to help. She's great at finding the right words," stated Red.

"Don't give up yet. We can do this," said Tater.

"I've got the first scripture," said Stick. "Everyone ready? Alma 34:32, 'For behold, this life is the time for men to prepare to meet God; yea, behold the day of this life is the day for men to perform their labors.'"

"Hey, this one is easy. The clue reads, *'As you travel in Alma 34:32, doing service for the Lord.'* Well, the only word in the scripture that references travel is the word *time*," said Squeaks.

"I think you're right, Squeaks. Good job," said Butch. *'As you travel in time, doing service for the Lord.'"*

"All right. What's next?" asked Red.

Butch read the second line. *"'Your Words of Mormon 1:8 will be tested; your return is the reward.'"*

"I've got that scripture," said Bear, smiling. "Words of Mormon 1:8, 'And my prayer to God is concerning my brethren, that they may once again come to the knowledge of God, yea, the redemption of Christ; that they may once again be a delightsome people.'"

"Maybe we don't need Bean," said Red. "I think either

knowledge or knowledge of God will fit."

"'*Your knowledge will be tested; your return is the reward,'*" read Butch. "That sounds right."

"Good, we're moving right along. What's next?" asked Tater.

"'*Take heed in the Lord's promptings, and remain 1 Nephi 3:16 in all things,'*" read Butch.

"I'm almost there," said Runt. "1 Nephi 3:16, 'Wherefore, let us be faithful in keeping the commandments of the Lord; therefore let us go down to the land of our father's inheritance, for behold he left gold and silver, and all manner of riches. And all this he hath done because of the commandments of the Lord.'"

"There the clues go again — talking about riches," said Stick. "I'm ready to find them!" he joked.

"Were all the clues this easy last time?" asked Bear.

"Not quite," answered Squeaks. "Some of them were really hard."

"I think this time the word that fits the sentence is faithful. '*Take heed in the Lord's promptings, and remain faithful in all things,'*" said Bear proudly, excited to be helping.

"Good," said Tater. "Butch, you're up. Read us the next line."

"'*The Liahona will direct you, providing the Alma 9:26 you will need,'*" read Butch.

"Red, will you read this scripture?" asked Tater.

"I'm already there," he replied. "Alma 9:26, 'And not many days hence the Son of God shall come in his glory; and his glory shall be the glory of the Only Begotten of the Father, full of grace, equity, and truth, full of patience, mercy, and long-suffering, quick to hear the cries of his people and to answer their prayers.'"

"Uh oh! A hard one," complained Squeaks.

"What can the Liahona provide from the scripture?" asked Butch.

"It can provide *glory*," said Stick.

"Not really, if no one can know about it, Stick," answered Tater.

"Oh, yeah. What about *grace?*"

"Nah, I don't think so," replied Runt. "How about *equity*, whatever that means."

"That means being equal or just, Runt. I don't think that is the right word. What about *truth?*" asked Tater.

"That works — providing the *truth* you will need," suggested Squeaks.

"Do we need the Liahona to provide *truth?*" asked Tater.

"I'm not sure about truth, but the next word is *suffering*. Could the Liahona provide *suffering?*" asked Bear.

"I don't think suffering is the right word. What if we try patience?" asked Red.

"Well *patience* works, but I'm not sure. Do we have any other possibilities?" asked Stick.

Scanning through every word in the scripture, everyone tried to fill in the blank with the best possible choice. Several minutes of silence was finally broken.

"I like the word *answer*," said Tater. "What do you guys think about that?"

"Let's see. *'The Liahona will direct you, providing the*

answers you will need,'" read Butch. "I like it."

"Me, too. The word just sounds right," said Bear. "Are there more scriptures to decipher?"

"Yep, quite a few," answered Red.

Without being asked, Butch read the next line, *"'The Book of Mormon is your Mosiah 2:36, at your side shows you the light.'"*

"Can I read another one?" asked Squeaks, quickly flipping through her scriptures.

"Sure," answered Tater, smiling.

"Okay, Mosiah 2:36," she said slowly. "'And now, I say unto you, my brethren, that after ye have known and have been taught all these things, if ye should transgress and go contrary to that which has been spoken, that ye do withdraw yourselves from the Spirit of the Lord, that it may have no place in you to guide you in wisdom's paths that ye may be blessed, prospered, and preserved.'"

"Nice job, Squeaks," said Red. Glad she had finally finished.

"Another hard one," complained Stick.

"Not really. The Book of Mormon can only be two things listed," replied Tater. "I think we should choose either Spirit of the Lord or Guide."

"'The Book of Mormon is your Spirit of the Lord or guide, at your side shows you the light,'" read Butch. "I like *guide.*"

"That sounds the best to me," agreed Bear.

"Good, that's settled. How many more do we have?" asked Tater.

"We're almost done with this clue. We've only got one left," replied Butch. "Ready? Here goes. *'Keep it with you as you Alma 37:41, setting back what is not right.'*"

"I've got it. Alma 37:41," said Runt. "'Nevertheless, because those miracles were worked by small means it did show unto them marvelous works. They were slothful, and forgot to exercise their faith and diligence and then those marvelous works ceased, and they did not progress in their journey.'"

"Well, the word is either *exercise* or *journey*," reasoned Butch. "And because I don't think they will need to keep the Liahona with them when they exercise, the word has to be *journey.*"

"Good job, Butch," said Tater. "If that was the last line, read us everything we've translated, Bear."

Bear, happy to be included, read,

> "'As you travel in time, doing service for the Lord,
> Your knowledge will be tested; your return is the reward.
> Take heed in the Lord's promptings, and remain faithful in all things.
> The Liahona will direct you, providing the answers you will need.
> The Book of Mormon is your guide, at your side shows you the light.
> Keep it with you as you journey, setting back what is not right.'"

"Great! We've deciphered the first clue. Let's move on to the next clue," suggested Squeaks.

"Butch, do you have the translation from Cheri?" asked Tater.

"Yep, are ya ready?" he asked, as he scooped salsa with his chip and took a quick bite.

Tater nodded as Butch looked up. Then he read,

> "*Your travels will begin when you hold Helaman 5:8 in your hand.*
> *Be prepared to take a journey into a long 2 Nephi 25:17 land.*
> *Three flashes start your mission, your adventure to the Mosiah 8:17.*
> *Without guidance from the 1 Nephi 3:7, your journey will forever Alma 37:41.'*"

"This clue is short!" exclaimed Red.

"And it sounds pretty easy," replied Stick. "I'll read the first line. *'Your travels will begin when you hold Helaman 5:8 in your hand.'* Okay! Wait, I've almost got that scripture," he said as he continued flipping through the pages. "Here it is. Helaman 5:8, 'And now my sons, behold I have somewhat more to desire of you, which desire is, that ye may not do these things that ye may boast, but that ye may do these things to lay up for yourselves a treasure in heaven, yea, which is eternal, and which fadeth not away; yea, that ye may have that precious gift of eternal life, which we have reason to suppose hath been given to our fathers.'"

"Holy cow, they don't get any easier than this!" shrieked Runt. "Your travels will begin when you hold *treasure* in your hand! I love that word."

"I agree," said Red. "Hey, if the clues are gonna be this easy, let me try the second part." Without waiting for a response, he started, *"Be prepared to take a journey into a long 2 Nephi 25:17 land."*

"Who has the scripture?" asked Tater.

"I've got it. Let me read it," replied Red. "2 Nephi 25:17, 'And the Lord will set his hand again the second time to restore his people from their lost and fallen state. Wherefore, he will proceed to do a marvelous work and a wonder among the children of men.'"

"Oooh, I know that one," said Squeaks, waving her hand wildly in the air.

"You don't need to raise your hand, Squeaks," chuckled Tater.

"Sorry, I forgot. But I think the word that fits is lost. They have traveled to a long-lost land."

"I think you're right, Squeaks. Good job. What's next?" asked Tater.

"I've got it. *Three flashes start your mission — your adventure to the Mosiah 8:17.'*" Without pausing for a breath, Bear read, "Now the scripture, Mosiah 8:17, 'But a seer can know of things which are past, and also of things which are to come, and by them shall all things be revealed, or, rather, shall secret things be made manifest, and hidden things shall come to light, and things which are not known shall be made known by them which otherwise could not be known,'" Bear finished.

"I think we are getting good at finding the words," said Red. "I think the word is *past*."

"Okay, let's move on to the last line," said Tater. "'*Without guidance from the 1 Nephi 3:7, your journey will forever last.*' 1 Nephi 3:7, 'And it came to pass that I, Nephi, said unto my father: I will go and do the things which the Lord hath commanded, for I know that the Lord giveth no commandments unto the children of men, save he shall prepare a way for them that they may accomplish the thing which he commandeth them.'"

"I can't believe how easy these have been," said Runt. "I think the word that fits is *Lord*."

Butch, read the entire clue, please," requested Tater.

> "'Your travels will begin when you hold treasure in your hand.
> Be prepared to take a journey into a long-lost land.
> Three flashes start your mission — your adventure to the past.
> Without guidance from the Lord, your journey will forever last.'"

"This is so cool! Guys, do you realized that Hero held the treasure in his hand, the Liahona flashed a number three times, and then they traveled to Book of Mormon time?" asked Stick.

"Now we have to hope they listen to the Lord so they are not stuck in the past forever!" said Bear.

"Do you think we are going to be able to talk to them again, Tater?" asked Squeaks.

"I don't know for sure, but I hope so," he replied.

"I wonder who they've met," Red said.

"I don't know, but I bet they aren't having much fun," said Runt.

"What do you mean? I think traveling in time would be a lot of fun," Tater replied.

"I mean — work! I bet that's what they're getting to do. No modern day conveniences to help them out, no lawn movers and stuff," replied Runt.

"That's true," said Tater.

"No bathrooms!" hollered Squeaks.

"No running water, ice or cold sodas," said Bear. "What about food? What are they having to eat?"

"Especially Hero — he won't even eat ketchup," said Squeaks.

The Team laughed and wondered how their teammates were doing without them.

The warm, humid nights caused by the unending rain formed drops of water that slid down the inside of the window in the Treehouse. Squeaks watched as the drops left streaks on the glass. Through the streaks of water, she noticed the brilliant color of the full moon shining in on the Team.

"I wonder if a full moon is shining where they are?" she asked.

"I can't wait to ask them," said Stick softly. "You know, I would love to be with them — even without modern conveniences."

"Me, too," added Tater, as he longingly looked at the moon.

"Has anyone noticed that the rain stopped as soon as they left?" asked Red.

"I wonder if it's raining where they are now," chuckled Bear.

"Yeah, maybe they took the rain with them," laughed Squeaks.

"We better hurry up and finish with the clues. If they get through on the walkie-talkie, I want to be able to tell them everything they need to do to get home," suggested Tater. "Butch, will you read the final clue?"

Without saying a word, Butch grabbed the paper and started reading.

> "'Once your journey is through, and you've completed the Jacob 2:10,
> Then hold the Liahona, and you will travel straight back.
> To the 2 Nephi 27:21 you have left, you will most definitely return.
> With the Lord's Mosiah 2:17 finished, you will have no concern.
> If the task is not complete, nowhere will you travel.
> What's wrong must be right, or your 1 Nephi 9:2 will unravel.
> Your time it is short; your journey only Mosiah 13:18 of the Lord's days.

To fix what's gone wrong, or remain forever
there to Mormon 8:26.'"

"I've found the first scripture. Can I read it?" asked
Squeaks.

Tater nodded.

Squeaks smiled and read, "'But, notwithstanding the
greatness of the task, I must do according to the strict
commands of God, and tell you concerning your wicked-
ness and abominations, in the presence of the pure in
heart, and the broken heart, and under the glance of the
piercing eye of the Almighty God.'"

"Why are the clues so easy?" asked Runt. "The word
that fits is *task*."

"I wonder if we will need to use these scripture references for something else in the future," said Bear.

"I hadn't thought about that. Good thinking, Bear,"
replied Runt. "Maybe the clues are easy to find this time,
because the word we use may not be all the scripture references are used for."

"The second line doesn't have a scripture reference,"
said Red. "Should I read the third line?"

"Yep," replied Tater.

"'*To the 2 Nephi 27:21 you have left, you will most
definitely return,*'" he started. "Hang on, let me read that
scripture, too. 2 Nephi 27:21, 'Touch not the things which
are sealed, for I will bring them forth in mine own due
time; for I will show unto the children of men that I am
able to do mine own work.'"

"The only word that goes along with something you have left is *time*. Does that sound right?" asked Bear.

"You're getting good at this, Bear," said Tater. "You'll have to think about hanging around us more often. If we find new clues, you could be a great help."

"Think about hanging around? No problem," he replied, grinning from ear to ear.

Runt shuffled through the pages of his scriptures and barked, "I've got this one!"

"You don't have to yell, Runt," said Tater. "You can read it."

Runt, excited to finish, said, "Sorry, we only have two left. *'With the Lord's Mosiah 2:17 finished, you will have no concern.'* Now, Mosiah 2:17, 'And behold I tell you these things that ye may learn wisdom; that ye may learn that when ye are in the service of your fellow beings ye are only in the service of your God.'"

"I know this one," shouted Squeaks excitedly. "*Service* — that's the word."

"Nice!" complimented Red. "We are doing so good."

"The next line has no scripture reference. So, can I read it?" asked Stick.

"Yeah, just read it," said Red, trying to be funny.

"*'What's wrong must be right, or your 1 Nephi 9:2 will unravel.'* 1 Nephi 9:2," he said, slowly flipping through the pages. "'And now, as I have spoken concerning these plates, behold they are not the plates upon which I make a full account of the history of my people; for the plates upon which I make a full account of my people I have given the name of Nephi; wherefore they are called the plates of Nephi, after mine own name; and these plates also are called the plates of Nephi.'"

"Could it be the word *history* that we are looking for?" asked Runt. "Our history will unravel?"

"That would be scary. I wonder what would happen," said Red.

"I never want to find out — ever!" exclaimed Squeaks.

"What's next?" asked Tater.

"'Your time it is short; your journey only Mosiah 13:18 of the Lord's days,'" read Butch.

"I've got the scripture," said Stick. "Mosiah 13:18, 'But the seventh day, the Sabbath of the Lord thy God, thou shalt not do any work, thou, nor thy son, nor thy daughter, thy man-servant, nor thy maid-servant, nor thy cattle, nor thy stranger that is within thy gates.'"

"They only have seven days!" said Butch.

"Seven of whose days? My mom is going to be freaking out when she finds out they have been gone one day," said Squeaks.

"Read the sentence, Butch," said Tater.

"'*Your time it is short; your journey only seven of the Lord's days,*'" he read.

"Time is different there, so how do we know how long that is?" asked Red.

"What happens if they don't figure out what they're doing in seven days?" asked Runt. "Does it say?"

"The last line reads, 'To fix what's gone, or remain forever there to Mormon 8:26,'" said Stick.

"Let me read that scripture," said Bear, turning the pages of his scriptures quickly. "Mormon 8:26, 'And no one need say they shall, for the Lord hath spoken it; for out of the earth shall they come, by the hand of the Lord, and none can stay it; and it shall come in a day when it shall be said that miracles are done away; and it shall come even as if one should speak from the dead.' What in the world? I have no idea which word fits."

"I do," said Squeaks quietly.

"What's the word?" asked Red.

"They are there to fix what has gone wrong in seven days or remain in the past to stay," she answered. Tears started to well up in her eyes.

"What?" asked Stick.

"She's right. The word *stay* fits in the sentence. *'To fix what's gone wrong, or remain forever there to stay,'*" said Tater.

"Some one read the entire translation," said Red.

"I will!" bellowed Bear.

> *"'Once your journey is through, and you've completed the task,*
> *Then hold the Liahona, and you will travel straight back.*
> *To the time you have left, you will most definitely return.*
> *With the Lord's service finished, you will have no concern.*
> *If the task is not complete, nowhere will you travel.*
> *What's wrong must be right, or your history will unravel.*

Your time it is short; your journey only seven of
the Lord's days.
To fix what's gone wrong, or remain forever
there to stay.'"

"We are sssooooo smart!" exclaimed Butch.

"I can't wait to tell our teammates everything we
know," said Squeaks eagerly. "They need to know what
the clues say so they aren't stuck there forever."

"Should we try to call them on the walkie-talkie
again?" asked Stick.

"I guess trying wouldn't hurt," said Tater. "Who has
the walkie-talkie?"

"I'll get it," answered Bear. "It's sitting on the charger." He ran to retrieve it, then turned back to Tater and
asked, "Did they have extra batteries with them?"

Stricken with a knot of sickness in the pit of his stomach, Tater laid down on his sleeping bag and softly said,
"I don't know if they did. What if we have no way to tell
them how to get home?"

Chapter Sixteen

The boys had traveled nearly three miles north, following the river and watching carefully for any Lamanites as they walked. The scenery around them seemed to change continually. They began their journey walking through a lush, heavily-forested jungle. As they continued, they moved through sparsely covered woods, and finally entered a beautiful meadow. The waist-high grasses floated back and forth in the wind. Spotting a city to the north, they crept tentatively through the open field toward what they hoped was the city of Mulek.

The city did not have the same protection as Jershon, but it was still somewhat sheltered. Posted at the gate to the city were several guards. As the boys approached the city, the guards stopped them and one asked, "What is your business here?"

Comonti boldly responded, "We are here to speak with the Prophet Alma."

Without another word the guards stepped aside and pointed toward the gate.

"We must look like we belong here," thought Hero, as the boys casually walked through the gates of the city. Unsure where to find Alma, they wandered deeper into the city and saw many children at play. Hero did not remember noticing any children at play in the streets of Jershon. These children ran to the boys and begged them to come play with them.

"We can't right now," said Hero. "Maybe later."

Disappointed, the children ran back to their game.

Comonti called after them, "Is this the city of Mulek?"

The children, busy at play again, ignored his question. The boys walked further into the city, hoping to find Alma.

One little girl with beautiful, long brown hair and tiny features, who was about ten years old, followed the boys for several minutes. She finally said, "You are the men the Spirit spoke to me about. You need to see the prophet, right?"

Comonti slowly turned around and said, "You're right. We're looking for the Prophet Alma. Can you tell us if we are in the right place?"

"Yes, you are. You have reached the city of Mulek. Are you the men visiting our land?" she asked.

"What do you mean?" asked KP.

"You are here for the Lord," she replied. "You don't belong here, right?"

Hero, surprised at her comments, knelt down on one knee and motioned for her to come closer. "How do you know that we don't belong here?"

"You are not from this time," she replied. "The Spirit told me to watch for you and take you to Alma quickly."

"The Spirit told you?" Bubba questioned.

"Yes. Now we must hurry or Captain Moroni will not have time to prepare. Follow me," she said, turning and starting to run.

The boys weaved in and out of buildings, down dark corridors, through alleyways with creepy shadows and finally into an empty marketplace. Quietly wondering where the adults were, they continued to follow her. Outside a building on the west side of town, the young girl finally stopped running.

"You will find Alma inside waiting for you. Good luck in your travels. I pray you will return home safely," she said.

"Thank you," said Bubba.

With that, she turned and disappeared into the shadows.

"That was weird," commented KP. "How did she know we're not from here?"

"Forget that, how did she know we needed to find Alma?" asked Bubba.

"I guess the Lord works in mysterious ways," replied Comonti.

"I think you're right, Comonti," added Hero. "I guess we better hurry."

Hero ran to the door and cautiously pulled it open.

The interior of the building was dark. The main room was lit with a small, flickering candle, which sat on the floor in a round, bowl-shaped pot. Hero moved timidly inside, hoping to see a friendly face.

"There's no one here," said KP loudly, as his voice echoed inside the empty building.

"Shhhh, quiet," snarled Bubba. "I'm scared enough."

The four boys wandered down a long hall in the pale light provided by the candle. No one seemed to be there.

"What do we do?" asked Comonti.

"Should we call for him?" asked KP.

"A prophet?" asked Hero. "Are you nuts?"

Suddenly a strong voice from behind them boomed, "What are you boys doing here?"

Bubba flipped around so fast, he could not focus on the man in front of him. His nerves, already on edge, shattered as he stood shaking, unable to speak.

Hero watched as his brother trembled. "We are looking for the Prophet Alma."

"I am Alma. What do you need?"

"We have been sent by Captain Moroni to see if you have received a revelation from the Lord regarding the strategies of the Lamanites," replied Hero.

"I have already given the revelations to his messengers," Alma replied.

"We believe the messengers, who came to you earlier, were spies for the Lamanites," said KP.

"And what would make you question them?" Alma asked.

"Well, Moroni thinks that his trusted spy is actually a

traitor. He is afraid the traitor has given him false information," replied KP.

"In fact, nothing in your previous seal made it to Moroni," said Bubba, finally able to speak.

"Why has Moroni sent you boys to me?"

"We are from another time — a time when the Lord has given the people a copy of the records you keep. We have read the prophecies that are to happen, and the message these spies gave to Moroni didn't match the messages we have received from the Lord."

"Am I to understand that you already know the Lord's strategies?" he asked.

"Yes, but only because you wrote them on a record that was translated for our time," replied KP.

"Are you from the future, too?" Alma asked, looking at Comonti.

"No, I have met you before. I am Lehi's son, Comonti."

Alma smiled and said, "I was aware that you were coming. The Lord revealed to me what has happened. I have prepared the correct strategies and a seal for Captain Moroni. Take this to him so that he knows that you speak the truth," he said, handing Hero a small leather cloth. It had writing drawn on the front that resembled the writing Cheri had translated for them earlier. "You must return quickly. Captain Moroni has very little time to prepare for this battle," warned Alma.

Alma moved toward the door. As he reached it, he turned to the boys and asked, "Was your journey here difficult?"

Bubba remembered the ride down the mountain, the jump of terror across the ravine, and the arrow scratch on his back. "It was horrible," he replied.

"I am sorry to hear that."

"Alma, he was scratched by an arrow," said Comonti. "Is there anything we need to do for him?"

"Where is the wound?" he asked.

Bubba turned around and lifted up his shirt. Alma saw the bright red, soft-ball-sized rash.

Alma rubbed his hand across Bubba's back and asked, "Was the area washed well?"

"I tried to clean the wound," replied Hero.

He quietly studied the area for several minutes. "This wound does not look deep enough to have caused a lot of damage. I believe it will be tender for several days, but it will heal," he replied.

Bubba pulled down his shirt, picked up his backpack and thanked Alma for checking the wound.

"Have you boys eaten?" Alma asked.

"No, our food was ruined as we slid down the mountain in a mud slide," responded Hero.

"A mud slide? That sounds interesting. Why don't we feed you before your journey home."

With that, he quickly moved out into the sunshine and walked rapidly through the city. Intrigued at how the boys came to visit his land, Alma asked, "Your faith must be great and hearts strong to be worthy to receive such a treasure from the Lord."

"Treasure?" asked KP, confused at his statement.

"Yes, the Lord must have great faith in you," Alma replied.

"I don't know why!" said Bubba.

"Do you not live in the last days?" he questioned.

"Yes, that is what we are told," answered Hero.

"That is when His strongest children are called from heaven. I wish I could have had as strong a testimony as you to have been alive at the end," he responded.

Quietly following Alma, the boys wondered if they were worthy to be walking with him. Alma reached a small cottage, opened the door and invited the boys inside. Exhausted from their travels, the boys sat down on the floor and rested for several minutes while Alma prepared a small meal. Bubba did not care what type of food Alma offered; he only wanted to fill his empty stomach as fast as he could. Alma handed each of the boys a bowl filled with all kinds of fruit, nuts and several pieces of jerky.

Alma sat on the floor next to the boys and said, "The Lord has shown to me a faster way back to the city of Jershon. As soon as you are finished and rest for a few minutes, I will show you the path to take."

Turning to Comonti, Alma asked, "How is your father?"

"He is doing very well," Comonti answered.

"And you mother — is she still sick?"

"Yes, but hopefully on the mend."

"That is good to hear. I am grateful that these boys were able to help her."

"How did you know that?" Comonti asked.

"The Lord showed me in a vision," he replied.

Bubba, completely exhausted from all the traumatic experiences of the day, laid his head on his backpack and closed his eyes. In a few seconds, he was fast asleep.

Alma turned to Hero and said, "Your time here is short — listen to the Spirit, and he will guide you on your journey."

"Do you know why we are here and what we need to do?" he asked.

"Ask the Lord, and He will help you. You have five minutes to rest and then you must go."

Hero nodded. He, too, laid his head on his pack and closed his eyes. Unable to sleep, he thanked Heavenly Father for the adventure and asked Him to watch over them and Bean. The five minutes passed rapidly.

Alma broke the silence and said, "It is time. You must leave now in order to give Moroni enough time to prepare." He walked to the door and opened it, revealing the late afternoon sun.

"Come quickly, boys," he instructed, as he walked outside.

Slow to move, Hero stretched as hard as he could, grabbed his pack and picked himself up off the ground. He grabbed Bubba's pack and said, "Come on, Bubba. We gotta go."

"Uuuummmmm, I'm too tired, and my entire body is sore," Bubba replied. "I'll just stay. Go on without me."

"Quit whining, and get up," Hero demanded. "Alma is waiting for us. You too, KP. Get up."

Comonti was the first out the door. Standing alone

with Alma, they waited for the boys.

Hero walked to the door and said, "Come on! Right now!" Then he quickly walked outside.

"I hate when Hero acts like Mom," complained Bubba.

KP chuckled and said, "Yeah, but he's right. We are making a prophet wait for us."

Bubba and KP stood up and wobbled to the door. Looking outside, they saw mysterious, dark clouds moving across the sky and slowly covering the suns rays. The clouds looked as though they were on a mission to destroy the rest of the evening.

"Looks like rain. We better hurry," warned Alma, as he headed south through the city.

Once outside, he took a sharp turn east. He walked swiftly through the long grass and the sparse trees, leading the boys approximately two miles to the base of the mountain. Passing the footpath up the mountain, Alma continued further east around the base. The foliage became so thick, maneuvering, even with a machete, was almost impossible. He stopped abruptly and climbed several feet up the mountainside to a small opening.

"This is as far as I can go. Crawl through the opening, and continue on your hands and knees until the tunnel opens. Then head directly south. Don't veer off the path at all. As long as you follow my instructions, you will remain safe. Your return to Jershon should only take you about two hours."

"Good, I'm not sure how much more I can do today," replied Bubba.

"You will be fine, Bubba," he replied.

"Will we see you again?" asked Hero.

"Not on this journey — maybe at a another time."

"Thanks for everything, Alma," said KP.

"Yes, thanks," repeated Hero and Bubba.

"Here are a few more snacks for your journey," he said, as he handed Hero a bag. "Move quickly, and remember to head south and never step off the foot path."

Bubba started crawling first, followed by KP, Comonti and Hero. As they entered, the tunnel was barely bigger than their bodies. They pulled on some roots with their hands to help move them through the hole. After roughly ten feet, the opening was big enough to allow the boys to crawl on their hands and knees. Then after an additional fifty feet or so, they were standing in an underground cave.

The inside of the cave was very unique, with an underground stream bubbling up a few feet away from where the boys were standing. The stream meandered south, further into the cave, and seemed to cast a glowing light that sparkled up from the sand. Vibrant green moss lined both sides of the stream. Two feet from the water was a sand and pebble footpath. Beautiful, lush, tropical plants and trees grew beyond the path on the south side of the stream. The cave seemed like its own perfect jungle ecosystem.

"That must be the path we follow," said Bubba, stating the obvious.

"Probably, since Alma said to follow the path, and it's the only path here," returned Hero sarcastically.

"Should we jump in the water and relax for a minute?" asked KP.

"We better not," replied Comonti. "Alma was specific about staying on the path."

"I'm not sure that I like caves all that much," added Bubba, nervously looking around.

"Everything will be fine. Someone must use this cave often. Look at how worn the footpath is," replied Hero, pointing to the ground.

"I hate it when you say everything's gonna be fine," said Bubba.

"Why?"

"'Cause I always seem to get hurt," replied Bubba, smiling.

"Come on, guys. We better hurry. Moroni needs this seal from Alma quickly," Comonti urged.

The boys headed south, following the path. They were amazed at the soft, warm glow of light cast by the sparkling sand. As they traveled deeper into the cave, their surroundings seemed quiet — almost too quiet — especially compared to the abundant noises they had heard in the jungle outside.

"I wonder where the cave ends," said KP.

"I don't know. But has anyone noticed that everything is getting darker in here?" asked Bubba.

"Yeah, it does seem darker in here. I wonder what that means," said Hero.

"Something feels wrong. The feeling is almost creepy," said Bubba, nervously looking over his shoulder. "Do you think animals or something could be in here?"

"I guess so," answered Hero.

The boys continued cautiously further into the cave,

walking as fast as they could. They listened to the nerve-racking quiet and watched their surroundings for any sign of life. A sudden rush of cold air rolled over their bodies, sending a chill up Hero's spine.

Panicking, he asked, "Did anybody feel that?"

"I did," replied Comonti nervously. "Something doesn't feel right."

"I wonder if we should turn around and return to Jershon by walking over the mountain," said Bubba.

"No, Alma told us to stay on the path and we would be safe. Besides, Moroni needs this information quickly," insisted Comonti.

Fearful of their unknown surroundings, the boys stayed close together. They noticed every shadow move, every leaf rustle, and every unexplained sound occurring around them. Their pace began to quicken as they heard a strange noise in the darkness behind them.

His heart pounding in fear, Bubba took off running as fast as he could, whimpering nervously. Scared he had seen something, Hero, KP and Comonti followed. They did not turn around, afraid something terrible must be behind them.

"What? What is it, Bubba?" called Hero.

"I'm not sure. I feel a…"

"A what?" interrupted KP.

"Stop! Nothing's behind us. Let's walk. I'm sure there is nothing here," Hero responded, as he slowed from a run to a walk.

"I can feel something," insisted Bubba, slowing only to stay with the others.

"Feel what, Bubba?" demanded Hero.

"An evil force or something," he answered.

"What, like Darth Vader?" asked KP.

"Oh, you're really funny," replied Bubba, mockingly. "I'm serious."

"I feel it as well," Comonti agreed.

Hero stopped on the path. "All right," he said. "Let's stay calm. Move quickly down the path, and watch for anything that could possibly hurt us, okay?"

Bubba, stopping only momentarily to listen to Hero, hesitantly agreed to his plan. As Bubba turned to continue down the path, he noticed something move in the bushes to the side of him. Squinting to focus on the moving object, he could not distinguish a definite color or shape — only a shadow through the bush.

"What is it, Bubba?" asked KP.

"I'm not sure. Look!" he yelled, pointing into the distance.

"Come on, Bubba. You're just seeing things. Let's get this over with already. If we don't get moving, were never gonna get this information to Moroni in time," said Hero, frustrated with Bubba's imagination.

"Uuuhhhhhh," gasped Comonti.

"Now what, Comonti? Bubba, you've got to stop. You're freaking everybody out," complained Hero.

Hero turned to see why Comonti had gasped, just in time to see the auburn glow of eyes, burning like coals, as they moved rapidly through the bushes.

"What is it?" yelled KP.

"I don't want to die in here!" screamed Bubba.

"Alma said we would be safe as long as we stayed on the path. Maybe whatever that is — is waiting for us to step off it," hoped Hero.

"We've got to get moving. Now!" ordered Comonti.

Quickly, the boys moved through the cave, knowing every step they took was being closely watched. Hero, last in line on the path, fought the urge to turn and look behind him. Several times, he could feel someone breathing down his neck.

"How long have we been traveling?" asked Bubba, shaking with fear.

"I have no idea — a long time. Time is moving so slow, it seems like we have been in here for hours," replied KP.

"Didn't Alma say our journey would only be about two hours?" asked Comonti.

"We must be getting close," encouraged Hero. "Keep going, and watch for an opening or some sort of exit."

The boys traveled another half mile and watched as the cave again started to narrow. It became smaller and smaller, forcing them to crawl fifty feet before having to lie flat on their stomachs. They pulled themselves by hand, using the roots and branches as anchors to finally free them from the terrifying cave.

As Hero, the last one to crawl into the fresh, cool air of the jungle, pulled his legs out of the cave, the boys breathed a heavy sigh of relief. They quickly looked around, still nervous from their experiences in the cave, to see if they recognized where they might be. Comonti pointed to Jershon, a quarter mile into the distance.

Relieved to be alive, they raced toward Jershon and Captain Moroni.

"Where can we find him?" panted Hero, nearly out of breath by the time they reached the city walls.

"This way, everyone. Follow me!" yelled Comonti, taking the lead. He raced through town, ducking in and out of alleys, and then straight through the bustling market place, filled with merchants and shoppers everywhere.

"Um, sorry," called Bubba, as he knocked a bundle of blankets from a woman's arms. "Wait! Don't lose me!" he called to Comonti.

Comonti noticed the army assembling in the field near his home. He knew Moroni would be waiting for their return at the command tent.

"This one! This tent!" screamed Comonti, pulling back the cloth covering of the door.

"We don't have much time," shrieked Hero, as he raced inside Moroni's tent.

Moroni, surprised at the boys' quick return and abrupt entrance, asked, "What are you talking about?"

"Here, read it fast," Hero insisted. "I told you the Book of Mormon was correct. The Prophet Alma has confirmed our story."

Moroni stood up quickly, knocking over the chair he had been sitting on. Reading every word of the letter three times, the expression on his face changed into one of disappointment and then horror. His young, boyish face looked hard and mean, as his muscles tightened. His body seemed to stand three inches taller than they remembered.

"This can't be," he muttered to himself, pacing

throughout the tent. "It's not possible. I can't have the men ready that fast."

Moroni stopped abruptly, looked up at the boys and placed the letter on the table. In a valiant voice, he said, "We have work to do, and we have very little time. Comonti, take these boys and find your father. Advise him you are home safely and that I need him in my tent — immediately."

"Moroni?" asked Bubba timidly.

"Hmm?" he answered, deep in thought.

"Are you going to leave the city?" he quietly asked, already knowing the answer.

"Yes."

"Are you going to help us rescue our friend before you go?" he almost whispered, afraid of the response.

"I can't boys. You know that if I don't move the armies now, we will not be able to save the city of Manti, and thousands of Nephites will be killed," he replied.

"But," Bubba stopped, looked down to the ground and finished weakly, "I understand."

As they turned to leave, Moroni stopped them and said, "I could feel the Spirit of the Lord with you. Thank you for your knowledge of the Lord's teachings."

Without a word, Comonti dropped the opening to the tent and raced toward home.

"We have to save her, guys," insisted Bubba.

"Don't worry. We will — even if we have to do it ourselves," said Hero.

As the boys drew near to Comonti's home, they yelled to announce their arrival. Lehi was elated to hear the boys' voices. He jumped and ran through the front door, down the cobblestone path and through the tall grasses to meet them.

"You've made it," Lehi yelled excitedly, throwing his arms around Comonti.

"Yes, Father. We're home."

"Have you seen Moroni yet?" he asked.

"Yes."

"And, what did he say?"

"He wants you to report to him immediately," Comonti answered. "I'm sorry, Father."

Lehi released his grip on Comonti, turned abruptly and walked toward the cottage. "Everything will be fine," Lehi replied, trying not to sound disappointed.

"Lehi, what about our friend?" asked Hero. "If you leave, no one will be able to help us save her."

"She will have to wait boys," he replied. "I'm sorry, but I must report to the Captain."

"But," Bubba protested.

"No boys — no buts. I forbid you to leave the city. If I am to leave for war, I want to know you are all safe," he warned.

"But," said KP.

"No, not another word. We will save her when I return and not before! Comonti, do you understand me?"

"Yes, Father,"

"Hero, KP, Bubba?" he asked.

"Yes, Lehi," each responded.

"There will be no more discussion of rescue now."

Comonti, trying to soften the sudden tension, asked,

"Father, how is Mother?"

Lehi turned and looked at Comonti. "Son, if you hadn't disobeyed me and gone into the jungle, finding these boys sent from the Lord," he paused and then continued, "your mother would have died. She is still weak, but feeling remarkably better."

Comonti smiled. Lehi turned and marched into the house. He changed his clothes, laced his sandals and grabbed his sword.

"I will be back, Loriah," yelled Lehi as he ran out the door. "I have to meet with Moroni."

Chapter Seventeen

Crickets chirped endlessly, birds sang sweetly and monkeys screeched continuously. The noise never faded during the night. The chatter made the jungle feel alive, Bean thought. She sat alone on the ground, listening to the sounds and watching the warriors prepare to leave the camp the next morning. She pulled her knees in tight to her chest and wrapped her arms around them.

Laying her head on her knees in despair, she wondered, "Do Hero, Bubba and KP even know where I am? Do they know the warriors, holding me prisoner, are moving in the morning? Are they planning on rescuing me?"

Unsure what the morning would bring, she struggled trying to decide what to do. Shaliah watched as Bean talked to herself.

"There is no way," said Shaliah, as she sat on the ground next to Bean. "It will never work."

"What will never work?" asked Bean innocently.

"I have tried to escape numerous times. Every time, I have been caught."

"I have to find my friends. Without me, they will be stuck here forever," replied Bean.

"And so will you! Life could be worse," said Shaliah.

"Oh really. How?" Bean snarled. "The Lamanites are leaving for war. They're planning to use me as a hostage, but the Nephite people don't even know I exist. I could be heading for death really soon."

"What do you think you can do?"

"I have been thinking," Bean replied. "The older warrior — the one that guards my side of the tent by the waterfall — he falls asleep every night about two a.m. What if we undo all of the stitching down the side of the tent and escape while he snores?"

"The other guards will not be asleep," protested Shaliah.

"I know, but I think if we are careful, we can escape," Bean said.

"Okay, it's possible. But once you're in the jungle — then what?"

"When my friends and I were traveling in the jungle, before I was kidnapped, we saw a city not too far to the southwest of here. I think we could try to make it to the city."

"This will not be easy, and they may kill you for try-ing," Shaliah warned.

"You won't come with me?" asked Bean, reaching for her shoulder.

"I don't know. My life has changed, and I have learned to accept my life as a maid servant."

"What about your daughter? She's worth trying for, isn't she?" asked Bean.

"I'm afraid the warriors will kill me if I try again," Shaliah admitted uncomfortably.

"I'm going to try, and you can come if you want," offered Bean, looking away.

Shaliah looked to the ground quietly for several min-utes before she finally responded. "I will try again. My Annah is worth trying for again."

Bean threw her arms around Shaliah and hugged her. "Thank you," she whispered. "Thank you."

Shaliah stood up abruptly and scolded, "Don't ever do that again, child."

Bean shot Shaliah a puzzled look. Then she realized, as Shaliah winked, that she was trying to mislead the warriors. Bean sat quietly, anticipating the night's adventure. She rehearsed in her mind the events that would occur as soon as the seam of her tent was pulled apart. Suddenly cold from the chill in the air, Bean crawled back inside her one room, no bathroom, no running water, no television, tent.

Every night, the warriors would tie the door closed, sealing Shaliah and Bean into the tent from the outside. Usually once that was done, the camp would settle down and the warriors would be very quiet. The prisoners knew that this time of night would be the best chance to escape.

Bean waited for the obnoxious snoring to begin. Then she wiggled apart the small hole she had made the first day she was captured. Carefully, she slid the thick, unbreakable thread out of every single hole. The process was slow, and at times, overwhelmingly hard. Nervously watching the slow progression, Shaliah found the string at the bottom of the seam and started helping.

The process was faster with two, but Bean was sure the sun would be up before they could finish. Working as fast as they could, they finally removed all of the thread, creating an opening large enough to crawl through.

"Are you ready?" asked Bean, her heart racing with excitement.

"If you are," Shaliah replied.

"Here we go," Bean whispered, as she pulled open the material and revealed potential freedom. The two moved slowly, only stepping as the warrior snored. They knew his snoring would cover any noise their footsteps might make.

Fifteen feet from the tent and half way to the jungle, Bean suddenly remembered she could not leave without her backpack. She looked up at Shaliah with a terrified expression on her face.

"Go to the jungle cover," Bean whispered. "Wait for me in the bushes."

Wanting to run back into the tee-pee for safety, Shaliah looked at Bean and replied, "I can't do this."

"Go. You can do this. I will be right there," Bean assured her nervous friend.

Watching Shaliah turn for the jungle, Bean moved carefully toward her backpack. The contents were still spread out across the log table. Her clothes were rolled up in a pile next to the bag. "I'm gonna need an iron," she thought, as she noticed their condition.

As she reached the canopy covering the tables where the Lamanites made their weapons of war, Bean could see her belongings. Her first aid kit had been opened and searched. Her Book of Mormon was still opened, and one page was slightly torn. She also saw some paper, two pencils, a brush, a handful of ponytail bands, several keys from the treasure hunt, and the precious treasure.

She quietly picked up her pack, trying to steady herself as her hands shook feverishly. One by one, she started to place her belongings back into the pack. All of a sudden, a warrior's cry pierced the silence. The sleeping warrior had woken up and noticed the hole in Bean's tee-pee. Instantly, warriors crawled out of their tents to find the cause of the commotion.

Bean knew her chance for escape was swiftly disappearing. She took her arm and slid everything on the log table into her pack with one big swipe. Making sure she had placed the treasure inside, she zipped up the bag and threw it over her shoulder. Then she sprinted toward the jungle and Shaliah.

The chaos caused by the screaming warriors allowed the two to race deep into the jungle, several minutes ahead of the warriors. Unsure of their surroundings, they did not know which direction to head and ran aimlessly for twenty minutes. Tired and scared, Bean located a small hideout in the bushes and trees. The two climbed into the bushes and prayed the warriors would not find them.

Bean held her hand over her mouth, hoping to muffle the sound of her erratic breathing. Suddenly a snake slithered through her arms and across her leg. Mortified, she wanted to jump up, throw the snake several hundred feet into the distance and scream at the top of her lungs. The slimy feeling was almost more than she could handle, but she knew the two would definitely be caught and possibly killed if she gave away their position. She closed her eyes tightly, and she prayed for Hero to save her from the snake. The snake was so long, Bean was sure it had taken three full minutes for its long body to cross her legs and slide out of their hiding place. When she opened her eyes, she was relieved to watch as its tail slid away and into the darkness.

Worried about the cunning warriors, and terrified about what might happen next, Shaliah tried to reassure Bean. She placed her hand on Bean's arms and whispered, "Trust in the Lord, and we will be all right."

Warriors searched and passed them every few minutes for nearly an hour, as the two sat in fear of being caught. In the distance, they heard leaves softly rustling together.

"Quiet child," warned Shaliah. "The sound of footsteps, are near. Here come the warriors again. Ssshhh."

Bean nodded and held Shaliah's hand for comfort. Shaliah had taken care of Bean and protected her while she had been held captive. And now she depended on her for safety.

The footsteps grew closer and closer — at least four

warriors based on the sounds Shaliah heard. Positive they would find them any minute, Shaliah dropped her head to the ground and prayed fervently for protection. Suddenly, Bean felt the weight of a knee crashing directly in the center of her back. Instinctively, she sat up straight and pushed the warrior's leg away from her.

"What in the world?" asked KP. "Something is in our hideout," he said.

Recognizing the voice, Bean jumped to her feet, popping up from the hideout and scaring the boys half to death. Bubba jumped back, tripped over a vine and landed on a rock.

With his spear pointed at Bean's chest, Comonti was ready to attack. When Shaliah saw the spear, she jumped to her feet and pushed it away from Bean.

"Let her go free," she demanded.

"Bean?" asked Bubba nervously. "Is that really you?"

"Guys?" she replied.

"Bean, it's me, Hero," he answered, almost yelling.

Elated and surprised, she started to scream in delight.

"Sssshhhh," said KP, as he climbed into the hideout. "The warriors are everywhere tonight."

Quickly, the boys climbed into the jungle hideout and hugged Bean. They were excited and relieved to see her alive and unharmed.

"How'd you do it?" asked Hero.

"Yeah. How did you escape?" asked Bubba, rubbing her arm to make sure she was really there.

"Shaliah helped me," she answered, pointing to her friend.

"We were on our way to rescue you," said KP.

"I told you I could take care of myself," she insisted.

"I knew you could," KP replied, grinning. "Hey, do you still have the treasure?"

"Right here," she answered, patting her backpack.

"Did you figure out how we can get home?"

"No, the warriors had my pack the entire time I was being held captive. I haven't had a chance to look at the treasure yet," she replied.

"That's all right. We'll figure out how to use it together," suggested Bubba.

"Everyone, meet Shaliah. She is my friend," Bean said, introducing the woman who helped her escape.

"Nice to meet you," replied the boys.

"This is our friend, Comonti," Hero said.

Comonti, more concerned about their situation than introductions, whispered, "We need to get back to the city before we are found. The Lamanites are good hunters, and it's only a matter of time before they locate all of us."

"Will you lead us back?" asked Hero.

Comonti smiled and replied, "Yes. Follow me."

Scouting the area quickly, Comonti stood up from his hiding spot. He stepped into the open jungle, crouched down slightly and pointed the way for everyone to follow. Bean and the others cautiously followed Comonti through the dense green jungle, grateful for the lush foliage that kept them hidden from the Lamanite warriors.

Relieved to be free, Bean pinched her arm three times — just to make sure she was not dreaming. Her new friend enjoyed each moment of freedom, hoping it would not be her last. Cautiously optimistic, she was unsure where and how she might find her people and possibly her daughter. She followed in silence, struggling through the vines with each step toward the unknown.

Comonti maneuvered effortlessly through the vines, though moving at a snail's pace. He hoped his constant motion would help relax the overwhelming sense of fear in the group. They traveled roughly a half-mile before Comonti stood up straight and said, "The city is not far now. We should be safe from here."

As he continued carefully toward the city, he noticed a small movement in the darkness. He was unsure what lay ahead, but continued to move forward. He could see the bridge to the city one hundred yards in the distance.

Comonti paused and held out his arms, motioning for everyone to stop. Afraid a Nephite warrior guarding the city might mistake him for an enemy, he called, "Who is there?"

No reply came, so he called again, "It is I, Comonti, son of Lehi. Are you a Nephite?"

Still no response. Comonti continued to lead the group, one timid step at a time. Suddenly, thirty feet in the distance, he saw it — the sleek, shiny coat of a jaguar. "Oh no!" he gasped.

"What? What is it?" asked Hero.

"A jaguar."

"I told you! I told you we would see a jaguar," stated Bubba nervously.

"What do we do?" asked KP.

"Run, right?" asked Bean, ready to bolt.

"NO! Don't move an inch. They can move too fast.

Besides, running would give him a reason to chase you," Comonti explained.

"What about the moat? It's not far. We could jump in because cats can't swim," said KP.

"This cat can," responded Comonti.

"Then, what? What do we do?" asked Bean, her voice trembling.

"Remain still. Let's wait and see what his intentions are first."

"We've got to move," replied Shaliah. "The warriors could find us any minute. I am almost free. Please don't let them find us and take me back."

"Sssssshhhhh!" demanded Comonti. "He's moving."

Shaking uncontrollably, Bean whimpered in fear. Hero slowly raised his arm and placed it on her shoulder. Comonti never took his eyes off the jaguar. As it circled their position, Comonti circled as well.

"What are you doing?" asked Bubba.

"As long as I keep eye contact with the cat, it shouldn't attack," Comonti quietly whispered.

"Shouldn't? That doesn't sound very convincing," complained KP.

Bubba was scared to death. He managed a small smile and said, "This feels like a science report. One where your teacher asks you to explain your experiment, and no matter how hard you try, you sound like a complete idiot. By the teacher's facial expression and comments of, 'Oh, really' and 'hum', you just want to cry out, 'Please, just slap an F on it, and let me go home!' I think we're failing this assignment, guys. Do you think I could ask the Lord to slap on F on this assignment and let us go home?" he asked. "Maybe we can do better on the next assignment."

Grateful for the slight break in tension, Hero put his hand on Bubba's shoulder and said, "Come on. Hang in there. We can get through this."

"How do we escape from a jaguar, Hero?" asked KP.

Suddenly, an arrow whizzed over their heads toward the jaguar — then another and another. From the distance they heard, "Move toward the bridge, quickly."

Comonti courageously continued to watch the jaguar, never taking his eyes off the animal as they moved closer to the city. The jaguar watched the group, ready to pounce at any moment.

"I think that jaguar wants to eat us for dinner," said Bean.

"Yes, he does," answered Comonti.

Again, another arrow flew toward the jaguar, but the animal maintained a consistent gap between the group and itself.

"Who's shooting the arrows?" asked Bubba, looking over his shoulder.

"I don't know," replied Hero.

"Do you know, Comonti?" asked KP.

"Yes," he answered.

"Who? Who is it?" asked Bean.

"My father," he answered.

The boys knew they were in serious trouble. Lehi warned them not to leave the city. In fact, he forbade them to leave the city.

"Oh man, we are in trouble," said Bubba.

"Trouble? We're dead," replied KP.

"I'm sorry, Comonti," said Hero.

Without warning, and when they least expected it, the jaguar started to run at full speed toward them. Bean screamed in terror, and chaos ensued. Everyone ran for their lives, praying they would make it across the bridge into the safety of the city before the animal could reach them.

With people running in six different directions, the jaguar chose one path and headed straight for Bubba. As he realized he was the cat's prey, Bubba dropped his pack, hoping the animal would stop for its contents. The jaguar did not even pause; it kept dead aim on Bubba. Bubba was running as fast as he could, but caught the top of his sandal on some vines and fell violently onto his face. Unable to wiggle his foot free, he closed his eyes, screamed in fear at the top of his lungs and waited for the cat to attack.

The group stopped running and watched in horror as Bubba lay on the ground waiting to be attacked. Hero, mortified at what was happening to his brother, raced toward the animal. He hoped to draw the cat's attention away from Bubba, giving him time to escape, but the jaguar's sights were set. Only a few seconds would pass before the animal's sharp claws and huge teeth sank into Bubba.

The jaguar jumped into the air, growling ferociously. It was ready to attack his prey. In that same moment, Lehi's arrow pierced the animal's heart, stopping the cat dead in mid air. As the animal fell down, its lifeless body landed on top of Bubba.

Unaware the jaguar was dead, Bubba screamed and pummeled the animal wildly — hoping to save his own life. Hero moved quickly to Bubba's side, untangled his foot and pulled him out from underneath the animal.

"He's dead, Bubba. You're okay," Hero assured him.

Bubba looked down at the animal, lying lifelessly on the ground. He dropped his head onto Hero's chest and sobbed.

Chapter Eighteen

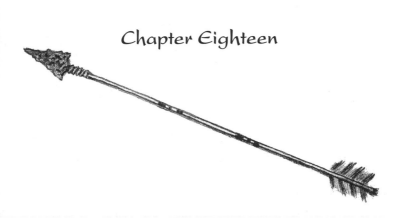

Lehi angrily crawled out from behind the bushes and marched toward the boys. Without saying a word, he picked up Bubba's backpack, stepped over the dead jaguar and handed the pack to Hero. He looked at the boys sternly, raised his hand as if to say something, and then stopped abruptly. He took a deep breath, causing his chest to rise, and then slowly he released the air. He turned without a word, picked up the jaguar, threw it over his shoulder and started walking across the bridge toward the city. Comonti, standing ready to accept his punishment, watched in disbelief as his father walked away.

"I'm sorry, Father," called Comonti, hurrying to catch him.

"Me, too, Lehi," said Hero. "This is my fault. I wanted to rescue our friend, and Comonti didn't think we should travel into the jungle without help."

Lehi remained quiet as they moved quickly through the early morning mist floating around the moat outside the city. They crossed the wide, dirt path that split the moat surrounding the city. Quickly they reached the city's second line of defense — the twenty-foot-tall fence constructed from trees. The trees were cleared of branches, sharpened to a point at the top and then laced together with leather to form a solid wall surrounding the city. Lehi paused at the fence and waved his hand to the guard posted above them. Then made a very strange noise that sounded like a chicken or bird.

"Gggrrrrrr, kuk, kuk, kuk, kuk. Gggrrrrrr, kuk, kuk, kuk, kuk," Lehi screeched.

Moments later, a small hidden door slid open and a guard motioned for the group to enter. Without a word, Lehi walked to the door and waited for everyone to follow. Closing and locking the secret door, the guard led them through a narrow hallway, up a flight of stairs and into the main street of town. Stepping into the safety of the city, everyone breathed a sigh of relief.

"What was that, Comonti?" asked KP.

"I don't know," Comonti shrugged. "I've never heard him do that, nor have I ever entered the city through that door."

Walking through the shadows of sunrise in the city, Lehi kept a brisk pace. A slight breeze swirled in the early morning air, and Bean shivered feverishly. Shaliah placed her arm over Bean's shoulder and tried to protect her from the cool air. The walk toward Lehi's home felt awkward to the boys. Lehi's silence was more than Hero could bear.

"Lehi, I know that you're angry with us, and I know that I disobeyed you. I will take the punishment for this alone. Please don't be mad at any of the others. I forced them to help me because I couldn't leave my friend with the Lamanite army any longer. I was afraid I wouldn't be able to find her again once Captain Moroni's army moved," Hero rambled.

Lehi paused and gazed at Hero. The scowl on his face softened a little, and he replied, "I have welcomed you into my home and treated you like a son. For that, you have disobeyed my every order and placed my family in danger. If I cannot control what happens in my own home, how am I to command an army with thousands of men?"

"I am sorry, Lehi," Hero quietly replied, looking down at the ground in shame.

"Boys, I am disappointed in all of you. Each one of you has your agency, and each one of you knew the right thing to do," Lehi scolded.

"Father, may I speak?" asked Comonti.

Silently, Lehi nodded his head.

"I will also take responsibility. I should have come to you when I learned what was planned. But, I wanted to help rescue their friend."

Lehi looked directly into Comonti's eyes and said, "What you have done is wrong, and you should have come to me. But boys, if I had been placed in your situation, I…" he paused, rubbed his chin with his fingers, and then continued, "I probably would have done the same thing. I'm sorry that I asked you to leave her," he finished tenderly.

Bubba, still reeling from the attack, looked at Lehi with swollen, red, tear-stained eyes. "Thank you for saving my life," he said. "I wouldn't be alive without your help."

Lehi smiled, put his arm around Bubba and said, "You are a special gift from heaven. I am grateful the Lord prompted me to find you and help."

"Me, too," added Hero. "I don't know what we would have done if you hadn't come."

They reached Lehi's home about an hour before dawn. Loriah was sitting in silent prayer next to the fireplace as they entered. Tears flowed quickly down her face as she saw Comonti enter the room.

"Comonti," she called.

"Yes, Mother. I am here," he replied, throwing his arms around her.

"Is everyone safe?" she asked, limping toward Lehi.

"Yes, Loriah. They're all home and safe," he replied.

"Were you able to save your friend, Hero?" she asked quietly.

"Yes. I'm sorry to have worried you," Hero gently answered. "Loriah, this is our friend, Bean."

Loriah smiled kindly. She reached for Bean's hand and said, "I'm glad you are here. Annah will enjoy having a friend her age. Now who is with you?"

"This is Shaliah. The Lamanites were holding her prisoner, too," Bean said.

"The Lord has blessed us all tonight. I'm glad you're both safe," Loriah replied softly.

"Thank you," whispered Bean.

"I have laid out blankets on the floor for all of you. We have but a short time for rest this early morning. But, see if you can find some sleep."

Holding Lehi's arm, she maneuvered her way into their room and crumpled into a heap on their bed. She was so relieved the Lord had blessed them and returned everyone home safely.

Morning seemed to come as soon as the boys' heads hit the pillow. Completely exhausted, they struggled to get out of bed. The boys knew Lehi would be leaving with Captain Moroni for the battle today, and everyone was sad to see him go. As Loriah entered the room, a slight smiled crossed her face. She enjoyed having her newly adopted family home. Moving into the kitchen slowly, she started to make breakfast for everyone.

"Loriah, if you do all of the work, then why am I here to help?" Annah questioned walking to the kitchen. "Please go sit down."

Annah pushed her out of the kitchen to the small rocking chair by the fireplace. She handed Loriah the baby and said, "Enjoy her while she sleeps."

"Annah, you are a heaven-sent child. I am grateful to have you here with us."

"Loriah," interrupted Hero. "We were not able to introduce Shaliah to the rest of your family."

"Let me," offered Loriah. "Shaliah, this is Isabelle, Kalia and Annah," she said, pointing to the girls. "I think you know everyone else."

"Nice to meet you, girls. Annah, you have a beautiful

name. I have a daughter named Annah. I hope she is as thoughtful as you are."

"Thank you," Annah said, as she smiled and walked to the door. "I'm going to collect eggs for breakfast. I'll be right back."

Loriah nodded at Annah and smiled. "Now Shaliah, tell me, what made you decide to leave the Lamanites?"

"Actually, I'm not a Lamanite. I'm from the people of Ammon," she replied.

"Why are you no longer with them? How did you end up with the Lamanites?"

"I was kidnapped in the jungle as we traveled to the city of Jershon. I hope one day to make it there and find my people."

"Shaliah, we live in the city of Jershon. You're here right now," replied Loriah.

Her face glowed with excitement. "Are my people still here?" she asked.

"They're not right now. They left a few weeks ago to go to the city of Mulek with the Prophet Alma. Captain Moroni did not want them to be here for the battle with the Lamanites. But I believe they will return soon."

"I'm eager to find them," she replied. "I believe my daughter lives among them."

Loriah quietly pondered for a moment, grinned and then said, "I have heard a story of a young girl waiting for her mother to return."

"Tell me of her," insisted Shaliah excitedly. "Is she kind? Beautiful? Is she... all right?"

"Yes, she is everything you hope for," Loriah replied.

"Should I travel to the city of Mulek? I'm not sure I can wait one more day to find her, now that I'm free. My only hope is that she remembers me. She was very young when I was captured," she responded.

"Traveling alone in the jungle is not safe, especially on the road to Mulek. Lehi will never let you go there alone."

"I'm afraid to leave the safety of the city anyway. I don't want to be captured again. I just want to be with my daughter. I guess I can wait a few more days for her to return."

"Do you have any other children?" questioned Loriah.

"Yes, I had one other son. He was killed in the battle along side my husband six years ago."

"I'm so sorry to hear that."

Annah stumbled as she walked into the house with a satchel full of eggs. Loriah watched her as she carefully placed the eggs on the table. Once the satchel was empty, Annah headed back outside to pick some mangos.

As she stepped back through the door, Loriah called, "Annah."

"Yes," she answered, as she leaned back inside the house.

"Would you come here for a minute?" Loriah asked.

Quickly stepping inside the house, she rushed over to her. "Can I take the baby for you?" Annah asked.

"No, dear. I have a question for you," she replied. "Sit here by me."

"Yes?" asked Annah, curious about the question.

"Tell me again, where did you lose your mother?"

Shaliah sat up straight with her eyes wide open, and she listened intently to every word of the conversation.

"I told you yesterday," she replied.

"Please, tell me again," prodded Loriah.

Annah shrugged her shoulders and started to tell her story. "We were traveling in the jungle when we were ambushed by warriors. Most of the people of Ammon escaped. A few were killed and three women were taken as prisoners. My mother was one of them."

"How long ago was it?" asked Loriah, smiling at the hopeful look on Shaliah's face.

"Six years ago," she replied.

"One last question, dear. Why didn't you leave with the people of Ammon as they followed the Prophet Alma to the city of Mulek?"

Annah smiled, "For two reasons. My mother knows to find me in the city of Jershon. What if I left and that was the day she came for me? Second, I didn't make the same covenant not to fight as my mother did.. Maybe I will go and rescue her from the Lamanites."

Annah stood up, ready to continue with breakfast.

"Annah, sweetie," Loriah said, taking her hand, "one last thing. Did you know that when the boys rescued Bean last night, they also rescued Shaliah from the Lamanite camp?"

"Yes, I heard you say that. Did you know my mother?" she asked, excited that Shaliah might have some information about her mother.

"Annah," interrupted Loriah. "I believe Shaliah is your mother. She was captured six years ago. Her husband was killed in battle, and she is searching for her daughter, Annah."

Annah looked longingly into Shaliah's face, hoping for a small spark of recognition. "I had a brother who was also killed. Do you know his name?"

"Yes, his name was Shiloah."

Annah smiled. "I knew you would come for me," she blurted, running towards her mother's outstretched arms.

Shaliah raced toward her daughter. She threw both arms around her and said, "I missed you so much. I never stopped thinking about you."

"Me neither," Annah replied, pulling back and looking at Shaliah's face. "Me neither, Mother."

Loriah stood up from her rocking chair and shuffled slowly toward the door, giving the women some privacy to enjoy the joyous moment and allowing them to reacquaint themselves with each other.

Outside, Lehi methodically prepared his horse for battle. The boys watched from the fig tree as he hooked the bridle in the horse's mouth. He pulled the reigns over its ears and patted his mane to comfort him. He threw a blanket over the horse's back, and then placed a dark-brown, leather satchel, with deep pockets on both sides, over the blanket. Lehi then hooked a round, wooden shield to the satchel on both sides of the horse. Inside the pockets, he placed a neatly-folded, tan skin that Bubba assumed was a blanket. He only carried one extra set of clothes and a small bag filled with jerky for his journey. In the satchel, on the other side of the horse, he placed a bow, curved at either end and masterfully crafted with fine engravings, along with a dozen arrows. He also included a machete-type knife with the blade sealed in a leather wrap and a sling.

Walking around the horse, he grabbed two leather straps from the ground. He flipped them over his shoulders and strapped them across his chest. Loriah shuffled her way to the door of the cottage and leaned against the door-frame, watching her husband prepare for battle. A tear trickled down her check. She selfishly wanted him to stay with her. Struggling for the strength to move, she worked her way to the fig tree. She handed Comonti the sleeping baby and moved toward Lehi's horse. She grabbed its reigns for support as she slipped a small bag into each side of his satchel. Lehi stopped preparing and walked to his wife. He picked her up, being careful of the cut on her leg, and carried her lovingly back into the cottage.

Once his father was inside, Comonti angrily said, "I want to go with him. I wish he would let me go. He has taught me well."

"My dad wouldn't want me to go either, Comonti," responded Hero.

"Why?" he questioned.

"He wants the best for me, I guess," replied Hero.

"Isn't fighting for liberty better than staying here and doing nothing?" Comonti asked. "He has taught me well, and I want to defend my family, liberty, land and freedom as much as he does."

"He defends his family, first and foremost, Comonti. And you are his family," said KP. "He wants you to be where he knows you're safe."

"Besides, he may want you here to help your mother get well," Bubba added.

Comonti stood up from the base of the fig tree, grabbed Hero's hand and helped him up from the ground.

"I know you're right. I only want to be with him."

KP and Bubba stood up with Hero and Comonti, and they casually walked inside the house. Shaliah and Annah attended to Kalia and Isabelle's needs, while Lehi knelt in prayer with his wife in the privacy of their room.

Disheartened, Comonti stood in the corner of the cottage. He warmed his hands over the meager red and yellow glow within the fireplace. Frustrated that he could not go to battle and fight with his father, and tired from the all-night adventure, Comonti stared silently into space.

Piercing the silence in the cottage was an unexpected call from Captain Moroni. "Brother Lehi! Brother Lehi! Are you ready? Our time runs short, my friend."

Throwing aside the skin hanging over the door to his room, Lehi strode confidently to the front door and answered, "Captain, I am ready."

"Good, the army has assembled in the city plaza. Friend, it is time to go," urged Moroni.

Lehi picked up his helmet and placed it on his head. He quickly tied on his arm and leg armor. Then he slid his axe into the strap on his chest, along side his sword. He grabbed his horse's reigns and pulled himself up onto its back. "I'm ready, Captain," he announced.

"Lehi, what about these boys?" asked Moroni, pointing to Hero, Bubba, KP and Comonti.

"They are too young, and they are not trained for

war," he insistently replied.

"We need every able man, Lehi — including these boys."

"Captain," Lehi started.

"Lehi, I will require their services only for the wounded. Will you agree?" Moroni asked. "Having them tend to the wounded will free others to fight."

"Captain, if you require their service, I will support your decision."

"Boys, prepare yourselves. Meet us in the plaza as quickly as possible," Moroni called, as he slapped his whip against the hindquarters of his horse. The horse took off with a vengeance, kicking up dirt with its hooves.

Lehi looked lovingly at his family and yelled, "Comonti, quickly do as the Captain orders." He turned his animal toward the city, waved at his family and commanded his horse to chase after Moroni's lead.

Bubba was panicked. "Does he mean all of us?" he asked.

"I think so, Bubba," replied Hero.

"You heard him. We only have to tend to the wounded. We won't be fighting any battles," exclaimed Bean.

"You're not going anywhere, Bean," insisted Hero.

"Well, you're not leaving me here," she retorted. "I'm going."

"They don't allow women to fight," Comonti informed her, as he pushed past and walked into the cottage.

"Well, I'm not going to fight. I'm going to tend to the wounded," she shot back. "So going shouldn't be a problem, Comonti."

Comonti hugged his mother and promised that he would return home safely as soon as he could. As she released his hand, Comonti watched as she tried hard not to cry. She could not control the tear falling down the side of her face as she replied, "Return home safe, son."

"I love you, Mother," he called, as he walked out of the house and headed toward the plaza.

"Wait! Wait for us, Comonti!" yelled KP.

Comonti stopped impatiently. "Hurry, I don't want to miss Captain Moroni's instructions."

"Hero, I hate blood and stuff. I can't even watch it on T.V. without getting sick. I really don't want to go," said Bubba.

"Bubba, it's your choice. I know you hate this stuff. I'm sure you can stay here with Loriah and the girls."

"I don't want to stay here either," he complained.

"What's it gonna be, then? We've got to go."

"I'm in," said Bean.

"Me, too," added KP.

Bubba stood silently. "With everything that has happened, do I go?" he asked Hero.

Hero shrugged and said, "It's up to you, Bubba."

"Come on, Bubba. I will protect you," offered Bean, smiling and showing her muscles.

"Cute Bean. Well, I guess I'm going. But guys, you heard Bean — she's gonna have to protect me," Bubba joked.

Hero, Bubba, KP and Bean hurried out the door and followed Comonti to town. As they arrived, they heard the sound of trumpets blowing. They were not playing a song, but several different blasts — some short and some long. Bean was sure they were sounding her arrival. They reached their destination as the soldiers assembled into groups.

Moroni had trained each of his soldiers to be specialists using all the weapons, but a master in one type of weapon. The men formed groups based on weapon mastery. Some groups were for the men who cooked, carried extra supplies, were physicians, and some were even repairmen for the armor. Moroni watched the hustle and bustle of the men assembling into rows and columns for several minutes.

The boys then watched Moroni raise his hand to signal the trumpeters, and again they sounded their horns. This time another series of blasts were played.

"Comonti, why are the trumpeters playing different sounds each time?" asked Bean.

"Each is a different signal telling the men what to do," Comonti answered.

"What do they mean?" asked Bubba.

"The first time the horns blew, they signaled for the men to assemble into their assigned groups. The second one, just then, signaled that Captain Moroni will be speaking soon. The last time they blow, they will signal we are leaving for battle."

"That's cool. This system works a lot better than trying to yell over the noise," replied Bean.

As they looked through the plaza, the sight was overwhelming. The sun climbed over the clouds and had started to warm the air. The mist covering the plaza offered a spooky view of the men, who were dressed from head to toe in full battle gear and holding weapons of every kind.

Captain Moroni walked to the steps of the central building and climbed to the highest point. From there, he turned his six-foot two-inch mighty stature and faced the enormous army. Holding his arm high in the air, he signaled for quiet. Then he began:

"Brothers, friends and soldiers, I am sorry to call you together today and tell you that we must again go to war with those who seek to destroy us. My personal messengers have delivered the seal of Alma. The Prophet has received a revelation from our Lord that the Lamanites plan to attack our brothers in the city of Manti. Without our help, they will fall into the Lamanites' hands. The enemy armies are traveling through the jungle as we speak. I estimate that if we leave this morning, we will come upon them in less than one night. If we are able to pass them, we will prepare to battle at the River Sidon where we will have the best chance to defeat them. I have already sent four scout groups that will advise me of the location of the Lamanites. Men, as we were steadfast in the protection of Jershon, so shall we be steadfast with the Lord's help in the protection of Manti.

"I have asked one-third of our army to remain here in the city to keep our families safe as we depart. I have asked the mighty soldier, Lehi, to be a captain and lead another one-third of our army. Men, Lehi is a man of God. Trust him, respect him, and know that he leads you with a sincere heart driven toward righteous desires for you and your families. And finally the remaining one-third will travel with me.

"We will travel to the River Sidon together and then part company as we put into motion the Lord's plan. Unfortunately, we will have to journey far tonight. We will suffer physical exhaustion and wake to face the enemy the next morning. But as we defend our families, liberties, and our God, he will give us the strength we need to be victorious — as we fight solely for His purpose and not for the purpose of gain.

Men, we have prepared well. We have trained hard. We have protected ourselves with our heavy clothing, head, chest, arm and leg armor, along with our shields and strong weapons. Have faith that the Lord will deliver the Lamanites to us, that we may convert them to the ways of the Lord. And if they will not be converted to the ways of the Lord, then by the hand of God will they be destroyed. As we leave our beloved city today, may we be protected in the course we must travel to uphold righteousness. Men, from this moment forward, we march as the Army of God."

The Nephite army cheered at his strength and courage.

Holding his hand up again, the soldiers quieted. "Alma, our Prophet, sent a letter with the messengers. He asked that I read it before we depart for battle.

"'Valiant soldiers of God: I am sorry that I am unable to be serving our God with you. But as I led the people of Ammon out of the city of Jershon to the city of Mulek, I am overwhelmed at what you have given them. They are blessed to have a land to call the land of their inheritance. They are eternally grateful for the protection you provide, that they may remain true to their sacred covenant they made with the Lord. And they so appreciate and are humbled by the sacrifices you have made on their behalf. The Spirit that resides in your hearts is greater than I have seen in any other people. May God grant you the strength you will require in your journey, as you march forward to defend our freedoms. I pray that each of you will return home safely to your families. And I pray that by His divine intervention, the hearts of the Lamanites will be softened, and they will repent and return to Him. May your captains be blessed with the Spirit of the Lord to guide you through this battle to safety, so that your rights, liberties, families and freedoms may be preserved. May your hearts be blessed with humility and faith to always remember the Lord's hand in all things. Stand as witnesses of God at all times and in all things and in all places. My heart is full, as I faithfully pray for your safe return. May God be with you, Alma.'"

"Men, may Alma's words burn in your hearts and grow strong as we depart on our journey," finished Captain Moroni.

Suddenly, the trumpeters blew their horns again, and the shuffle of thousands of feet shook the ground. As the soldiers moved, Moroni ran down the steps into the plaza. He grabbed his horse's reigns and jumped onto its back. With his helmet firmly in place, he took his position at the front of the army. At his command, he righteously led nearly four thousand men toward the gates of the city.

Chapter Nineteen

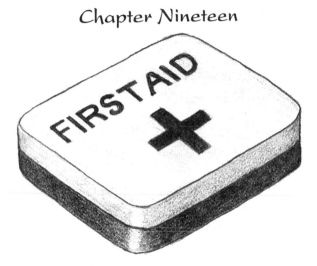

The road to the River Sidon was a dangerous one. Not only did the Lamanites have a lead over the Nephites to the city of Manti, but they also had scouts watching for any movement of Moroni's army. Moroni's only hope was that the traitor he had trusted for so long would advise Zerahemnah that the Nephite army was traveling toward the city of Mulek, not Manti.

Moroni attributed his leadership skills at such a young age to his faith in the Lord. He prayed now, more than ever, that he would make the right decisions on how to lead his army. Leading the army through the cover of the jungle would be difficult, but not impossible. He also knew that traveling through the jungle, rather than on open roads, would take an army four thousand strong twice as long. His only hope was that the jungle would ultimately be safer for his men.

He led the army at a slow, jogging pace for nearly an hour, before he let them slow to a walk. He entered the cover of the trees as they neared the road north of the city of Lehi. The army remained in the cover of the trees most of the day, slicing their way slowly through the jungle. Moroni stopped the army about midday for lunch, after reaching the base of the Hill Amnihu. The cooks brought around dried figs and jerky for the men to eat.

The boys fell to the ground as the army rested. They were hot and sweaty from the day's travels.

"How much farther do you think, Comonti?" asked Bubba, winded and struggling for air.

"We're maybe half-way there," he replied.

"What? Are you kidding?" Bubba squealed. "I'm not sure I have enough strength to continue for another four or five hours."

Bean, trying to lift Bubba's spirits, asked, "Do you want me to give you a piggy back ride?"

The boys laughed hysterically, as did several of the soldiers listening to their conversation.

"Really funny, Bean," replied Bubba gruffly. "If you're not careful, I might take you up on that offer."

Resting only about thirty minutes, Moroni again ordered the army to continue on toward the River Sidon.

The sun drifted through the clouds and hung barely over the western horizon as the army reached the river.

While the soldiers rested, Lehi sent a messenger to the kids, and asked them to join him at the front. As the kids reached Lehi and Moroni, one of the scout groups scurried down the banks of the river toward them.

"What have you found?" asked Moroni.

"Zerahemnah and his men," answered the scout.

"Where?"

"You have passed them. They're two hours behind you," replied the scout.

Moroni quickly separated the army — two thousand would follow Lehi, and the remainder would follow him. As Moroni viewed the terrain, he advised Lehi to take his army south of the Hill Riplah, and he would take the remainder of the men into the jungle on the other side of the river. As Zerahemnah's men entered the river, Lehi was to attack and force them to head directly toward Moroni's awaiting army. The two armies of men would be able to pin the Lamanites in the middle of water. Moroni ordered the boys and Bean to stay with Lehi and tend to the wounded.

Lehi reached out and took Moroni's hand. "Brother, may the Lord be with us. May you return in safety," he said.

Moroni, almost tearful, hugged Lehi for a brief moment. Then he turned to advise the men.

Lehi turned to his army and said, "Men, we will wait for the enemy behind the mountain. As they begin to enter the waters of Sidon, we will attack. We will force them to cross the water right into the arms of our great Captain. Follow me," he yelled, waving his arm high in the air.

Bubba looked at the mountain referred to as a hill, and he sighed at the thought of the walk they still had to make.

"Come on, Bubba. We're almost there," said KP, slapping him on the shoulder.

He cringed in pain as KP hit the tender scab where the arrow had pierced his shoulder the day before.

The trek over the hill was easier than the boys thought. They moved swiftly through the tall grasses and trees. Reaching the crest of the hill with all the men and supplies, Lehi told the men to continue over and head to the bottom of the hill. He told the men to hide in the trees and set up camp. Exhausted from the double-time walk and ready to collapse, the men hurried into the trees and set up their tents.

Standing at the top of the hill, looking toward the east where Zerahemnah's army would enter the valley headed toward the river Sidon, Lehi spotted two Nephite scout teams crawling toward camp.

"Captain Lehi, Zerahemnah's army has stopped to camp for the night. The Lamanites are a mile further to the east, barely out of our sight," announced one of the scouts.

Lehi, relieved for the night's rest, told the scout teams to cross the river and advise Moroni of the situation.

"Comonti, find Pahoran and Limher. Tell them I request their presence," instructed Lehi.

"Yes, Father," Comonti said, glad to help.

He hurried to find the men, and told them to report to Lehi.

"Men, the Lamanites have stopped for the night. Advise the troops to eat quickly and retire early, so they can be rested for the battles that will begin at sunrise," he instructed. "No fires tonight; the enemy is close enough to see them."

Pahoran and Limher both nodded and left to advise the troops.

"Father, may I help?" asked Comonti.

"Son, you may help with the wounded," he replied.

"But Father, I have been trained well," Comonti protested.

"Comonti, I promised your mother I would bring you home safely. I can't control what happens in battle, but I can prevent you from fighting."

"This is not fair," Comonti complained.

"Comonti, find us some food, and then go to sleep. If we have time, we will discuss you fighting in the battle in the morning," replied Lehi.

Comonti turned to find the cooks for some food. Visibly upset, he wandered slowly down the hill toward the other warriors. He stared at their weapons and knew he was more skilled than several of the other young men. He worked his way through the multitude of men, and retrieved cold, flat corn shells, jerky and more dried figs. Then slowly meandered back toward his father's tent.

KP watched as Comonti walked aimlessly. He wondered if Comonti was looking for them.

"Comonti, are you sleeping over here tonight?" he asked.

Comonti looked up when his name was called and said, "No, I will stay with my father tonight."

KP waved in acknowledgement and yelled, "Have fun."

Comonti reached his father as he was praying for guidance from the Lord. "How can such a righteous man be so mean to his son?" he thought, feeling sorry for himself.

As Lehi finished, Comonti somberly handed him the food. He quietly snuggled into his bedroll and faded away into sleep. Sleep came quickly because he had been deprived of sleep the night before when they had rescued Bean. Lehi watched as his son fell asleep, hoping by morning, after the fighting started, that Comonti would understand why his father did not want him to fight in the battle.

The morning light came early — way too early for the boys' liking. Bean watched as they pulled their bedrolls over their heads and tried to sleep a little longer. Meanwhile, across camp, Lehi rose before the sunrise, and was already preparing for the army's attack. As he planned the day's events, he was interrupted by the scream of a familiar voice.

"Father! Father! They're coming!" yelled Comonti, racing toward camp. "Thousands of them — more than we expected."

"How far away are they?" Lehi impatiently asked.

"With as many men as they have, the scouts think they can reach the river in an hour," Comonti replied.

"Find Pahoran, quickly," Lehi commanded. "Then find yourself a safe place to hide."

"Hide?" he replied.

"Yes, Comonti. I told Moroni I would allow you to care for the wounded. Not fight!"

"But, Father, I'm really good."

"No! Comonti, not now. Go and find Pahoran. I need him immediately," Lehi demanded.

Comonti angrily ran through the sleeping warriors, searching for Pahoran's tent. Tears welled up in his eyes as he thought about the words his father had spoken. Comonti ran past Hero, Bubba, Bean and KP, not even noticing them.

Hero could see something was wrong. He stood up from his comfortable spot in the grass. He watched Comonti maneuvering his way down the hill into the valley of soldiers who were securely hidden in the trees at the base of the mountain.

"Something must be up," said Hero. "Should I go see if I can find out what's happening?"

"Sure," answered Bean. "Hurry. If the Lamanite troops are close, I want to make sure we have a safe place to hide."

"Hide? Really?" asked KP. "I want to watch the battle."

"I figure if I am helping tend to the wounded, I will see more than enough," she replied.

Hero, still keeping a close eye on Comonti, now observed Comonti and Pahoran racing toward Lehi's tent.

When they reached it, Pahoran threw open the cloth door.

"This must be it," thought Hero. "The battle must be close at hand."

As Hero approached Lehi's tent, the conversation was tense.

"Pahoran, wake the men and have them suit in Moroni's armor. When they are dressed and ready for battle, inform me so that I can give further instructions."

"Yes, Captain," he replied, as he swiftly returned to the valley of tents to inform the men.

"Lehi, what is happening?" asked Hero, interrupting his concentration.

"The Lamanites are only an hour away. Ready yourself, Hero. Make sure you have prepared a secure location for you and your friends. When the time comes, tend to the wounded. No matter what happens, do not try to battle anyone. Is that clear?"

"Yes, Captain."

"Go now, Hero," demanded Lehi.

As Pahoran readied the men for battle, Hero took his teammates to a secure location at the top of the hill.

Suddenly, Lehi heard a scream. Afraid the Lamanites might have heard the scream, he rushed to see what would cause one of his men to make so much noise and place the entire army in danger. Lehi could see a group of soldiers circled around something on the ground. As he arrived, he could see Pahoran rolling back on forth, writhing in pain.

"What has happened here?" he demanded.

"I am sorry, Captain," said one of the soldiers. "I was checking the tension on my sling. The sling slipped out of my hand. It was an accident; I didn't mean to hit him," he explained.

Carefully helping Pahoran to sit up, Lehi could see that the baseball-sized rock had hit and broken Pahoran's forearm.

"Bring me the visitors from my home," he demanded. "Quickly."

A soldier hurriedly ran up the hill to where the teammates were hiding. Nearly out of breath, he announced, "Lehi needs you immediately."

"What's the matter?" asked Bubba.

"Pahoran is hurt, and Captain Lehi needs you now."

The four ran swiftly down the hillside toward Lehi. As they reached him, they heard Pahoran moaning. Lehi lifted Pahoran's arm to show them, and Pahoran passed out from the pain.

"Lehi, set his arm down softly," instructed Bean. She wiggled her way around the soldiers, and then she kneeled at Pahoran's side.

"Can he fight?" Lehi asked, worriedly.

"His arm is broken," she replied. "He will not be able to fight today."

"Can you fix it?" he asked.

"I can bandage it and take care of him, but his injury will take four to six weeks to heal," she replied. She opened her pack and rummaged through it for the first aid kit. As she searched, she noticed the small, shiny, brass plates.

"Where did those come from?" she wondered. "I don't remember putting those in my backpack."

Suddenly brought back to the moment by Lehi's commanding voice, she looked up — a little startled. She slid the records to the bottom of her bag and tended to Pahoran's arm.

"Hero," Lehi called glancing up, "did you find a safe location to hide?"

"Yes."

"Good. Take Pahoran to your safe place. Keep him there and tend to his arm," instructed Lehi. "Where is Comonti?" he asked impatiently.

"I'm here," Comonti replied, standing behind the circle of soldiers surrounding Pahoran.

"Son, I will need your help. Carefully find Zerahemnah's army, and advise me how much time we have before they reach the river."

"Yes, Father," answered Comonti. "Are you sure you want me to help?"

"Yes, I need your help. But please be careful. Your mother would never forgive me if you got hurt. Now go!"

Comonti took off running toward the Lamanite army.

Lehi quickly scanned the surrounding men and called, "Limher, make ready the troops at the base of the mountain. Be very quiet. We will move in behind the enemy army and attack by surprise."

"Yes, Captain," the warrior replied.

Captain Lehi returned to his post as Hero, Bean, Bubba and KP helped Pahoran to the safe location. Limher made ready the army, and Captain Lehi watched for the Lamanite army to appear.

The teammates watched and waited as the beating footsteps of two thousand men grew steadily louder and louder. They were hidden in the tall, green grasses on the crest of the Hill Riplah. They looked down toward the dark, tiny figures in the distance. With every minute that passed, the figures in the distance grew bigger. Finally, the Nephites could see the faces of the enemies.

The Lamanite warriors were dressed in loincloths. No other clothing was visible except sandals wrapped around their feet. Some of the men had tied brown leather bands around their head and arms.

Lehi's army waited patiently, hidden in the trees, for the call to arms. Almost an hour after the first sighting of Lamanite warriors, they all had finally reached the River Sidon. The Lamanite army had no idea Captain Lehi's army was anywhere near them.

Chapter Twenty

At daybreak, just above the horizon, the sun's glare behind the wispy clouds cast a beautiful, golden glow over the deep-blue sky. Bean was reminded of home. The longing and worried expression on her face concerned Hero. Bean had been through so much, and the anticipation of going home was burning in her heart.

"We've got to figure out why the Lord wants us here," Hero thought to himself, as he watched a tear trickle down Bean's face. He took a deep breath and released the air slowly, contemplating what else he could do.

Noticing Hero watching her, she looked up to him and said, "I miss my family, Hero."

"I know. Me, too," he quietly replied, as he sat down next to her in the soft, wavy grasses. "I even miss Squeaks. I haven't been tattled on forever."

Bean softly smiled, looked at the ground and said, "I know my mom is going crazy."

"I know, Bean. I'm sure mine is, too," he replied.

"What are we missing? What aren't we doing?" she asked. "We must be missing something."

"Maybe we should try the walkie-talkies again," suggested Bubba, as he joined them.

"What?" asked Bean. "You talked to the Team with the walkie-talkie?"

"We did," answered KP, walking toward them.

"How in the world is that possible? Were you dreaming?" she quizzed.

"No! No dreaming going on," answered Hero.

"Did they say everything was all right back home?" Bean pressed.

"We only spoke for a minute. Tater said something about us not being gone very long. But, when we talked to them, we had been gone about eighteen hours," replied Hero.

"So then, time is different here?" she asked.

"It must be," Bubba answered.

"I wonder how long we have been gone back home?" asked KP.

"Well, if we could get home, we could find that out," she whined. "What else did he say?"

"They had Cheri come to the Treehouse and translate the writings inside the tree. They were gonna try to figure them out for us. Other than that, we didn't keep the signal very long," replied KP.

"Have you talked to them since then?" she asked.

"No, we haven't had a chance," answered Hero.

"Look!" said KP, pointing toward the river. "The Lamanite army has started to cross the river."

"It won't be long before Lehi attacks," said Pahoran, watching from the cover of the trees.

"I'm not sure I want to see the battle," said Bubba.

"According to the scriptures, the battle is fierce, and a lot of men die," added Hero.

"So, should we try the walkie-talkie?" asked Bubba. "Maybe they have some answers for us, so we can get back home."

Hero took the walkie-talkie from Bubba's hand. He turned on the power, checked the number to see if it was set to the right channel, and then he slowly turned on the volume.

He looked at his friends and said, "Here goes nothin'!"

He pressed the TALK button and nervously yelled, "Tater! Squeaks! Anyone there?"

Several tense moments passed with nothing but static on the other end.

Again he called, "Team! Anyone there?"

As he released the button, they listened for an answer. Again, the small, black, handheld box was silent.

"This isn't looking very good guys," said Hero, as he glanced up and frowned.

"Should we try one more time?" asked Bean. "The

third try might be the charm."

"Sure, Bean. We can try one more time," responded KP. "Right, Hero?" he asked, lifting his eyebrows.

"You betcha', guys. Let's try one more time," said Hero. "How can it hurt?"

Picking up the walkie-talkie again, he looked at the anxious expressions on everyone's faces. He knew they were hopeful. He hoped they could reach the Team so that their spirits did not drop further into despair. Hero started to push the button and then paused.

"Bean, why don't you try this time? Girls always seem to have better luck," he declared, holding out the walkie-talkie to her.

Delighted, she accepted the walkie-talkie. She located the TALK button and held the walkie-talkie three inches from her mouth. "Is anyone there?" she yelled.

"I don't think you have to yell," said KP.

"Talk normal, Bean," suggested Bubba.

Bean looked at the boys, smiled and again pushed the TALK button. "Red! Stick! Anyone?" she cried out.

Static was the only sound they could get the walkie-talkies to make. She looked disappointedly at Hero and said, "I hoped the walkie-talkies would work! I'm not sure that I'm ready to see this war."

As she handed the walkie-talkie back to Hero, they heard in a tired, worn-out voice.

"Hero, is that you? Hero? Hero?"

Bean grabbed the walkie-talkie and called out, "Squeaks, it's me, Bean. Is everything all right?"

"Bean, is that you? I can hardly hear you," Squeaks

said, screaming into the walkie-talkie on the other end.

"Yes, Squeaks. It's me," she responded. "I sure miss you."

"I miss you too, Bean," Squeaks answered through a yawn.

"What time is it there?" Bean asked.

"About three in the morning, I think. What time is it there?"

"About seven a.m.," Bean answered, looking at the sun's position in the sky. "How many days have passed back home?"

"Days? No days — only hours so far," Squeaks answered, yawning again. "By the way, you're gonna have to hurry up and get home. I talked to your mom and got permission for a sleepover, but she wants you home in the morning to do some chores."

"Chores? Great!" replied Bean. "I want to hurry home so I can do chores."

"Is Tater available?" asked Hero, as he grabbed the walkie-talkie from Bean.

"Let me try to wake him," Squeaks said.

Several long minutes of silence passed as Squeaks tried to wake Tater.

Finally, Tater answered, "Hello? Hero, is that you?" he asked, half asleep.

"Yep, it's us, Tater," replied Hero. "I'm afraid we are going to lose the signal again, so I'll hurry. Were you able to take the clues Cheri gave you and solve them? We can't figure out why we're here or what we're supposed to do to get home."

"Sure, we got them figured out. The clues describe exactly what has to happen," he explained.

"Do you have them with you?" asked Hero.

"Yes, but I can't see in the dark. Hold on a minute while I find a flashlight."

Tater quickly set the walkie-talkie down on the ground. He rummaged through his huge backpack for the flashlight and then called back to his missing teammates.

"Okay, there are three separate clues involved. I will start with the first, okay?" he asked.

"Yep. That's great, Tater. Just hurry. I really want to come home," answered KP.

"Okay, clue number one," he started.

"'As you travel in time, doing service for the Lord,
Your knowledge will be tested; your return is the reward.
Take heed in the Lord's promptings, and remain faithful in all things.
The Liahona will direct you providing the answers you will need.
The Book of Mormon is your guide, at your side shows you the light.
Keep it with you as you journey, setting back what is not right.'"

"Wait!" Bean interrupted. "We don't have paper or a pencil. Hold on a minute," she insisted.

Bean tore through her pack, looking for a pencil or

pen and paper to write on. She finally found them and instructed Tater to repeat the clue, As he did, she wrote down every word he said.

"Okay, we're ready for the second clue," KP yelled into the walkie-talkie.

Tater started reading.

> "'Your travels w... begin when ... h.. treasure in... hand.
> Be prepared to .... a jou.... into a ...g l..t land.'"

"Wait! Wait, Tater," interrupted Hero. "We can't understand what you're saying."

"What? I can't hear you," Tater yelled into the walkie-talkie.

"Start over. We lost the signal for a minute," replied Hero.

"From the beginning?"

"Yes."

Tater started again,

> "'Your travels will begin when you hold treasure in your hand.
> Be prepared to take a journey into a long-lost land.
> Three flashes start your mission — your adventure to the past.
> Without guidance from the Lord, your journey will forever last.'

"Did you get all that?" he asked.

"Yeah. Hang on a second while Bean finishes writing it down," replied Hero.

Tater waited patiently for an okay to continue before he began reading clue number three.

"Sorry for the delay, Tater. The pencil lead broke, and we had to sharpen it with Pahoran's knife. Go ahead now," Bean said.

"Okay, just a minute. I can't read Butch's handwriting." Tater deciphered the clue and then said, "All right, I have it. Are you ready?"

"Yep, go for it," called Bubba.

"Okay, clue number three," he started.

> "'Once your journey is through, and you've completed the task.
> Then hold the Liahona, and you will travel straight back.
> To the time you have left, you will most definitely return.
> With the Lord's service finished, you will have no concern.
> If ... task is n.t c..p...e, no.... w... you travel.
> What's w...g must .. r...t, or your ..... un..vel.'"

"Tater, we lost you on the last two lines. What do the last two lines tell us we have to do?" asked Hero.

As the teammates listen for a response, all they could hear was static. Frustrated that the walkie-talkie cut out again, Hero shook it furiously. Jumping to his feet, he started moving through the trees, trying to find a signal. Bean shook her head, stood up and walked over to Hero.

"Give me that!" she said, grabbing the walkie-talkie from his hand. "Before you break it."

She walked cautiously back to her hiding spot on the ground overlooking the river, and watched momentarily as the Lamanites slowly tried to maneuver through the river's mighty current. Sure Lehi would sound the attack at any moment, she turned the static on the walkie-talkie louder.

"Bean, whatever that is, the noise is too loud. You are going to give away the army's position," warned Pahoran.

Bean smiled and quickly turned down the volume. "Tater! Squeaks! Anyone there?" she called.

Only a few seconds passed before she heard Tater reply.

"Bean, is that you?"

"Yes, I'm still here," Bean answered. "Will you re-read the last two lines of the third clue? We lost you. Hurry, before we lose you again."

Without saying another word, he reread the last part of the clue.

"'If the task is not complete, nowhere will you travel.
What's wrong must be right, or your history will unravel.
Your time it is short; your journey only seven of the Lord's days,

To fix what's gone wrong, or remain forever
there to stay.'

"Did you get that?" he asked, hoping the signal had not faded.

"Oh, my goodness. These clues tell us exactly what we need to do," replied Bean. "We got it. Thanks, Tater."

"Is everybody okay?" asked Tater. "Do you think you can figure out why you're there now?"

"Figuring everything out will be easier now. Thanks, Tater," called Bean.

"If you can, let us know when you are coming home!" Squeaks yelled into the walkie-talkie.

"I don't know if we will be able to, but I will try," answered Hero. "Wish us luck, Tater."

"We m...s y.., hu ..k," Tater replied.

Again static filled the air as they listened. Hero turned off the walkie-talkie and said, "I hope we didn't miss any information."

"Let's get started," said Bean.

"Where do we start?" asked Bubba.

"Yeah, tell me what I need to do," insisted KP, trying to take the clues.

"Just a minute, KP!" she protested. "First, let's read them and see what we have done." She read the first two lines,

'"As you travel in time, doing service for the Lord,
Your knowledge will be tested; your return is the reward.'"

"We've traveled in time. I hope we've done some service while we've been here. Our knowledge has been tested more than once. Keep going," said Hero.

> "'Take heed in the Lord's promptings, and remain faithful in all things.
> The Liahona will direct you, providing the answers you will need.'"

"I think we have followed the Lord's promptings, but we haven't even looked at the Liahona," said KP. "Where is the treasure, anyway?"

"In my backpack. Do you want me to get it or finish with the clues first?" she asked.

"Finish the clues. Then we will know what to do with the Liahona," suggested Bubba.

She started reading,

> "'The Book of Mormon is your guide, at your side shows you the light.
> Keep it with you as you journey, setting back what is not right.'"

"Well, the Book of Mormon has helped us several times," offered KP.

"We'd be in a lot of trouble right now if we didn't have it," answered Hero. "Bean, is there anymore to that clue?"

"No, that's all of it," she replied.

"Please read the second clue, Bean," requested Bubba.

"Okay, clue number two,

> "Your travels will begin when you hold the treas-
> ure in your hand.
> Be prepared to take a journey into a long-lost
> land.'"

"Well, that is totally how the Liahona worked," stated Hero. "I held it in my hand, and away to a long-lost land we traveled!"

Bubba smiled and said, "Oh, so this is all your fault. You are responsible for ant bites, mudslide heart attack, swinging vine of terror, jaguar, and who knows what else. This means I can blame everything on you."

Hero slapped Bubba on the back, and said, "Yep, I guess it is all my fault."

"Ow, Hero. That hurt. You did that on purpose," squealed Bubba, cringing in pain from the arrow scratch. I forgot, the arrow is also your fault. I'm gonna get you for that one," he said, as he jumped to his feet and started to chase Hero.

"Bubba, did you really have all that stuff happen to you?" asked Bean.

Bubba stopped running after Hero. He knew everything that happened was not Hero's fault. Bubba walked back to where Bean was sitting and replied, "All of that, and a few other things I didn't mention."

"Well, if you weren't such a klutz, most of that stuff never would have happened," teased Hero.

"You're so gonna get it, Hero," laughed Bubba, holding up a fist. He pretended to jump to his feet again, and Hero took off running.

"Come on, guys. I want to go home," pleaded Bean. "Quit messing around."

Bubba shrugged his shoulders, mischievously grinned and said, "Sorry, Bean. Go ahead and finish reading the second clue."

She continued,

"'Three flashes start your mission — your adventure to the past.
Without guidance from the Lord, your journey will forever last.'"

"Three flashes happened for sure," said KP.

"I think we have had guidance from the Lord, too," said Hero. "Read more, Bean."

"That's it on that clue," she replied.

"Isn't there one more clue?" asked Bubba.

"Yes, I'll start reading that one," said Bean.

"'Once your journey is through, and you've completed the task,
Then hold the Liahona, and you will travel straight back'".

"Hey, none of this has happened yet," said KP. "Read some more."

Bean smiled and continued,

"'To the time you have left, you will most definitely return.
With the Lord's service finished, you will have
no concern.'"

Bean paused, and KP cried, "Keep going! Keep
going!"

"Okay, okay," said Bean.

"'If the task is not complete, nowhere will you
travel.
What's wrong must be put right, or your history will unravel.'"

"History will unravel? What does that mean?" asked
Bubba.

"The clue suggests that we have come to fix something specific. The Lord wants us to fix whatever that is,
or time in the future will change, and could possibly cause
our history to unravel," explained Hero.

"Well, have we fixed anything while we've been
here?" asked Bean.

"I think so," said KP. "We told Moroni about a traitor,
we helped Lehi's wife, and we helped Pahoran when he
was hurt before the battle."

"Were any of those things what the Lord wanted us
to fix?" asked Hero. "The clue states, 'With the Lord's service finished…'"

"I don't think we were doing all of this for our own
benefit," insisted KP.

"I know that, and I wouldn't change anything we've done. What I am asking is, have we done what the Lord sent us here to do?" asked Hero. "Is there any more to the last clue?"

"Yes," said Bean.

"'Your time it is short; your journey only seven of the Lord's days,
To fix what's gone wrong, or remain forever there to stay.'"

"Remain here forever? No way," said KP.

"I guess we better figure out what we need to do before we have been here seven days," said Bubba.

"Why don't we see if the Liahona tells us anything? Doesn't one of the lines from the clue say something about how the Liahona will guide us and provide the answers we need?" asked Bubba.

"Yeah, it does," said KP. "Where is the Liahona?"

"Right here. I'm getting it. Hang on a minute," Bean replied. She unzipped her backpack, located the Liahona and showed it to the boys.

"Safe and sound, like I told you I would keep it," she said, grinning at KP.

Hero took the Liahona and set it down on the grass so everyone could see. Then he asked, "If our task is finished, it will take us home now, right?"

"Nothing is happening," KP informed everyone.

"If the Liahona guides us, what are we missing? The spindles are steady, so we must be in the right location.

Nothing is flashing. What is it?" asked Hero.

"Hero," said Bubba. "Wasn't the writing on the ball in Egyptian before?" he asked, pointing to the writing above where the numbers had flashed.

"I think so. I don't remember seeing anything I could understand before," he answered.

"Isn't this a scripture reference?" Bubba asked, still pointing.

"Yes, it is. Good job, Bubba," said Hero. "Anyone got their scriptures close?"

"You were the only one who had scriptures with us on this trip, Hero," replied Bean.

Hero walked over to his pack, unzipped it and searched for his scriptures. He quickly located the blue, leather-bound book, and smiled as he remembered that Comonti thought the leather was from a blue cow.

"Here they are. Now, what's the reference, Bubba?"

"Alma, Chapter 18, Verse 36," he replied.

Hero flipped through the pages of his scriptures and quickly located the reference. "Everyone ready?" he asked, smiling.

"Start already, Hero," demanded Bean.

"Okay, Alma 18:36, 'Now when Ammon had said these words, he began at the creation of the world, and also the creation of Adam, and told him all the things concerning the fall of man, and rehearsed and laid before him the records and the holy scriptures of the people, which had been spoken by the prophets, even down to the time that their father, Lehi, left Jerusalem.'"

"Do you think the scripture is talking about the records that were stolen?" asked KP.

"Yeah, maybe our task is to find the stolen records and return them," said Bubba.

"Man, I wish we'd have known this information before. We could have been looking for them this entire time," said Hero. "Next time we go on an adventure, we will know to watch for clues from the Lord."

"What records are missing?" asked Bean.

"The records of the people of Ammon were stolen from the city of Jershon a few days before we arrived," replied Hero.

"What do they look like?" she asked.

"I have no idea," replied Hero. "I bet they are small, metal plates of some sort — kinda like the gold plates."

"So, does everyone think the Liahona's purpose is to take us wherever the Lord needs us to fix something that has changed that will cause the outcome of the Book of Mormon to change?" asked Bubba.

"That is what the clue means to me," answered Hero. "What do you think, Bean?"

"I think I know why we haven't gone home yet," Bean quietly responded.

"What do you mean?" asked Bubba.

"I know you guys did a lot while I was being held captive, but I think I know why we haven't gone home yet."

"Probably because we haven't found the records yet?" said KP. "But now that we know, let's go start investigating."

Bean did not move. She sat perfectly still, staring nervously at her backpack.

"No, wait guys. I have to show you something."

Bean retrieved her backpack, unzipped the main pocket, and slowly reached inside. She rifled around for several moments and then pulled out the brass plates. Nervously, she held them up for the boys to see.

"What are those?" asked Bubba.

"I took them on accident from the Lamanites when they were holding me hostage," she replied.

"How?" asked Hero, as he dropped to his knees to get a better look.

"The night I escaped, they had the contents of my backpack spread out all over a table. When I grabbed my backpack, I swept everything off the table into my pack. These must have been on the table with all of my things," she explained.

"Why didn't you tell us?" asked KP.

"I just found them when I was searching in my backpack for the first aid kit when Pahoran got hurt."

"Why didn't you tell us then?" asked Bubba.

"I was afraid I had stolen the Lamanite records on accident. I didn't want anyone to be mad at me. I didn't take them on purpose," she explained.

"I bet those are the records of Ammon, not Lamanite records," said Hero.

"Are you sure? I don't want Captain Moroni or Lehi to be angry with me," she asked warily.

"They wouldn't be mad at you, Bean," answered Pahoran, joining the conversation. "Even if they are stolen records, Lehi and Moroni would help you get them to the right place."

"We should take these to Lehi right now," suggested Hero. "Everything will be fine, Bean. I promise."

She slowly zipped her backpack, stood up and threw it over her shoulder. Hero grabbed her hand and said, "Quit procrastinating. Let's move. I only hope we can get to him before the battle begins."

They started running through the trees and brush toward Lehi's command post. They tried to stay low and hidden so they would not be spotted by any of the Lamanite warriors. Desperate to find Lehi before he sounded the attack, they ran as fast as they could.

Calling to the warriors, Bubba asked, "Where is Lehi?"

The warriors pointed toward Lehi, hiding at the crest-line of the hill. Crawling toward him, Hero called, "Lehi! Lehi, we need to speak to you. It's important."

Lehi looked down at the kids and motioned for them to go back. Hero shook his head and continued toward him.

"Hero, you should be hidden," scolded Lehi. "Why are you here?"

"Lehi, when Bean was captured, she mistakenly found these," he said, as he showed Lehi the plates. "She was afraid they belonged to the Lamanites. But Pahoran believes they might be the records of Ammon that were stolen from the city of Jershon," said Hero, handing Lehi the plates.

Lehi took the plates and inspected them closely. A huge grin spread across his face. He looked to Bean and said, "These are the plates of Ammon. We weren't sure if we would ever get these back. You have all truly been a blessing from above."

"What should we do with them?" asked Bubba.

"The Prophet Alma is traveling, as we speak, toward the city of Jershon to search for these records. We can't run the risk of Alma being hurt while searching, or having the plates stolen or lost out here on the battlefield," exclaimed Lehi. "I need you to return them to the city."

"Now?" asked KP. "I wanted to stay and see the battle."

"This battle is going to be terrible, KP, with a lot of bloodshed. I would rather you return them now, and keep our prophet from danger," said Lehi. "I will assemble guards to accompany you home. Follow me quickly. The battle is about to begin."

Lehi led the kids on their hands and knees off the hillside, until they could stand without being seen. As they reached the bottom, Lehi motioned for Limher. The warrior moved quickly to him and Lehi said, "Limher, I will return in a minute. Keep watch on Zerahemnah's army, and signal me when half of the men have entered the river."

The warrior nodded and ran to the top of the hill where Lehi had been watching. Lehi grabbed Bean's hand, started running and said, "Where is Pahoran?"

Bean pointed to a group of trees and bushes on the west side of the Hill Riplah. "He is waiting for us there," she said.

"Come, we must hurry," he said, running faster.

"Pahoran?" whispered Lehi. "Pahoran?"

"Yes, Commander?" he replied, carefully climbing out of the bushes.

"I need you to pick two body guards and escort my friends home. They must return to the city of Jershon safely. They have located the plates of Ammon, and Alma is traveling to the city to search for them. Because these records are sacred, only Bean may touch them from this point forward. I do not want the plates here on the battleground. We cannot afford to lose them again. Can you do that, and protect them as you would me?"

"Yes, Commander. But why me?" he asked.

"I cannot risk losing you in this battle. You are in no condition to fight, and I must return to lead the army. Pahoran, I leave my friends in your capable hands. Remember, no one is to get near them," whispered Lehi.

Chapter Twenty-One

Hero, Bubba, KP and Bean knew this would be the last time they saw Captain Lehi or Comonti. They knew as soon as the plates were given to Loriah and they held the Liahona, they would be going home. Sad to leave their new friends, but excited to see their families, they watched as Lehi ran back to camp. They longed to say goodbye to Comonti, who was still scouting Zerahemnah's army. Pahoran and two bodyguards were assigned to take the kids back to Jershon. With a strenuous half-day walk ahead of them, Pahoran was anxious to get started.

"Let's go. If we don't go now, we will be traveling after the sun goes down," Pahoran said.

Hero looked at Pahoran and thought, "He just does-n't want any of the soldiers to see him crying because he has to leave. I didn't know the commitment to fight for freedom was so strong."

The walk home was anything but easy. Pahoran commanded the kids as though they were his own personal army. They jogged through the brush for an hour at a time, alternating with thirty-minute walk breaks in between. Three hours into the journey, Hero was dying of thirst, but Pahoran would not allow a break. Frustrated, tired and thirsty, Hero stopped. He grabbed a vine and sliced it open. He turned it upside down and drank almost every bit of water inside, and then he dripped a little water down his face and on his clothes.

Bean watched in amazement. "Hey, how did you know to do that?" she asked.

Hero looked over and smiled. "Comonti taught me," he replied. "Would you like a vine?"

"Yes, please," she replied.

Hero grabbed another vine, sliced through the thick, round core and handed it to Bean. She gulped the water.

"Now, if I only had a cup and some ice, life would be perfect."

Pahoran and the guards were fifty feet in the distance. One of the guards turned around and noticed the team-mates had stopped. Pahoran waited impatiently for them to finish. As he stared at the kids, he noticed two shadows in the distance. Remembering Lehi's counsel to stay in the cover of the trees and avoid confrontation with the Lamanites, Pahoran motioned for them to hurry.

"What is Pahoran doing?" asked Bean.

They started laughing, watching him wave his unbroken arm wildly in the air above his head.

"I don't know. Maybe he is trying to swat at a bee," suggested Hero.

"He looks like he wants us to start running again," groaned KP.

"No way! I need a couple minutes of rest," complained Bean, sitting down in the grass.

"He looks like he's trying to tell us something," said Bubba.

"Tell us what?" asked KP. "To hurry up? I need a break."

Hero called to Pahoran, "What? What's up? Can't we have a few minutes to rest?"

Pahoran angrily motioned to them to follow.

"Come on, guys. Something must be wrong for him to freak out and have a guard run to get us," said Bubba, pointing to the guard headed their way.

"Come now, quickly," demanded the guard. "We are being followed."

They immediately jumped to their feet and searched the area behind them. Several seconds passed before Bubba spotted two dark shadows.

"There, look — two men," Bubba whispered.

"Who are they?" asked KP.

"I don't know," answered Hero. "Could they be Nephites?"

"With Pahoran so upset — probably not," replied Bubba. "Come on. Let's move."

They quickly ran to catch up with Pahoran.

Bean asked, "Do you know who they are?"

"No! If I am to protect you, you must listen to me," he heatedly exclaimed. "Follow me, and stay close!"

Pahoran knew with his injury and the kids' inexperience, they would never be able to outrun the men behind them.

"Any chance they could be Nephites, Pahoran?" asked KP.

"That is possible, but very unlikely."

"Why?" asked Bean.

"The Nephites are needed to defeat Zarehemnah's army. But, the Lamanite army is so large, I'm not sure a few missing warriors would matter."

"What do we do?" asked Hero.

"We've got to find shelter," replied Pahoran.

"Shelter? We need to escape!" shouted Bean.

"There are seven of us traveling. Because of the jungle terrain, and the fact that I am unable to use my arm for balance, I am slower. You are unfamiliar with the terrain. Lehi trusted me enough to accompany you back to the city. Believe me when I say that we cannot outrun them," Pahoran explained.

"Fair enough, Pahoran. What are we looking for?" asked KP.

"Something large enough to hide all of us, but discrete enough that those men will not find us."

"Oh great. We're looking for something impossible! That makes our situation even easier," Bean said sarcastically.

"Come on, guys. We can find something. We are so close. Stay focused, please," insisted Bubba.

Not another word was spoken as they raced through the trees and vines. Not unexpectedly, the rain began to fall. The rain poured down hard for nearly twenty minutes. Everything became more difficult — walking, seeing, even hearing. And still, no hideout had been found.

Feeling the presence of the two men bearing down on them, the group hurried faster. With adrenalin pumping through their bodies, they raced through the dense brush of the jungle.

"I can't see anything that might work," complained Bubba, frustrated and scared.

"Keep looking. We'll find something. The Lord always provides a way," replied Pahoran.

Bubba, afraid he would be the one caught or killed, ran ahead of the group. He searched everywhere, even in the trees, for a place to hide. With the rain still coming down, he was surprised as a ray of light shined on a small willow tree.

"Pahoran, what about under the canopy of that willow tree?" asked Bubba, pointing toward the now-faded ray of sun.

"You mean the Canopy Fig? That might work," he replied. "Let's check and see."

They hurried over to the tree. Pahoran slid his hand into the hundreds of branches hanging to the ground and moved several to the side. The branches formed a circle around the trunk of the tree, providing a perfect place to hide.

"The tree is wet inside, but it just might work," Pahoran said.

They all crawled through the branches and sat in the mud. Pahoran was the last to enter. As he did, he allowed the branches to fall back into place.

"I wonder how far behind us they were?" whispered Bean.

"Not far," replied one of the guards. "Ssshhhh."

They had been hiding for only a minute or two before they heard the rustling of the brush. Pahoran held his finger to his mouth, reminding everyone to remain silent.

Hero, unable to control the urge to see who it was, slid a few willow branches slightly to the side and peered through them. To his surprise, twenty feet away stood the traitor who might have stolen the plates, kidnapped Bean and lied to Captain Moroni. Shocked, he placed his hand over his mouth and watched as the man continued searching for them.

Several minutes passed before Hero whispered, "I saw the same warrior who kidnapped you, Bean."

Her face drained of all its color. She felt sick and asked, "Do you think they will find us?"

"I hope not," whispered Bubba.

Pahoran again held his finger to his mouth and whispered, "They're back. Ssssshhhh."

They listened as the men angrily searched for them.

Chapter Twenty-One

"Where could they be?" asked Coninihah.

"I have no idea. Why don't we go back? Why are we worrying about those children anyway?" asked Matoki.

"Because of them, I have lost everything — the plates of Ammon, the girl, and probably my status with Moroni," Coninihah snapped. "Not only will I find them, but I am going to kill them."

"Kill them?" asked Matoki. "Why not take them captive?"

"I tried that once, and the girl made a fool of me. I will not make that mistake again," answered Coninihah.

"They're not here. Let's look a little further west," Matoki suggested.

Coninihah agreed, and the two men walked westward.

"We are in trouble," said Pahoran. "This warrior is the traitor. We saw him with Moroni, remember?"

"Yes," replied Bubba.

"He is the same warrior who captured me," said Bean.

"They will find us if we stay here. We have to go," said KP.

"We have nowhere to go," protested Pahoran. "They will only find us faster if we leave."

"Then what do we do?" asked Bubba, trying not to sink in the mud.

"There is nothing we can do, other than prepare for them to find us," said Pahoran dejectedly.

Then Pahoran suggested they pray to the Lord for protection. Suddenly, without warning, the dirt under Bubba's feet began to give way. He frantically tried to pull his feet loose, but they were stuck in the mud. Hero watched, wondering what Bubba was doing. But by the time he figured out the problem, Bubba was in trouble. Hero had no time to save him.

Bubba squealed as he disappeared through the mud into a tunnel hidden below. He hit the ground with a thud. Unable to see anything, he frantically looked around.

"Oh, please not again!" he screamed.

"Where did Bubba go?" asked KP.

"He was right there," replied Hero, moving over to check the area.

As Hero stepped into the mud, he too was mysteriously sucked into the tunnel below. Pahoran watched, completely mystified by the strange events.

"What an escape!" he whispered to himself. "The Lord always provides a way." He said as he turned to the others and said, "Hurry and step into the mud."

Pahoran watched for the warriors to return while he made sure everyone escaped. Certain they had not been seen, he was the last to disappear through the mud into the tunnel below.

"Where are we?" asked KP.

"In a tunnel," replied Bubba, grinning.

"Oh, you're cute, Bubba! Really cute," said KP. "If I could see, you'd get it."

"You think I'm cute?" asked Bubba, getting under KP's skin. "Gross!"

"Bubba!" exclaimed KP.

Pahoran, who had been quiet, said, "Feel around on the ground for wood to make torches."

"I can't find any wood on the ground. We may have

to feel our way through the cave in the dark," suggested one of the guards.

"Don't we have a flashlight?" asked Bean.

"Yeah, I think so," replied Hero. "Hold on. Let me see if I can find it."

"A what?" asked Pahoran.

"Oh, it's something from our time," replied KP.

"Here it is!" shouted Hero, as he flashed on the light.

Pahoran stared at the light in Hero's hand. "What kind of magic is that?" he asked.

"No magic, Pahoran," replied Hero. "In the future, we have more technology than what is available in your day."

Pahoran, leery of the flashlight, walked behind Hero and watched the light as though it were the enemy. The air was humid, wet and sometimes hard to breathe. The group, cold and tired, could see no end to the tunnel.

"Do you think this passageway is one of Moroni's escape tunnels?" asked Bubba.

"No, I have never guarded this tunnel. I'm sure Moroni would have said something to me about it," replied Pahoran.

"Well, where did it come from, then?" asked Bean.

The group walked a mile or more in silence, contemplating Bean's question.

Bubba finally had the nerve to say, "Do you think the Lord created this tunnel for our safety?"

"I was thinking that," replied Hero. "I bet He did. Otherwise, where in the world did it come from?"

"Can I tell you how glad I am that those two warriors did not catch me again?" asked Bean.

"I'm sure they also stole the records of the people of Ammon," said KP.

"What if they found out that because of us, Moroni learned they were traitors?" asked Bubba.

"We wrecked their deceitful lives. I bet they're pretty angry!"

Pahoran and the guards quietly listened to the team-mates, surprised at everything they had done. They had walked at least three miles underground before Pahoran finally spotted a light.

"Look!" he called.

"Hey, I wonder where this tunnel ends?" asked KP.

"I don't care — as long as we are away from those warriors," said Bean.

"Let's go find out," suggested Hero, running toward the light.

A small opening, about the size of a laundry basket, was hidden behind leaves, vines and bushes. As they pulled the leaves back, they could see they were still in the cover of the jungle. As they each climbed out, they searched their surroundings for something familiar.

"Look!" exclaimed Hero. "Isn't that the road where Moroni had the army enter the jungle?"

"Good work, Hero," smiled Pahoran. "We are only a few miles from Jershon."

"The sun is starting to set. If we run, we could get back before dark, couldn't we?" asked Bean.

"Yes, let's hurry," answered Pahoran.

As they started to run, they struggled to breath. The

air was so moist, they felt like they were breathing water, not oxygen.

"We're gonna get wet again — I can feel it," said Bean.

"Yes, I can feel the storm, too," replied Pahoran. "We are almost to the city walls. Keep running. We can make it."

As the odd group of Hero, Bubba, KP, Bean, Pahoran and the two bodyguards reached the defenses of Jershon, Hero breathed a cautious sigh of relief.

"I don't know how we survived that trip," he said.

"We are not safe yet," warned Pahoran. "We still have to find a way into the city."

"Won't they open the gates for us?" asked Bubba.

"No, not without the full army to protect them."

"We can't climb the fence with all those spikes at the top!" shrieked Bean.

"Lehi said there was a secret entrance," replied Pahoran. "We just have to find it."

"We know where that is!" exclaimed Hero.

"How? It's a secret entrance."

"I'm serious. He had to use it last night when he was with us," Hero insisted.

"Well, show us, before something else happens," demanded the bodyguard.

"Relax, Haltium. Everything will be fine. Nothing is going to happen now," reassured Pahoran.

"Pahoran, why does everybody keep saying that? Every time anyone does, something doesn't happen to us — it happens to me!" complained Bubba.

Enjoying the laugh and the relief from tension, they circled the city, looking for the secret entrance.

"There it is," said Hero, pointing to the walls.

"How do we open it," asked Pahoran.

"Lehi waved at the guards above and then made some funny bird noises," replied KP.

"What were the sounds?"

"Kinda like 'Ggrr, ku, ku, ku'," answered KP.

"No, not like that. I remember them sounding more like, 'Gggggggg, ku, kuk, ku', I think," said Hero.

"Do you mean, 'Ggggrrr, kuk, kuk, kuk. Ggggrrr, kuk, kuk, kuk'?" asked Pahoran.

"Yep, that was it," said Bubba.

Suddenly the secret door opened, and a guard invited them inside.

"That is Lehi's personal call," said the guard. "Why do you know it, and where is he?"

"He is still at the battle front," answered Pahoran. "I was assigned as a bodyguard to bring these children home for him."

Remembering Lehi had used the entrance the night before with the group of kids, the guard accepted the explanation and led them up the stairs and into the plaza.

"Thank you," said Pahoran.

The group walked quietly into the darkness of the city. The kids were not afraid of the warriors standing guard, but they were nervous about the journey they would be taking shortly. Upon reaching the fence to Lehi's home, Pahoran thanked Bean for her assistance with his arm, and bid them all farewell. He turned and disappeared into the night with the two bodyguards at his side.

Excited to see Lehi's family, they ran to the door and pounded several times.

Kalia screamed with excitement as she watched everyone walk in the door.

"You've made it home. Where are Father and Comonti?" she asked, obviously disappointed that they were not with the teammates.

"The battle had barely begun when we left," replied Hero. "They were still needed for the battle."

"Oh," she said sadly.

Loriah entered the room. She placed her arm around Bean and said, "I am glad you are home. The battlefield is no place for young girls."

Bean smiled and walked with her into the kitchen.

"Are you hungry?" Loriah asked.

"Yes, starved," replied Bean.

"Loriah, I'm hungry too!" added Bubba, holding his stomach.

Loriah smiled as Bubba made hunger noises and rolled around on the floor, putting on a show for Kalia. She quickly pulled jerky and dried figs from the shelf and handed them to the boys.

"Eat these while I make you something else," she said.

"Where are Annah and Shaliah?" asked Bean, looking around.

"They will be back to help me tomorrow. I sent them home to be together," Loriah responded.

"How are you feeling?" asked Hero, truly concerned.

"Much better. The wound is finally healing, thanks to my Hero!" she replied, smiling.

Hero, instantly embarrassed, turned a beautiful crimson color and stared down at the floor. Even his ears were burning red.

"Now, tell me why you have returned home so quickly," she demanded.

Hero was excited to show Loriah what they had found. He looked to Bean and motioned with his eyes for her to retrieve the plates. Loriah watched Bean carefully unzip her backpack and search through its contents. A moment later, she pulled out something carefully wrapped in cloth. She handed the package to Hero and said, "These are your responsibility now."

Hero smiled and replied, "You mean Loriah's responsibility now!"

Hero handed the cloth to Loriah and said, "Bean found these by accident when she was being held captive by the Lamanites. Lehi said they were important enough for us to leave the battlefield and return them to you, where they could be kept in safety until they can be returned to Alma when he arrives."

Intrigued, Loriah set the bundle on the table and started to unwrap the cloth. Suddenly, an unexpected scream startled everyone, including Loriah. Bean ran into Loriah's room and quickly picked up Isabelle, quieting her screams. As Bean walked back into the room, Bubba held his chest.

"Holy cow! I thought for sure that Lamanites had found us," he said.

Chuckling, Hero replied sarcastically, "If your luck got any better this trip, we'd be caught for sure."

Bubba smiled, shrugged his shoulders and made a funny face. Then he said, "All right. Open the package, Loriah, but don't take the contents out of the cloth."

She carefully unwrapped the cloth to reveal the plates of Ammon.

She gasped in excitement. "You found these, Bean?"

Bean nodded.

"Were Lehi and Captain Moroni excited?"

"Captain Moroni had already crossed the river before I knew we had them," responded Bean.

"Lehi told us to bring them to you for safe keeping until he and Comonti returned from the battle," added KP.

"And I will do just that," promised Loriah. She entered her room and placed the records in a safe location. "Well done!" she exclaimed as she returned. "The people of Ammon could never have replaced those."

"That is what Lehi said," stated Bubba.

"Do you have to return to the battle, or are you staying until they return?"

"Neither," replied Hero. "We are going home."

"What? How?" Loriah sadly asked.

"The treasure that brought us here is ready to take us home," said Bubba excitedly.

"And I bet with all the excitement you've had, Bubba, you're ready to go," she said, smiling.

"Yes, and I really miss my mom."

"I understand," she said, hugging each teammate as though they were one of her children. "Do Comonti and

Lehi know you will not be here when they return?"

"No, the beginning of battle is not the best time for goodbyes," Hero said.

"Then I will tell them for you. But, that will require another hug," she demanded. "Kalia and I will be sad to see you go."

"We will never forget you," whimpered KP.

"Nor I you," she replied, wiping a tear from her eye. "Will I ever see you again?"

"We don't know where the Lord will have the treasure take us next," Bean replied.

"I will thank the Lord every night for the time I got to know you — my very own heavenly miracles."

Suddenly a bright light shined out the top of Bean's backpack, filling the house with warmth. Bean stood up and handed Bubba the baby. Then she carefully opened her pack.

"Hero, the panel on the Liahona is flashing again!" exclaimed Bean.

"What number is flashing?" asked Hero.

"No numbers — just a solid red panel."

"Loriah, it's time for us to go!" hollered Bubba. He handed Isabelle to her, blew her a kiss and moved closer to Bean. "Stay back! We don't want you to get stuck in the future."

Loriah smiled and watched as the Liahona flashed the brightest light she had ever seen. And then, before her very eyes, Hero, Bean, Bubba and KP disappeared.

Chapter Twenty-Two

The panel and light suddenly went dark. The teammates tried to look around, but their surroundings were pitch black. With the bright flash of light, their eyes took a minute to adjust.

"We didn't make it home, did we?" asked Bean quietly.

"I can't tell where we are," replied Hero. "Everything is dark."

"Do I dare try to move?" asked KP.

"I suppose you could try, but don't get hurt," said Hero.

"This doesn't feel like home," said Bean.

"Hey, wait a minute. Don't we have a flashlight somewhere?" remembered Bubba.

"Yeah, hold on. I've got one in my pack," answered Hero.

Hero slid off his pack, unzipped it, and rummaged around until he found the flashlight. He pointed it toward the ground and clicked on the light.

Moments later, as their eyes adjusted, Bean squealed, "I know where we are!"

"So do I," replied Bubba.

"I should have known the treasure would bring us back inside the tree," reasoned Hero. "We are home!"

"We must be back home. The air doesn't smell as clean as it did back in the jungle," declared Bubba.

"Come on! Let's go find our Team," shouted KP, shaking from excitement.

The teammates climbed out from inside the tree and ran to where the ladder should be.

"Oh great! They pulled up the ladder," said KP. "Now what?"

"We'll do what Squeaks did. I'll climb to the top from inside the tree and throw you down the ladder," said Bean matter-of-factly.

"You amaze me, Bean," said Hero. "How did you remember that?"

She smiled and climbed back inside the tree. The boys only waited about five minutes before Bean kicked the ladder down. Hero grabbed hold and started climbing toward the Treehouse.

"I wonder what time it is," said Bubba.

"I wonder what day it is," said Bean.

"I don't wonder anything. I'm just glad to be home," replied KP.

As they reached the Treehouse, Bubba carefully opened the door and walked inside. He was followed by KP, Bean and then Hero. They looked fondly at the familiar surroundings.

"Do we wake them?" asked Bubba, looking at the Team fast asleep on the floor.

"What time is it?" asked Bean. "I want to see my mom."

"I set my watch to Book of Mormon time," said Hero. "I don't have any idea what time it is here."

"Hey guys," said Bean. "If they wake up right now, I bet we give one of them a heart attack."

"What? Why?" asked Bubba.

"Look at our clothes! We look like Indians or something."

"I hadn't thought about that. You're right. We'd scare them to death," replied KP.

"Especially coming out of a deep sleep," agreed Hero. "Bean, we will go out on the balcony to change if you want to change in here. Okay?"

"Yeah, that will be fine. But hurry. I don't want anyone to see us in these strange clothes," she replied.

The boys moved to the balcony to change into their normal clothes, and Bean changed inside the Treehouse. When the boys returned, Hero looked at the watch on Tater's arm.

"It's almost six a.m. Do you want to sleep for a while or wake the Team?" he asked.

"Sleep!" yelled KP.

"No, wake the Team," replied Bean. "We have to let them know what happened before we talk to anyone else. And they should probably let us know what has happened around here."

"Man, I hate it when you're right!" said KP.

They moved around the Treehouse, trying to wake their teammates. Almost five minutes passed, with nothing more than a, "Stop it, Hero," from Squeaks.

"What now, Hero?" asked Bean.

"You got any water?" he asked jokingly.

Right then, Squeaks lifted her head and yelled loudly, "Hero! Bubba! Everybody, they're back!"

"Sssshhhh, quiet Squeaks. You'll wake Mom screaming that loud," said Bubba. He picked her up and gave her a teddy-bear hug.

"I am so glad to see you," she said, refusing to let go.

"Me, too," whispered Bubba.

"Hero?" said a scratchy, rough voice. "Is that you?"

"Yep, we're home Tater."

"Oh boy. Our prayers have been answered," he said, almost crying. "I thought we were in real trouble."

One by one, the teammates woke up to the excitement of the return of their friends. Everyone was excited to hear everything that had taken place. The sun rose as Hero told them about the events that had just happened. He finished by showing everyone the clothes Kalia had purchased for them in the market. But Hero's favorite stories were those about the terrible things that had happened to Bubba. By nine a.m., Hero, Bubba, Bean and KP were ready to go see their moms.

"Remember Team, nothing that has happened with the treasure leaves this Treehouse," reminded Hero sternly.

"Where are we going to put the Liahona?" asked Tater.

"Good question. Let me see," said Hero, looking around the Treehouse.

"I know!" yelled Squeaks.

"Where?" asked Hero, glad to be talking to his little sister.

"We brought the treasure box up from inside the tree. How 'bout in there?"

"Yep, that works. Now, where do we put the box?" he asked.

"How 'bout in the trophy case?" asked Red. "We don't have a trophy for it yet."

"Perfect! Good thinking, Red," Hero declared. He slid open the glass door and placed the small box inside. "Now remember, no one gets into the box ever — unless we are all here together. Does everyone agree?"

The Team nodded in agreement.

Everyone quickly climbed out of the Treehouse and ran toward the house. They discussed the many events that had happened in the Book of Mormon. They knew that they would have to become experts on the book if they were going to go on any more adventures.

"Team, I was about to call you, but I can't find my walkie-talkie. Any ideas?" asked Mom.

"Mom!" yelled Bubba, running to hug her. "I missed you."

"All right, Bubba, what are you buttering me up for?" she asked suspiciously.

"I'm not buttering you up — really. I'm really glad to see you this morning."

"Me too, Mom," said Hero, a little more in control. "I guess you were really busy yesterday."

"Well, I missed you too, boys. Now get ready to eat. And the walkie-talkie?" she asked again.

"Oh, yeah. Sorry about not returning it to you. We were playing with it last night while you were gone," said Tater. "I'll run get it."

"No, Tater. Wait until after breakfast. The pancakes are hot and ready to eat right now."

"I've got to get home, Mrs. M. Sorry, I can't stay for breakfast," said Bean.

"Me, too. I've got some chores to do before I get in a lot of trouble," said KP.

"No problem. I hope you had a fun sleepover. Be careful going home," said Mrs. M.

"See ya later, guys," waved Hero.

"So Bear, how was your sleepover?" asked Mom.

"Great! Thanks for inviting me," Bear answered through a mouthful of pancakes. "I'm gonna hang out for a few days, if that's okay."

"If it's okay with your mom," she replied.

The Team sat quietly, enjoying every bite of pancakes and syrup. Hero, grateful for real food, would be happy if he never had to eat another dried fig again. He savored every bite.

"Hey, Mom," Bubba said. "What kind of food do you think people ate in Book of Mormon times?" he asked.

Chapter Twenty-Two

Hero about choked when he heard the question. He shook his head back and forth.

"What?" asked Bubba, shrugging his shoulders.

"Oh, I don't know. Why?" she asked.

"I don't know — just wondering," he replied.

"Probably because of the Moroni's treasure map," replied Hero. "We have been reading a lot in the Book of Mormon."

"By the way, boys," said Mom, "I saw your room."

"Y...Y...Yes," stuttered Hero. "And did you like it?"

"Yes, I have never seen it that clean. Nice job," said Mom.

Runt, Bear, Red and Stick finished their pancakes.

They excused themselves from the table.

"We're finished already. We'll go up to the treehouse and grab the walkie-talkie. Then we'll meet you all back here," said Runt.

"Thanks, boys," replied Mrs. M.

"Remember, don't touch anything," whispered Bubba.

"We know," replied Bear, smirking. "We're not three years old."

"Tater, where is the walkie-talkie?" asked Stick.

"In my backpack," he said, looking up for a moment before taking another bite of pancakes.

"Bear, will you also grab my backpack?" asked Butch.

"Sure."

Hero smiled and said, "Hurry back, boys."

The four boys ran to the Treehouse and climbed up

the ladder. They reached the top in record time. Then they ran to the trophy case and stared at the box.

"What would happen if we took the Liahona out of the box?" asked Bear.

"We could end up on an adventure like Hero, Bubba, KP and Bean," replied Runt.

"Should we check it out?" asked Bear.

"No, we better not. I don't want to do any of that stuff Bubba had to do!" exclaimed Stick.

"Come on, Stick. It's not like anything is going to happen," begged Red.

"No, let's just get the walkie-talkie and go," replied Stick. "Now, where is Tater's backpack?" he asked.

"Over in the corner — next to mine and yours," replied Red.

Stick looked to the far corner. He spotted the backpacks, grabbed them and brought them over to the table. He handed Red his and slid his own on his back. Then he opened Tater's bag, looking for the walkie-talkie.

"Stick, can we look in the box if we promise not to touch the Liahona?" asked Bear.

Stick nervously agreed. "I guess, but don't touch anything," he warned.

Red excitedly grabbed the small box and carefully carried it to the table. Looking at his friends with a mischievous expression on his face he asked, "Are you ready?"

Even Stick was a little anxious to have a better look at the treasure they had searched so hard to find.

Red carefully lifted the lid and laid it on the table. The

boys surrounded the box, trying to see every detail.

"Where is the panel that flashes the numbers?" asked Bear.

"You can't see it very well," replied Runt, pointing just below the material lining the box.

Bear tilted the ball to its side to see better, and then quickly set it straight after he had looked at the shiny panel. "Well, it's not flashing anything right now," he said.

"Look at this writing on the top. The figures seem to be changing, don't they?" asked Stick.

"How can the engravings change, Stick?" asked Red.

"I don't know. But they do seem to be changing slightly," Stick insisted, closing his eyes and shaking his head. "Come on. We need to put the Liahona away before anyone knows we took it out," he said. He placed Tater's bag on the table and continued searching for the walkie-talkie.

"Oh, Stick, you're so paranoid," teased Runt.

"Hey, look. The material over here seems to be shining red," noticed Bear.

"What?" yelled Stick. "Oh, no!"

Without warning, the brilliant white light flashed again.

"What was that?" asked Mom.

"What, Mom?" replied Hero.

"I don't know. I thought I saw a flash of light outside — almost like lightning."

"What?" asked Hero, abruptly sitting up in his chair. He opened his eyes as big as golf balls.

"I thought I saw something," said Mom. "I guess with all the rain, we are going to have an occasional flash of lightning," she reasoned.

"I'm gonna head up to the Treehouse for a minute. Is that all right, Mom?" asked Hero. He had a sick feeling in the pit of his stomach.

"Me, too," said Bubba.

"And me, Mom," said Squeaks.

"Sure, Team. Everybody can go. And thanks again for cleaning your room so well."

"No problem. Anytime, Mom," yelled Bubba, as he closed the sliding glass door.

"Do you think they got into the treasure box?" Bubba asked Hero, as they ran toward the ladder.

"If they did, I'm gonna be so mad," answered Hero. "I thought they could leave it alone for one minute."

Nervously climbing, Hero, Bubba, Squeaks, Tater and Butch crawled step by step up the ladder. Hero threw open the door. They found no one and saw nothing but the empty treasure box. Hero's heart sank. Runt, Stick, Red and Bear were gone.

"How are they ever going to get home?" he whispered, on the verge of tears. He pulled a chair away from the table and sat down. He placed his head in his hands and said, "They have no idea what's in store for them."

The Titan's have a date with destiny…Where will they end up next?

About the Author

Although born in Provo, Utah, Tina spent most of her life in San Diego, California. Her writing is strongly influenced by her hometown experiences and her large family whose flair for story telling never ends.

As a direct descendant of Heber C. Kimball and Orson Pratt, the stories told to her by her parents about them encouraged a fascination with the Book of Mormon, Church history, and the adventures of the early saints.

Tina Storrs Monson currently lives in Draper Utah, a suburb of Salt Lake City. She attended Brigham Young University where she met her husband, Kreg. They have been married for sixteen years and have four children.